NEPHILIM

BOOKS by JEB KINNISON

The Substrate Wars:

Red Queen

Nemo's World

Shrivers

Relationships and Attachment, Nonfiction:

Bad Boyfriends: Using Attachment Theory to Avoid Mr. (or Ms.) Wrong and Make You a Better Partner

Avoidant: How to Love (or Leave) a Dismissive Partner

Other Nonfiction:

Death by HR

NEPHILIM

Jeb Kinnison

NEPHILIM

This is a work of fiction. All the characters and events portrayed in this book are fictional, and any resemblance to real people or incidents is purely coincidental.

8 February 2018, First Edition

ISBN: 1984915169
ISBN-13: 9781984915160
Library of Congress Control Number: 2018901145

Noumenal Publishing

Cover art by Augusta Scarlett, www.scarlettebooks.com
Cover Copyright © 2018 Jeb Kinnison

1 - Sara: Gone West   1
2 - Jared: Bishop Snow's Office   3
3 - Sara: New Kid in Town   17
4 - Interlude: Incipient Rift Zone   27
5 - Randy: First Class   29
6 - Jared: Seminary   37
7 - Sara: Lailah   47
8 - Randy: Police Blotter   55
9 - Jared: Project with Sara   65
10 - Sara: Mine Hike   78
11 - Jared: Study Session   86
12 - Sara: Spellbound   90
13 - Randy: Enlightenment   93
14 - Jared: Family Dinner   100
15 - Sara: Predator   108
16 - Randy: Class   116
17 - Jared: Bishop Snow   122
18 - Sara: More Minions   128
19 - Randy: Lost   131
20 - Jared: Thanksgiving   137
21 - Randy: Seeking Help   143
22 - Jared: Betrayal   149
23 - Randy: The Noumenal Foundation   162
24 - Sara: Lunchroom Fight   173
25 - Jared: White Knight   176
26 - Randy: Disciplinary Hearing   180
27 - Sara: The Stick   183
28 - Jared: Attacked   192
29 - Randy: Truant Officer   196
30 - Sara: Dance   199
31 - Jared: Defender   202
32 - Randy: Cracking Up   206
33 - Sara: Escape   209
34 - Jared: Lost   213
35 - Sara: In Las Vegas   218
36 - Jared: Summoned   222
37 - Sara: Penthouse Suite   229

38 - Randy: Rumblings 233
39 - Jared: Graduation 236
40 - Randy: The Chase 240
41 - Sara: Labor 249
42 - Jared: Submerged 253
43 - Randy: Standoff 261
44 - Sara: Crowning 263
45 - Jared: Compulsion 264
46 - Randy: Intervention 271
47 - Sara: Revival 273
48 - Jared: Woke 275
49 - Randy: Debriefing 276
50 - Sara: Recovery 279
51 - Jared: New Mission 282

More by Jeb Kinnison 286
Further Reading 286
About the Author 287
Acknowledgements 289
Author's Note 290

1: Sara: Gone West

Sara Horowitz got a good view of Salt Lake City from a mile up. Through the scuffed plexiglass of the jet's window she could see Temple Square below as the airliner banked to make its final approach for landing. Off to the west was the Great Salt Lake itself, in shades of aquamarine set against the surrounding white and tan of salt flats and sand.

The businessman trapped in the middle seat next to her had tried to engage her in conversation. She had shut him down by giving him the briefest polite response to his questions about where she was going, then put on her headphones to listen to music. He was just a bit too interested, and she imagined that if she'd told him she was alone and headed to a hotel, he'd have asked her if she wanted to have a drink later. He was at least thirty—ewww!

He probably didn't realize she was only sixteen. She tried to give off a jaded, knowing vibe, and her goth style of dress and pale makeup helped.

So where was she going? She thought of herself as independent and in control, but when her parents divorced, she had only been pretending not to care—she could see now that it had disturbed her more than she had wanted to admit. And now her mother had taken a job in a small town hospital, and Sara's whole world was upended. It was either move to Utah with her mother or live with her father and the hated new stepmother. That was out of the question, so Utah it would be.

Sara's mother had scouted out the town and set up their apartment, but Sara had stayed behind in New York—she had never been west of Newark. She imagined Utah was very white and very Mormon, though you couldn't tell that by the people on the plane. It would all be very boring and she'd have to get through the last two years of high school in a backwater town without dying of dullness.

Far below her, beneath the mountains, watchers stirred as they sensed her presence.

2: Jared: Bishop Snow's Office

πορνεία, ας, ἡ — transliterated as **porneía** (the root of the
English terms pornography, pornographic; compare *pórnos*
(male prostitute) which is derived from *pernaō*, "to sell off")

1) The *selling off* (surrendering) of sexual purity; *promiscuity*
of any (every) type.
2) Metaphor: The worship of idols.

Jared Spendlove thumbed through the magazines on the
coffee table while he waited. Someone had neatly arranged the
LDS magazines in age order: *The Friend, New Era,* and *Ensign.*
The local Mt. Hermon *Times* newspaper occupied the center,
with the *Wall Street Journal* and the Sunday *Deseret News* on the
left. The bank offices were cool and modern, with slate floors,
grasscloth-covered walls, and glass-enclosed offices. Bishop
Snow's office was the only one you couldn't see into from the
lobby.

He paged through another magazine. The first article
stopped him—"Wives of Pornography Addicts Share What
They Wish They Had Known." Argh! Was God trying to tell
him something?

He had been struggling with his addiction to pornography
since he was twelve. His parents had bought him a laptop for
schoolwork, but quickly he had discovered online games and
porn. He knew it was wrong to spend so much time and energy
in game worlds, but that at least was clean. He hated himself for
jacking off several times a day to the porn he found free online.
As his addiction increased, he moved from pictures to videos,

from wholesome to kinky. He learned to browse in incognito mode to erase all record of his habits.

Finally it got so bad he stopped going to church and missed school. His mother thought it was the game worlds—she was the one who had suggested spiritual counselling. And so Jared was here, waiting to face the bishop.

He told himself this was the honorable course. The church was supposed to be an extended family, and any member suffering temptation would receive a sympathetic hearing and get support. At least he wasn't gay—he dismissed the few times his fantasies had gone that direction. And the one time his best friend had come on to him. Well, so he was only ninety-nine percent non-gay. *Almost* pure. But he certainly wasn't going to bring that up.

The office door opened, and Bishop Snow motioned him in.

Bishop Thomas Snow was a fixture in the community, head of the local bank and head of the local LDS ward. His suit was expensive-looking, his desk cleared of all but a computer and a picture of his family. Behind him through the window, Jared saw maple trees in fall colors of orange and red set against the dry foothills beyond, with Spirit Peak looming above. The stepped white buildings of the abandoned Zion Mine spilled down the side of the mountain.

"Take a seat," the bishop said, motioning to the chair in front of his desk. "Can I get you some water?"

Jared sat down. "No, thanks."

The bishop steepled his hands and looked straight into Jared's eyes. "It's been eight months since we talked last. Your mother asked me to speak to you. She's a lovely woman, and she's worried. Your grades are down and you're missing out on life. We understand there are many temptations for a young man. Tell me what you're struggling with and we'll help you deal with it."

Jared looked down at his hands. "Mom thinks it's games. But..."

"All of us have had to struggle with temptation, son. The first step is saying out loud that you have a problem. I've talked to hundreds of young men like you. Have the courage to talk about it."

"It's the porn. I can't stop looking at it. It's got the best of me..."

"Your mother is not as oblivious as you think. She washes your sheets and your underwear. Did you think she didn't notice?"

Jared started to sob. "I know it's wrong. I'd give anything to stop."

"The power of prayer and repentance can give you the strength to resist temptation, son. Ask for guidance from our Savior. He will answer." The bishop opened a drawer and pulled out a pamphlet. "We see this problem so often we have a written program. First step is to reduce temptation by avoiding the source—stay off the internet when you're by yourself. Get your computer out of your bedroom."

Jared took the pamphlet. On the cover was a pair of ghostly hands reaching out from a computer screen to grab a boy. "I've tried that. I just give up after a day or two and I can't get any school work done with my sister around."

"Tell your parents to set up a filter so you can only go to sites you need to use for school."

Jared grimaced. "I know how to get around any filter. No

one can help me but me."

"And God. Explain yourself to him and pray for strength. Resist the urge to abuse yourself."

"I will, Bishop Snow."

The bishop read from a passage of scripture. "'Verily, verily, I say unto you, ye must watch and pray always, lest ye be tempted by the devil, and ye be led away captive by him.'" He looked up at Jared, then continued to read selections about resisting temptation through prayer. When he had finished, he sighed and leaned back in his chair. "And you have missed too many Sundays, I hear. We gather together to seek the strength of our fellowship, and in times of great temptation our family and friends can help us find our own strengths. Through prayer and reaching out to others. Don't face your struggles alone."

The bishop typed at his computer, then began to write on a pad. "I've spoken with your father as well. He says that school isn't challenging enough for you. You're very bright, but unless you find a healthy outlet for your intelligence, you may be in more danger than the less gifted. We're a small town, so we don't have programs like they do in the city—our seminary leaves a lot to be desired. I have a teacher in mind for you—to help you gain the spiritual strength you need through study and prayer. At BYU—she teaches a new online seminary for advanced high school students. Lisa Atwater—former Marine, doctorate in religion, a formidable woman. Call her." He tore off the page and gave it to Jared.

"Thank you, sir. I will."

"I'll let her know you're coming. It's probably not too late to get you in for this term. And, son," the bishop said, turning to look out the window, "I have struggled with a similar problem.

Don't look so surprised, your elders were young once, too. I had to learn to step away from lust, to save God's gift of sexual pleasure for my wife. If you waste your seed you will never have the strength you need to court a real woman. Stop masturbating —you need to use that energy to create a life for yourself and your family."

Jared didn't know what to say. "I'll do my best. And thank you again."

They shook hands, Bishop Snow gripping his hand tightly and then pulling him into a hug. "I know you are good, Brother. My door is always open to you—let me know how you are doing with it in a few months. I want to hear that you have spent your time praying and learning, and not abusing yourself." The bishop smelled faintly of Old Spice and money.

❖   ❖   ❖   ❖   ❖

Jared was driving his older brother Connor's worn-out Corolla. It took three tries to start it, but finally the engine caught and he eased out of the bank parking lot and down Main Street toward home. On the right he saw the state liquor agency, the only store in town where you could buy alcoholic beverages —the parking lot was almost full. On the left, he passed City Hall and the police headquarters where his father was likely getting ready to leave work. The radio was set to the local station, usually dominated by crop reports and phone-in talk shows. His brother had left a few scratched CDs in the glove compartment, but nothing Jared particularly liked. Jared turned up the radio when the news started.

"The search for Bella Harris and Justin Lopez continues

today. The two college students from Provo were last seen a week ago headed into the National Forest trails on Spirit Peak. Their car was left at the trailhead parking, and searchers led by park rangers, the Sheriff's Office with dogs, and volunteers have turned up nothing. Today a helicopter with infrared scanners will overfly the area looking for signs. There's a five thousand dollar reward for information on their current whereabouts. Their families are holding a fundraiser in the trailhead parking lot tomorrow at noon before heading out for another search. All are welcome to join them." Then a tape of the distraught parents asking for help. An ad for the Salem Ford car dealership followed, then a list of missing pets, then the weather.

A thunderhead was building over the mountain as Jared pulled into the driveway. Lightning flashes illuminated the dark clouds below the sunlit anvil of white cloud above, but he could barely hear the distant rumble of thunder above the noise of a lawnmower across the street. He waved at the mower's operator, a younger student at his high school, before heading in.

The house was older but comfortable, with knotty pine paneling from the 50s in the living room and orange laminate counters and newer stainless appliances in the kitchen, where he found his mother putting away groceries.

"How'd it go?" she said. His mother was thin and birdlike, her hair permed and graying.

"Okay, I guess. I have my orders. He was very… understanding."

"You know you can always talk to me about anything that's bothering you. But I know you'll listen to him when you might not listen to me or your father. When you were a Scout—"

"That was a long time ago."

"Just two years. You looked up to him then. I never understood why you stopped going."

"It just seemed like a waste of time to me. I have more interesting things to do." Jared opened a cabinet and got out a box of cheese crackers.

"Like spend all your time online playing games. While you let the real world pass you by."

"I tried to get a job. There's nothing out there. I get my schoolwork done. What am I missing out on?"

"How about girls? Since Melissa you haven't even tried. You're handsome. You should be going out more."

He chewed on the handful of crackers. Bringing up Melissa was a low blow—she had dumped him when he backed away from her pressure to commit to marrying her. "I go out enough."

"With Preston. To play more games."

"We work on our music, too," Jared said. "Our YouTube videos get lots of views."

"Let me know when you start making enough money to cover your game fees," his mother said, arching one brow. "It may not seem like much but they add up. Your father thinks we should stop the charges."

"I can get by without buying anything. It's free to play."

"Yet somehow you spend ten or twenty dollars a month on it."

"That just makes it cooler and faster. But I'll stop buying stuff if that's what you want."

"That's not really the point here. The point is that you need to focus on your schooling and your real life, not this false life inside a machine. Other kids are passing you by, getting into the best colleges, meeting the right people to start a family someday. You're just *present*. Some of the time." His mother leaned down to put vegetables in the refrigerator lower bin. Her voice was muffled. "This is the time to get out in the world, before you have a family and responsibilities. You may never have the opportunity again. What you do now determines what you can do for the rest of your life. Do you want to be a cop like your dad? Even that means college these days."

"Dad did okay. He didn't go to college."

"The competition is much tougher now. Sure, you can go to community college and do okay, but you're much smarter than that. We want you to use your gifts wisely. You should go to BYU, like your brother."

Jared got a glass out of the upper cabinet and filled it with milk. "As it turns out, I will be, soon. Bishop Snow referred me to a BYU professor for advanced seminary. Online, so I can do it from here. And I was thinking I'd do my mission before college."

"But you still need the best grades to get into a good school. You used to get mostly A's, now you get B's, and I'm hearing you're distracted."

"I'll do better. The bishop has me on a program of prayer and abstinence. You'll see."

It had grown darker outside, and a bright flash of lightning followed by a clap of thunder heralded the beginning of heavy rain.

❖   ❖   ❖   ❖   ❖

After dinner Jared excused himself and went upstairs to

brush his teeth, then sat down at his desk with the laptop. His room was small, with sunshine yellow walls and a hand-me-down maple twin bed that had been part of a bunk bed set he'd shared with his brother when they were little, before they'd moved to the larger house. He'd recently replaced the Call of Duty poster over his desk with a Morpheum Online poster showing most of the character types in a fantastic battle.

He felt a little guilty since he had promised himself to tell his parents he would move the computer downstairs where he wouldn't be able to use it for porn, but he'd start that tomorrow. He got out the paper the bishop had given him. At the top was the name, phone number, and email of the online seminary professor, Lisa Atwater. Below that the bishop had written, "And look up NOFAP on Google." He typed it into the search bar.

A half hour later, he had read up on NoFap on Reddit and Wikipedia and knew he was far from alone in being hooked on porn. The leaflet the bishop had given him was entirely religious—recommending prayer, faith, struggle, avoiding temptation. The NoFap people came at it from the more pragmatic and practical angle of whatever worked. If he just stopped, it seemed to say, he would conquer the habit, and be more energized to do what had to be done to get a real girl to have sex with him. He was sure he had seen people joking about it online but never realized what they were talking about. But now he had some hope—others had been there before him and fought back successfully. He would win, too.

Jared logged into Morpheum Online, the latest online game world to gather millions of players. The world opened up to the last place his character—Starclaw, Thane of Falconhurst—had been, near the Falls of Eredon. Starclaw was a hulking giant,

Thor on steroids with exaggerated muscles and his signature
battle-axe, with leather and plate armor; Starclaw moved more
slowly but packed more strength than all but a few of his foes.

The comm channel had messages received after he had left,
so he quickly replied to each and checked on the squad leader's
location. Action had moved down the ridge to the Vale of Sher,
so he teleported to the nearest drop point and started moving
toward the front line where his squad was defending a small
fort. He stopped to collect a glowing pouch of unicorn horn
dust, then reached the battle in time to confront a giant orc
clubbing one of his mates. One blow of his axe took off the
giant's head, green blood gushing from the stump of its neck
before it collapsed and dissolved. He gave his teammate a
healing potion and moved on.

He had wanted to check in and then log off, but his squad
needed him. It was an hour before the first wave of attackers
had been dispatched. In a lull, he messaged his squad, "Going to
be busy for awhile, won't be on much."

Replies varied from "Okay, man," to "Bye for now."

Before logging out he got a notification from the location
add-on—he had installed it to allow other players to find him if
they were close in the real world. He was usually careful not to
reveal too much online, but he wanted to recruit players close
enough to have low-latency connections to him, for faster
command communication. Jared clicked on the sender and a
popup showed a newbie's record—no battles, one quest, low
strength ratings. The avatar was an anime boy elf with pointed
ears and sparkling eyes. His age was shown as 99 years, which
seemed unlikely.

Lanarick: Hi

Starclaw: Hi back. I see you're new.

Lanarick: New to this game, old hand elsewhere. You live in Mt. Hermon?

Starclaw: Born and raised here, yes. You?

Lanarick: Just moved here. My mom took a job at the hospital.

Starclaw: You in high school yet? What year?

Lanarick: Junior. Just enrolled, first day will be Monday.

Starclaw: Great! I'm a senior. Look me up. Jared Spendlove. Found a team yet?

Lanarick: You mean for the game? No

Starclaw: Take a look at mine. We welcome newbies. If you're smart.

Lanarick: I will. How will I recognize you at school?

Starclaw: Tall, blond, geeky. Ask anyone to point me out. What do you look like?

Lanarick: I'm a girl. Short, dark, goth. :-)

Starclaw: And your name?

Lanarick: Sara Horowitz

Starclaw: Good to meet you, Sara. I have to go to bed now. See you Monday, I hope!

Lanarick: Nice to meet you as well. G'night

He left the game world and rubbed his eyes. He Googled Sara's name and stared at pages of results—too many to figure out which one might be her since the name was so common. He ended up on a website called "Jew or Not?" looking at the Vladimir Horowitz entry. It seemed likely Sara was Jewish—if so, she would be not quite the only Jew in town, but still very rare. She might be either beautiful or disgusting, though most people into online gaming tended to be, umm, not lookers. Or at least more casual about hygiene and appearance. On the other hand, most of the girls who worked hard to look good would brush him off. He wasn't on their radar.

It was after midnight and well past time for bed. The house was quiet so everyone else had already gone to sleep. His habit was to take the laptop to bed with him and jack off to the free porn sites he had found—Pornworld, XXXTube, and the others.

He'd taken to using hand lotion as lube and cleaning up with one of his white cotton gym socks, which he then threw under the bed, being careful to retrieve them and put them in the closet hamper every morning before his mother could come in and find them. He had noticed yellow stains on his socks even after laundering, so that habit was going to have to go—he shuddered to think his mother had noticed. But if he didn't jack off at all, there'd be no tell-tale stains to deal with....

He resisted the urge and went to bed without the laptop. It took a lot longer than usual to get to sleep. He tried praying but ended up thinking about Sara before he drifted off.

❁　　❁　　❁　　❁　　❁

The dream started off with a search for something. He was looking for a key—literally a key to the house, then a door. He was with his older brother, then a beautiful dark girl—he couldn't see her face but everything about her was graceful. He was underwater, holding his breath, trying to find the key in the bottom ooze. He found it! The girl was back, by his side—he felt her there and wanted to be strong for her. They approached the massive oak door bound in dark metal bands. He was about to put the key in the keyhole when Bishop Snow grabbed his hand.

"Son, don't open that unless you want to know more than you should," the bishop said. His voice was like the rumble of thunder.

The dark girl was gone, replaced by another girl wearing a white wedding dress with a veil over her long blond hair. She smiled at him knowingly as they stood side-by-side under a golden bower covered with white flowers. Then they were looking into each other's eyes as they kneeled on either side of a wedding altar, Bishop Snow standing at one side. Then they were in bed, naked, his bride reaching around his neck and pulling his head down toward her swelling breasts. He started to get hard. He felt something behind him and suddenly the bishop was in the bed behind him, still in a wool suit which scratched Jared's bare back. He looked up to see his parents watching from the stands, grandparents above that, and great-grandparents and the other ancestors rising in ranks above them, disappearing into the haze. He felt sick and his stiffness subsided, but then his bride pushed his head down further down to her warmth and wetness. His hands and feet were tied, but somehow then he was on top of her, pushing himself into her. She bit his neck as he penetrated her further. An old man's hands reached from behind him, holding her pelvis and pushing him in all the way. The world rumbled and gushes of warmth splashed over him.

Then he was face up, straddled by his naked bride. Her perfect breasts bounced as she rode him and fingered herself, her hair wild, stray blond tendrils plastered across her breasts. He thrust in rhythm with her movements.

His new bride shrieked and clawed at his chest as he erupted. Everything went black.

A high, pure tone pierced the quiet of his room. Then he felt a presence—swelling to fill all space, pushing back the dark and the shadowy dreamscape.

"Jared!" a musical voice announced. Jared was blinded by a brilliant light. When he could see again, a man in flowing translucent robes stood before him. Emerald green light streamed from his shoulders and head. His hair was copper-red.

"Attend me."

"I'm here."

"I am Raphael, sent by our Lord God to guide you. You would destroy yourself with your lusts if you do not grow beyond them. Beware the Harlot, for she will tempt you into sin with false visions. The path upward is narrow and steep, but you can climb it to glory if you have faith. Do not be afraid, do not be turned from the path. God is with you at every step."

The light and the presence faded, and he dropped further into sleep. When morning came, he only remembered the sense of warmth and shame, then forgiveness. It had stormed through the night, but the dawn sky was blue and clear.

Monday morning. Sara Horowitz made coffee while her mother showered. The orientation packet instructed her to be in her assigned homeroom at the high school by 7:30 AM, but at least she could walk instead of taking the bus since their new apartment was only two blocks away. Her mother had been at work at her new job as administrator at the community hospital for a week, and no one expected her to be in until 8:30.

Sara made some toast and buttered it. Her mother came down the stairs in a bathrobe and poured herself a mug of coffee. "Excited about going to a new school?" she asked, sitting down at the table and picking up a slice of toast.

"Kind of. Not as big as Manhasset, less pressure. Less diverse. It'll be easier to stand out here, but harder to get into a good college—kids here don't leave the state." Sara sat down with a bowl of cereal.

"I know. But this job is the opportunity I was looking for, so I had to take it. You could have lived with your father—"

"Yuck. Then I'd have to put up with Missy." Her new stepmother, brittle and robotic. Why her father took up with her... Dad had shrugged when asked. Missy looked a lot like Sara's mother, just younger and less worn with anger and regret.

"So here we are for a few years. Make the best of it. There are some cute boys..."

"Jesus Christ." Sara rolled her eyes. Her mother had no idea what boys Sara might like since Sara had never admitted to liking any.

"You'll be in college before you know it. Whoever you meet

here, you'll forget about there. So relax and have a good time getting to know the locals."

"I did chat with one last night. Online. He's a player in Morpheum, seems cool."

"There you go, already making friends. Does he go to your school?"

"Yes. But a senior, so I probably won't have any classes with him."

"Still, it's a start. I had to change schools many times because of my dad's career. Each time it gets easier to make new friends. Just be yourself."

"I'm hoping not to frighten them." Sara rinsed out her cereal bowl and put it in the dishwasher. "I'm late, still have to dress. Have a good day at work." She leaned down to kiss her mother's neck.

"You too," her mother said, looking at her phone. "Text me if you need anything."

✧   ✧   ✧   ✧   ✧

The high school was a modern red brick and green glass building set on a grassy corner lot with parking lots on one side and bus lanes on the other. Sara crossed the street at the light, dodging a group of runners before making her way into a crowd of students waiting for the doors to open. She was proud of herself for getting there early.

A group of girls chattered by the doors. Sara knew they would be less diverse than she was used to, but they were almost all blond, with one redhead standing out. They radiated health and had bright white teeth. *And I used to feel invisible.*

Here I stand out. There were banners in the school windows, one about the upcoming GENERAL DEER HUNT (whatever that was) and others about sports teams. Most of the girls and almost all of the boys wore blue jeans, with a scattering of shorts and hoodies.

There was an empty space at the end of one of the concrete benches, so she brushed off the fallen leaves and sat down to wait. The girl sitting closest to her looked over and smiled. "You're new here, right?" She was another blond, but with shorter-than-average hair, freckles, and a pug nose that made her seem more comic than intimidating.

"This is my first day, just moved to town last week."

"Oh, great! We need some fresh meat here. You're from back east?"

"How could you tell?" Sara laughed and exaggerated her accent. "From 'Lawn Guyland.' My mom took a job at the hospital."

The girl smiled brightly and turned further toward her, holding out her hand. "I'm Brandy Hansen."

"Sara Horowitz. Good to meet you."

Sara began to relax as she realized that however different these kids looked from what she was used to, they were mostly friendly and kind. Brandy chattered on, extracting more information from Sara—homeroom (they had the same one!), boy likes and dislikes, past boyfriends and creeps to watch out for. Brandy nodded toward a group of mostly boys on the other side of the entranceway.

"See those guys?" she said. "Jocks, mostly. And those girls over there..." she nodded to the left, "Our mean girls. Not

Hollywood mean, but competitive. Watch your step and stay out of their way and you'll be fine."

"I have no intention of … *competing*."

"Well, you're very pretty and very different. How do you keep your skin so pale? And your eyes—striking, the green with such dark hair. And those long, dark lashes!"

"Thanks. It's my genetic heritage, I guess. Wandering Jews." Sara laughed nervously. She was sharing maybe too much too soon?

"Oooh, exotic! We're mostly the dullest of whitebread-and-Jello-salad Mormons here, with a few Catholics and Methodists." Brandy looked over at a more distant group of boys. "You're already turning heads. Don't look! But you have at least three guys watching you and talking to their friends about you. You'll be turning down dates before you know it."

The front doors opened and students shuffled into the building.

❂   ❂   ❂   ❂   ❂

Sara found her locker and stored her backpack inside, keeping only a notebook and her phone. The homeroom was on the second floor not far from her locker, and Brandy had already saved a seat for her near the front. The room quickly filled, and since these were the kids she would see every morning of the school year, Sara examined them for clues.

A clump of rowdy boys in the back. A cluster of geeks looking at their laptops. Girls who were probably cheerleaders out of uniform. A few lost souls sat quietly, but her eyes slid past them without noticing anything memorable.

"What's on your schedule?" Brandy said. "Maybe we've got classes together."

Sara pulled out the printed schedule from her packet. "Next up, PE. Have to go back to the locker to get my gym clothes. After that, AP US History and Politics. The counsellor said that was usually a senior course but she said my record made the regular class a waste of time."

"Impressive. Your school probably makes us look sad."

"It was very competitive, but the kids there had lots of issues. Suicides, ulcers."

"No way!"

"The town is very rich and the kids were mostly from families of doctors, lawyers, and finance people. If you weren't one of them, you didn't stand a chance. Summers in Europe and all that."

"Just a few rich kids here. I'm looking forward to the big city —Salt Lake!"

"It's all relative, I guess… then there's Chemistry, then English, lunch, then Chorus, finishing up with Algebra II."

Brandy looked up from her own printout. "Aha! We have Algebra together. Mr. Olsen again, I had him last year. He's great."

"Classes end at 2:40. Why so early?"

"I guess because we used to be mostly farmers. And then there's seminary. The law says we have to go to a separate building with no tax money to study LDS topics. Some kids go in the early morning, some after school."

"Ah," Sara said. "A few kids went to Hebrew school after school. Same idea."

"I suppose. I enjoy it but being a Mormon means hardly

getting any time to yourself. If you're not being run ragged by your family, you're in some program or other, then being sent off on your mission. Not great for introverts."

"Good thing I'm not a Mormon, then." Sara sighed.

An older gray-haired woman in a flowered sweater came in and sorted some papers at the desk in front. She looked around until everyone quieted, then said, "I'm Mrs. Grimes, your homeroom teacher. We only have five minutes to take attendance, so listen up. You will be here every day at 7:30 sharp, or report in at the Office before going to class if you are tardy for any reason—the state requires we take attendance because our funding depends on the daily count. I'm going to read the list of students registered to this homeroom, and I want you to sound off when you hear your name. Jason Anderson?"

"Here."

"Stonewall Ballard?"

"Yo."

The reading of the list went on while Sara tried to associate each name with a face. When her name was called she was surprised and blurted, "Yes!" She flushed red. The worst thing in the world was to feel people staring at her, whether they really were or not.

When attendance was finished, they waited for the bell.

"So if you're Jewish," Brandy said, "where will you go to church? What do they call them, synagogues?"

"Usually we say temple. But we aren't very observant—I haven't been in years. So we'll be fine."

"We have to go. A lot. Besides, we don't have that much else to do here, so that's where your friends are."

"I do some study on my own. My parents had me going to

classes and I had my bat mitzvah when I was twelve, but then they divorced and we stopped going to temple."

"That seems sad, somehow."

"Oh, it's fine. I read Torah and study Talmud, I read up on the Kabbalah—at least Kabbalah for Dummies—and I've read some of the Christian Bible, I should look at your Book of Mormon. They all say the same thing. Be kind, the Golden Rule, blah blah blah."

The bell rang.

"Well, see you in Algebra!" Brandy said.

Sara made her way down the main stairs and down the hall toward the back of the school. The gymnasium, auditorium, and performance rooms backed up to the athletic fields and visitor parking. She found the girls' locker room, already crowded with girls changing. She spotted an open space near the back and an empty locker.

Undressing made her anxious and she tried to face the lockers while she changed. She had taken off her shirt when the blond girl closest to her said, "Hi! You're new here?"

"Yes, we just moved here from New York." This was going to get old fast.

"Oh, I heard about you!" The girl blushed—she had long straight blond hair and freckles scattered across her nose. "Welcome to Mt. Hermon. I'm Kaylee."

"I'm Sara. And thanks." Sara turned to cut off the conversation and hoped Kaylee hadn't noticed anything.

"If you don't mind my asking—what happened to your arms?" Kaylee pointed to the scars. They had faded over the years since The Episode, but still stood out as raised welts, six or seven on each wrist.

Sara always wore long-sleeved shirts when she could. Her mother had tried to get her to see a doctor for plastic surgery to disguise the scars, but Sara didn't want to erase them, and it would have been costly. Her friends back East knew about them, but no one here knew—yet.

There was no choice but to plunge ahead. "I had an accident with a mirror when I was a kid. Sliced up my arms where I was trying to protect myself."

"Oh! That's terrible. I'm so sorry." Kaylee looked at her with her blue eyes wide.

Sara could detect no malice in Kaylee. Cutting was apparently not a thing in Mt. Hermon. "That's okay, it was a long time ago and it didn't hurt that much."

The gym class assembled on the bleachers and the teacher—an athletic young woman in sweats with close-cropped hair and a whistle—spent most of the hour talking about the activities they'd be doing, including gun safety training—with parental approval—and lots of cross-country. Inside sports like volleyball were scheduled for the winter months. Then the teacher led them on a run on the outdoor track, a paved loop around the football field.

Back from the run, the coach released them. Sara wiped the sweat off with paper towels and avoided the shower. She could see too much pink flesh and hair in the gang shower room and the loud voices echoing from the tiled walls repelled her. She changed quickly and left.

The next class was History. The kids were mostly seniors, and several boys were staring as she entered the room. She looked down at the floor and found a seat. Two boys entered, laughing and talking loudly, so she looked up to make sure she was no longer the center of attention and relaxed enough to look around.

Her eyes stopped on a tall boy sitting off by himself in the back corner. His hair was shaggy and almost gold in highlights, his shirt rumpled brown like he had just stepped in from a forest. He caught her looking and started, before a slow smile lit his face. One hand went up to tip an imaginary hat her way.

Time stopped. What was the name?—Jared. Her pulse began to race and she flushed—he was hot, in a geeky way that felt right. She nodded back.

A throat-clearing from the front of the room signalled the arrival of the teacher. He looked like a refined biker—black leather jacket, blue jeans, military high-and-tight haircut, graying at the temples.

"Good morning, all. This is AP US History and Politics, so if that was not the class you were expecting, you should find another classroom." When no one moved, he continued. "I'm Randy Wright." He wrote it on the whiteboard. "Please do not call me 'Mr. Wright.' My wife is very tired of that joke. You can call me sir, or Randy if we're talking outside class. If you're here, you've signed up for hard work and a lot of reading. If you do well on the AP exam, you may be able to get college credit for this course. But we're going well beyond the usual syllabus— this will be a true college-level course that covers more than just what's on the AP exam. Any questions?" No one stirred. "Is a... Sara Horowitz here?"

Sara raised her hand. "Here."

"Welcome to Mt. Hermon, Sara. Your counsellor tells me you've already had much of the material in the standard American History course so she felt you would benefit from taking the

AP version. Are you comfortable with that?"

"Yes, sir."

"Good. The rest of you volunteered, so here we go." He turned back to the whiteboard and began writing.

Sara looked back toward Jared. He smiled and gave her a thumbs-up.

4: Interlude: Incipient Rift Zone

The Wasatch Fault runs from north to south down the center of Utah. On the east side of the fault are the upthrust Wasatch Mountains, riding atop the ancient North American continental root, or *craton*. On the west side of the fault is the Great Basin, filled with layers of sediment. The Great Salt Lake is the remnant of a much larger Ice Age lake that once filled the basin. Since there is no outlet to the sea, water with dissolved minerals enters from the surrounding catchment area and leaves only by evaporation, leaving the lake to grow saltier over time. Layers of salt laid down by the lake as it shrank created the Bonneville Salt Flats.

Volcanic activity in the mid-Cenozoic covered large areas of Utah with volcanic ash, and deposits of silver, gold, and copper were injected into existing fault zones as dikes. Heat from below wells up under the crust, spreading and thinning it. The Yellowstone hot spot, a fixed plume of intense heat from the mantle, created volcanoes in a line starting in eastern Oregon 16 million years ago, moving through the Snake River Valley of Idaho to its current location under Yellowstone as the North American plate moved west above it. The disruptive effect of the mantle plume began a rifting of the continent along the Wasatch Line as the additional heat and stress softened the thin crust.

Faulting along the incipient rift valley runs roughly along the route of Interstate 15 from Los Angeles through Las Vegas to Salt Lake City and then north to Yellowstone. The segment of the Wasatch Fault near Salt Lake City has been locked for 1200 years, and a magnitude 7.5 earthquake could occur there at any time.

The mantle hotspot plumes rise through the mantle from the magnetic field dynamo that operates in the Earth's fluid outer core. The tremendous energies released by decaying transuranic elements in the core produce heat that runs the convective dynamo that generates the Earth's magnetic field.

Since long before the time of Man, the dynamo in the Earth's core has supported a form of life, patterns of magnetic energy that can live indefinitely in the fields generated by convection in the liquid outer core. Some of these life forms evolved on Earth, but some were exiles from the stars. The strongest of them were able to observe and influence the electrical activity in the brains of the primitive humans, who learned to worship them as gods.

5: Randy: First Class

Randy Wright remembered his first years of teaching, when each new group of kids had seemed full of potential and he felt a rush of adrenalin before taking his place in front of the class. After a decade, though, it was routine and he could slot most of the new students in a few bins based on his first years of teaching—that boy will turn out to be a cruder version of Jason Stone, that girl will be a chattier Heather Andersen. There were few surprises and he didn't need to rehearse his classroom performances—he could wing it unless he modified the syllabus.

The classroom had been remodeled over the summer, freshly painted a sage green, and the fluorescent tubes in the ceiling had been replaced with warmer LED versions that were a lot easier on his eyes. The new whiteboards covered the entire front wall of the room and slid back and forth on rollers. He had asked for more AV support, and now there was a big LCD monitor behind a whiteboard and connectors on the desk for a laptop.

His back was turned to the class while he underlined the "No Late Homework" line he had just written on the whiteboard. "If you're late getting homework in, you'll get a zero for it. That doesn't mean you shouldn't do it—if you don't you'll miss some important material which will be on the exam. You'll find in life that no one gets points for being a day late and a dollar short."

The kids in front looked suitably cowed. Randy had noticed the looks passing between the transfer student, Sara, and the local boy in the back—the police chief's son, Jared. Some devil in Randy made him pick on her. "Sara?" Her head turned back to the front. "Sara, I understand your last school was ranked one of the best in the country. Did they let you hand in late homework?"

Sara looked back at him. "No, sir, mostly. I remember one teacher would, but he took off points for every day late." Her green eyes really were quite striking against her pale olive skin.

"That's more special treatment than I have time for. If you miss an occasional assignment you can still get an A, so perfection is not expected or required." Sara kept her eyes forward, so he had achieved his goal of establishing control. "But reading all the assigned material is. If you don't read the textbook and the readings, you won't do well on the exams. The syllabus and reading list are on the class web page. You're responsible for buying the books—other than the primary text—or getting the readings from the library. Much of the public-domain material is linked to the class page."

He wrapped up the ground rules and started on the overview.

"Who can tell me what is meant by 'American exceptionalism?'" Hands went up. "Okay, umm—" he looked at the seating chart on the desk. "Claire."

"God blessed America and chose us to be an example to other nations?"

"That would be one religious perspective, but it's not necessary to invoke religion to discuss the idea. Let me ask a different question to shed some light on this discussion—why do you think the US has more churchgoing and professed religious citizens than most of the countries in Europe that immigrants came from?"

A few hands went up. "Sara."

"We were the first country to establish freedom of religion? So the US attracted those who had been persecuted for their religion in other countries?"

"There may be something to that, but most of those new immigrants came here several generations ago. Why would there still be a difference?" He looked toward the back. "Justin."

"Most of the European countries had one powerful church?"

"Yes, that's what I'm getting at. Europeans resented their established churches and the reaction was to support government as a countervailing force. So during the French revolution priests and nuns were executed and Catholic church property was expropriated. Here only a few colonies, like Massachusetts, had government-supported religion. In Massachusetts, authorities were hanging heretics and burning witches for a hundred years before freedom of religion was established. By the time the Constitution was written, most educated people understood that the bloodshed and war that came from religious differences could be avoided only by separating belief from civil government. And so we got the First Amendment, establishing freedom of speech and religion—really the freedom to think differently from the majority without being jailed or punished."

Jared had his hand up and Randy nodded toward him.

"What about the persecution of the Mormons?"

"We'll have a reading on that topic after Thanksgiving. Since many of you are descendants of the group of Mormons driven out of the Midwest before the Civil War, you'll be interested in hearing how that *pogrom*—a word I don't use lightly, which while it was never as systematic as the pogroms against Jews in Europe, sprung from the same tribal hatreds—led to the founding of the independent state of Deseret, which was eventually—and mostly peacefully—was incorporated into the United States as the state of Utah.

"Those persecutions were contrary to the law, much as lynchings were never legally authorized actions, but the result of mob sentiment. While there were some shameful government actions, like the official order from Missouri's governor authorizing extermination of all Mormons, these were widely seen as unlawful even at the time."

Jared crossed his arms, clearly unconvinced. "So some religious beliefs weren't really protected."

"Minority religions that practice what is viewed as sinful by dominant religions are naturally going to be viewed with suspicion by majority populations. The Latter Day Saints were seen as a cult suddenly flooding towns to take land and business from settlers who'd already set up there. Of course this led to bad feelings. You have to remember how isolated communities were in those days—there might be a local newspaper, but there were no telephones or mass media, and news came by riverboat and mail. Over a period of a few months a community could be flooded with new residents who stuck together and seemed organized to dominate the original residents. How would you feel if thousands of Scientologists, say, moved in and bought up half your town?"

Jared shrugged. "Not so happy, I guess. Sounds like what's happening in Europe lately."

"And that's why we study history—to understand how natural human tendencies lead to big political movements and changes over time. Mormons were refugees when they came here to get away from hostile interference. That's the story of the United States—move to the frontier to gain freedom for your religion, then when your area gets crowded, look for the commonalities in your beliefs and accommodate the differences."

Randy turned to the whiteboard and began to write. "Americanism. What could be called the secular religion of the United States, the Enlightenment ideals of the Founders and the willingness to accept as American any person or group of people who behaved in accordance with those ideals, a kind of belief system not attached to any particular territory which could expand to the western frontier and into the minds of people all over the world, spread by pop culture like music and movies. We'll look at how this bundle of ideals took root and grew here, and the competing ideologies like Communism that contended with it around the world for power over minds and hearts. We'll also talk about the challenges of issues like slavery, which resulted in the Civil War. The ideal of equal treatment under the law was only realized after a long and costly struggle—which continues even today."

Randy went on to outline the themes to be covered and the requirements of the AP exam. His phone beeped to warn him he had only a minute left to wrap up before the bell.

"Read chapter one of the main textbook and the readings on pre-Columbian peoples and the era of discovery. If you want to read ahead, start in on the Colonial-era readings. By next month we'll be looking at the sources of the ideas in the Declaration of Independence and Constitution. There'll be a pop quiz sometime next week."

Someone groaned softly.

"Sorry. I want to be sure that if you need to goof off in a class, it won't be this one—you can't put off the reading until later and cram before the final."

The bell rang and Randy opened the door. "See you all Wednesday."

Randy noticed Sara was talking to Jared, hanging back while everyone else left. Randy collected his notes from the desk and pretended to scan them while he listened, but they were talking too softly to be understood with all the noise from the hall outside. Sara smiled and nodded, then left. Jared came forward and hesitated until Randy looked up.

"Mr. Wright—Randy. But that feels odd," Jared said.

"Don't worry about it. If it makes you feel more comfortable, call me Mr. Wright. I was joking about that bothering me."

"Okay. I just wanted to ask, you talk like you're not a Mormon."

"I'm not. I married one, but I was raised Methodist. I admire the Mormon community spirit but would be afraid of community pressure as well. It can be both good to have lots of people who care about you, and bad—when they push you to conform. Shouldn't you be off to class?"

"Next period is study hall, almost next door—but I wanted to ask you about that. Sometimes I don't feel like I belong here. But then I'm afraid to leave. You hear so many stories about people who leave and go haywire, drugs and suicide."

"You're not having any thoughts in that direction, I hope?"

"No, just—wondering where I belong."

"That's the human condition, Jared. It's just worse when you're your age. Keep learning and questioning. Don't throw away what you have for what's on the other side of the fence. Take your time and talk to your family and friends. It'll sort itself out."

"Okay. Thanks." Jared turned and left.

◊   ◊   ◊   ◊   ◊

That afternoon Randy went home early since he had no grading yet to do. The sun was still high in the sky and the mountain loomed over the town, the bright white buildings of the mine shining against the green and brown of the mountainside. He was still thinking about Jared and Sara as he parked the car in his driveway and went inside. They were striking together, light and dark, male and female, yin and yang. Were they going to be a couple? It wasn't often he speculated about students' personal lives. Something about them....

He relished this time to himself—his daughter was still at school and his wife would come home from work around six, so he was supposed to make dinner by then. He sat down in front of his computer and answered a few emails before starting up an online war game, where he lost himself for an hour directing a tank battle.

After dinner their daughter excused herself to do homework. Randy and his wife Stephanie lingered at the table.

"So how did the first day go?" Stephanie asked, starting to clear the plates.

"Same old same old. We have an interesting new student, a Jewish girl from New York named Sara. The other kids are talking about her."

"No wonder. She's an exotic creature from foreign lands

seen only on TV." Stephanie laughed.

"She was flirting with Roger Spendlove's son, who's Mormon through and through. I predict sparks." Randy helped by washing the pans while his wife put the dishes in the dishwasher.

Stephanie smiled. "I remember when that was us." She sighed and picked up a towel to help him dry the rest of the pans.

Randy remembered. They had met in Iowa City at the university half a lifetime ago—he was the dark one, she the light. Twenty years, two children, and a shared history of troubles overcome and joys shared. Nothing like his youthful dreams of being a crusading journalist, but he wouldn't trade any of it for the glory he had imagined.

That night he dreamt. Something was expected of him, and he tried to comply, but couldn't move. He was tied down by thousands of threads, unable to get free. He watched as Jared and Sara walked unaware toward him. They stopped and he watched them embrace, then undress. He tried to speak but nothing would come out—something horrible was about to happen but he couldn't warn them.

6: Jared: Seminary

When the bell rang at the end of History class, Jared moved forward to introduce himself to Sara.

"Hi," he said. "Jared Spendlove. We talked in Morpheum." He bowed slightly.

"I figured that out. Sara Horowitz."

"Good to meet you in the real world. It's great to have someone interesting turn up."

"Thanks, likewise. But listen, I need to go—Chemistry next. The science labs are on the other side of the building, right?"

"Yes, turn right and all the way down the hall, then left. The labs are all on that side."

"Thanks. Be seeing you. You have a phone?"

"You mean, on me?" Jared pulled out his phone.

"Open it." Sara took it from him. "Here's my number." She typed in her number and hit dial. Her phone rang once before she ended the call. "Call me, I don't know anyone here."

"I'd be happy to show you around." Jared took his phone back and started filling in Sara's address book entry.

"Gotta go," she said, and smiled at him before turning to leave.

Jared was as happy as he had ever been—no ambiguity there, she was inviting him to go out. He wasn't in a rush so he approached Mr. Wright to ask him a question….

◊   ◊   ◊   ◊   ◊

The first day of school dragged on. His mind kept drifting

back to replaying Sara's voice, face, and movements, but he
didn't see her again all day. When the last bell rang, he was out
the door and waited a bit by the bus loading area, hoping she
would appear, but she didn't. He gave up and went to his car,
disappointed.

Once home, he went upstairs and started up his computer.
He tried a web search on Sara's name again, then her phone
number, but the area code—631—was for cell phones over a
large area of Long Island, and didn't have any useful search hits.

Soon it was four o'clock and time to log in to the online
seminary class—his father had called the number Bishop Snow
gave him and explained the situation, so arrangements had
been made to enroll him.

Jared had done a web search on the professor. "Capt. Lisa
Atwater, USMC, Retired" had been appointed to her position at
BYU last year with some fanfare—a press release and a lun-
cheon. She had served in Iraq—both wars—and studied religion back East before coming back to Utah. She was supposed
to liven up the moribund all-old-white-male Department of
Ancient Scripture since she had been recognized for her studies
of Hebrew and Greek biblical texts. "An original, a soldier-
scholar," the press release described her.

The class was live and interactive only once a week, Thursday afternoon, but every school day he was supposed to log in
and work through the canned lesson plan for the day, so today
he logged in for the first time. There were assignments to be
done, with a video and some readings. The instructions suggested he sing a hymn along with a video and pray afterward before
starting the lesson. He felt a bit foolish, but he got into the spirit
of "An Angel from on High," and prayed silently—for strength

to resist temptation, for Sara to be his… well, that was probably an improper thing to pray for. But it would be good.

He was finishing another video—this one on Joseph Smith and the ferment of the Second Great Awakening of the early nineteenth century. Western New York where Smith had come of age was then experiencing a revival of belief and interest in religion and the supernatural. Jared's Sunday School had glossed over this cultural history, focusing on the founding of the LDS church—Mormonism—as a unique event. But Smith had been inspired by the boom in evangelical religions in the newly-settled inland areas of the US, and the video explained that he was one of many religious leaders to gather converts and found new institutions during the period. Related movements fed the Abolitionist cause, with its moral fervor against slavery, and Spiritualism, the belief that the spirits of the dead could be contacted through séances. The video quoted Smith:

> … I kneeled down and began to offer up the desires of my heart to God. I had scarcely done so, when immediately I was seized upon by some power which entirely overcame me, and had such an astonishing influence over me as to bind my tongue so that I could not speak. Thick darkness gathered around me, and it seemed to me for a time as if I were doomed to sudden destruction.

> But, exerting all my powers to call upon God to deliver me out of the power of this enemy which had seized upon me, and at the very moment when I was ready to sink into despair and abandon myself to destruction… I saw a pillar of light exactly over my head, above the brightness of the sun, which descended gradually until it fell upon me.

> It no sooner appeared than I found myself delivered from the

enemy which held me bound. When the light rested upon me I saw two Personages, whose brightness and glory defy all description, standing above me in the air. One of them spake unto me, calling me by name and said, pointing to the other— This is My Beloved Son. Hear Him!

My object in going to inquire of the Lord was to know which of all the sects was right, that I might know which to join... I was answered that I must join none of them, for they were all wrong; and the Personage who addressed me said that all their creeds were an abomination in his sight; that those professors were all corrupt; that: "they draw near to me with their lips, but their hearts are far from me, they teach for doctrines the commandments of men, having a form of godliness, but they deny the power thereof."

... Some few days after I had this vision, I happened to be in company with one of the Methodist preachers, who was very active in the before mentioned religious excitement; and, conversing with him on the subject of religion, I took occasion to give him an account of the vision which I had had. I was greatly surprised at his behavior; he treated my communication... with great contempt, saying it was all of the devil, that there were no such things as visions or revelations in these days; that all such things had ceased with the apostles, and that there would never be any more of them.[1]

The study materials gave him the unsettling sense of his own church as one of many, started in reaction against more established churches and their denial of direct personal revelations. Smith had talked directly to angels and God, and brought back a personal understanding of spiritual truth. But anyone who claimed that today would be excommunicated or committed.

Jared imagined his church as a great family on a ship in a

storm-tossed sea, like Noah's Ark, sheltering them from the flood drowning the world around them. Its leaders steered as best they could, hoping for guidance from above which never came. He shivered and felt alone.

He wrapped up the unit and aced the test at the end. He was heading down the stairs when he heard his sister Kristi come in. Kristi was ten and had blonde ringlets and pigtails.

He found her peeling a banana and drinking a glass of milk at the kitchen table. "How was school?"

Kristi looked up. "Okay, I guess. I have Mrs. Hamilton this year."

"I had her. She was okay but she got cancer, so they gave us a substitute most of the year."

"She looks fine now. She sent Jimmy Henke to the principal's office for texting."

"Hah. She never much liked boys. I had to work to stay on her good side."

"So did you meet that girl you met online?"

"Sara. Yes, turns out she's in my History class."

"Is she pretty?"

Jared thought for a moment. "Not quite the right word. Beautiful is closer." The look on his face must have been funny, since Kristi's eyes grew wide and she vibrated in her seat.

"You've got a crush! Don't you!" she said, grinning.

"We'll see. I'm … intrigued. She gave me her number." Jared blushed, remembering.

"Bring her by for dinner. I promise I'll be good."

"We'll see. I'd rather keep it casual for now. I'm headed over to Preston's house for some music work."

"Oh, okay. Mom should be home soon."

"Yeah, that's why I need to go. She'll want to talk and I'm already late." Jared left through the front door since his car was parked on the street so his parents could use the garage. He looked at his phone before starting the car and fought the urge to call Sara immediately. He wanted to wait so as to not look too eager, and he was reminded of how Melissa had insisted he respond to her every text—if he didn't, she would send increasingly angry messages until he did. So this time he was going to play cool even if he wasn't.

❖　　❖　　❖　　❖　　❖

Preston lived a half-mile away in a fancier neighborhood—the houses had grandiose two-story entrances with columns. His father was Bishop Snow's younger brother. Jared and Preston had been friends since grade school since they liked the same games and music. Two years ago they had been in Preston's basement, sitting side-by-side on the bench while Preston played honky-tonk piano on the old upright—Preston had added thumbtacks to the felt hammers to give it that janky metallic sound. Preston had brought out a flask of illicit rum to share, and they laughed and talked until the suddenly serious moment when Preston leaned in close and tried to kiss him. He was shocked and angry and left in a huff. After he cooled off, he realized he had overreacted, and wasn't really mad at Preston. After all, he himself had done things in private he wouldn't have wanted anyone to know about. It was more about the shame that would come if anyone found out—the reflex display of anger was intended for onlookers. There weren't any onlookers and he understood Preston was lonely and trusted him with his secrets, so he was ashamed of himself more for hurting Preston further than for any implied insult.

Later, when he ran out of new straight porn online and it all seemed boring, he tried jacking off to gay porn—some of it, anyway. He had locked that fact away in a mental compartment and dismissed it. He often did things in his porn-fueled fantasies that he would run away from in real life. He felt degraded, but that was not Preston's fault.

Things had not been quite the same between them after that incident, and he had tried to apologize for his angry rejection and explain to Preston that he wasn't interested but still wanted to be friends. Jared had avoided Preston for months, but gradually returned to visiting after Melissa had dumped him—his other friends lived too far away to see after school.

Jared went around back to the basement door. He knocked and could see Preston beckoning him through the window, so he went in.

"Hey," Jared said.

"You're just in time. I've got the cam set up and ready."

Jared took the guitar and Preston sat at the piano while they played a few practice sets. Preston adjusted the sound and lighting until he was satisfied. They finished a good set.

"I was a little stiff on that one," Jared said. "One more warmup?"

"Let's record this one. We can toss it if it's bad. Ready?" Preston saw Jared's nod and pushed the record button.

Jared begged off when Preston invited him to dinner, and he

got home just in time for it—everyone was at the table, about to start. His father sat at the head of the table.

"Good of you to join us." Roger Spendlove was middle-aged, his brown hair going gray and his waist thickening. He had worked his way up to police chief after two decades on the local force—but since Mt. Hermon had only six officers, he still worked shifts some evenings to cover for others. Tonight he was home. He said grace quickly, then spooned mashed potatoes onto his plate.

Jared's mother passed him the green beans. "How did it go at school?"

"Okay, I guess."

Kristi was squirming in her seat. "Tell them about the girl!"

Jared rolled his eyes. "I met a nice girl, just moved here from New York. Sara."

His mother glanced at his father, then said, "Oh? Is she…"

"She's Jewish. I think. Does it matter?"

Jared's father pointed at him with his fork. "Not at all. Right, honey?" he said, looking at Jared's mother.

"Well, of course not," she said. "It's just…"

Jared sighed. "We're not getting married. We've barely talked."

"That's how it starts, though," his father said. "You wouldn't be talking about her if you didn't think she was important." His laughter rumbled.

"I might ask her out. She gave me her number."

"Well, don't wait too long," his father said. "New girl in town, you'll have competition." He sat back in his chair and his eyes unfocused. "I remember when we were young." He took his wife's hand. "Young people in love. Which reminds me—those missing college kids. I was out looking with the search party today, on Spirit Peak. Nothing's turning up. This is the third disappearance up there this year—you shouldn't go hiking up there until we've figured out what's going on."

"Not even tempted, Dad." Jared took another bite of meatloaf. "She doesn't seem like the hiking type."

✧   ✧   ✧   ✧   ✧

After dinner, his mother shooed him upstairs when he offered to help clean up. Jared turned on his computer and logged into the Morpheum server to see who was on. Nothing much was going on, but he had received another message from Sara—"You look better in person!"—which he assumed was a joke since his avatar as Starclaw was inhumanly handsome and muscular. He tapped back, "I'll call you," then stopped before hitting send; why not just call now?

So he did. Her number rang four times before she answered, "Jared?"

"It's me. You are quick on the caller ID."

"I was hoping you'd call, so yes, I entered you in my address book."

"I'm honored, fair lady. Just read your message on Morpheum so I figured I'd reply this way. I enjoyed meeting you, too."

"I haven't signed up with your team yet."

"No rush. With school on, most of us are too busy to play as often anyway," Jared said. He wasn't as interested as before in having her on his team. Or now he wanted her on a more intimate team, in the real world.

"Okay. I'm not going to have too much time, either," Sara said. "What did you think of Mr. Wright in History?"

"Cool guy. I need to start reading soon."

"Maybe we could study together?"

Jared laughed. "Read together? How would that work?"

"Okay, not read. Just hang out." He could hear her pout.

"I think that would be great," he said. "How about tomorrow after school? I have to work through a unit in online seminary, but you could come over and do it with me."

"Seminary? You're studying to be a priest?"

"Technically, yes. Most respectable, married men of my church are priests."

"That's a lot of priests. What kind of church can afford that?"

"They're unpaid. In fact, we pay to be members. It's very democratic in that way." And he had heard a lot of complaining about the tithes, with the expected amount being ten percent of each family's income.

"This is fascinating. Okay, sign me up for tomorrow after school."

"It's okay with your parents?" Jared asked.

"With my mother—Dad's long gone and remarried. My mother won't be back from work until dinner, or later—she often works late."

"Well, if she's working late you can stay for dinner and meet my folks."

"I'd like that. I'll tell her where I'm going. I'm sure she'll be fine with it."

The next day Sara sat next to Brandy in Algebra class. The teacher lectured about functions and equations. Brandy took notes while Sara's mind wandered—she knew most of the material already. She listened and drew doodles in her notebook. She wondered if the teacher would let her jump into self-study calculus to keep up with her friends back in Manhasset.

The teacher finished the lecture and gave them an assignment five minutes before the end of the period, so they were free to talk while they waited for the bell.

"Did you hear about the missing kids?" Brandy whispered.

"No."

"There are search parties on the mountain every day. A couple from BYU disappeared while out on a date, hiking. Every year people go missing up there. Then there are the kids who break into the mine."

"I read some of the warnings. Do not enter, deadly drops, old timbers giving way?"

"That's the one. They've blocked up all the entrances, but that just makes it more of a challenge. My brother and his friends got in by cutting the fence when they were seniors. Found a lot of broken liquor bottles and trash, dropped some rocks down the shafts. No gold, no Nephites."

"No what?"

"Nephites. A tribe of Israelites who migrated to the New World before Jerusalem fell to Babylon. They were supposed to have left a huge trove of gold under the mountain. Mormon mythology, I guess. Embarrassing to the church nowadays since there's absolutely no evidence they ever existed." Brandy looked around, apparently afraid someone would hear.

"So your holy book says Jewish guys sailed across the Atlantic before Columbus and the Vikings, and populated the wilderness? Doesn't sound like the Jews I know."

Brandy rolled her eyes. "Much as we love our church and believe in it, some parts of the Book of Mormon seem… unlikely. More a parable than a history."

"And my people have the same sort of problems with the old books. Even the Christians—some people think Jesus was made up, too. It's the lessons you draw from the books that matter."

"Anyway, if you go up on the mountain, don't get out of cell phone range. If you fall and crack your head, they might not ever find you. Too many rocky slopes and crevices."

"I'll keep that in mind. I haven't even explored town, much less the mountains."

"Part of our complete natural lifestyle package. You'll end up hiking sooner or later—there's not that much to do around here."

Sara's phone chirped—it was a text from Jared: "Meet west door after school."

Jared was leaning against the blue-enameled steel exit doors when Sara arrived. He wore a navy-blue hoodie over a green plaid shirt and blue jeans—Sara appreciated that he had made an effort to look good. His shaggy hair was combed back but golden locks had escaped to stand out against the dark blue of the hoodie.

"Hi," Jared said, opening the door for her. "Our chariot awaits." The old Corolla was parked at the far end of the lot.

"Very impressive." Sara eyed the trash in the back seat and the dents in the side door panel.

"Hey, this is clean. You should have seen it when I inherited it from my brother."

They got in and Jared started the car. Music blared.

"Oops, sorry. I like it loud."

"So do I, when I like the music," Sara said. "But I'd rather talk to you."

The drive to Jared's house took ten minutes. Jared led her up to his room.

"My sister gets home in an hour. We ought to be able to finish the seminary lesson by then."

"Is it a live lecture?"

"No, it's canned. But I can ask questions and the instructor is on the chat for the hour. That makes it interactive."

"So they won't see me."

"Nope, no camera for this part. There's a live videoconference one day a week but you're safe for today."

Jared put a folding chair next to his desk for her. He opened the unit on the screen and they started to read. Sara asked about unfamiliar words, but they made good progress. Sara felt him lean closer to her. When she didn't pull away, he put his arm around her and pulled her close while they laughed at the sight of some especially hokey illustrations of the angel Moroni appearing to the young Joseph Smith.

They worked through the lesson together. Jared dropped in wry observations about Mormon doctrines and his own failings. She felt—home with him.

But they reached the end of the lesson, and Jared broke contact with her when he heard noise out in the hall.

"Kristi?" He stood and opened the door. "I have a guest."

Kristi appeared in the doorway and brightened. "Oh, you must be Sara. We've all been dying to meet you!"

Dinner was reheated chicken casserole and steamed broccoli.

Jared's mother apologized. "We're eating healthier for Jared's father. Doctor's orders: low salt, low fat—"

"And low flavor," Roger Spendlove finished. "I spend too much time sitting at a desk these days, so this is my punishment for the sin of sloth."

"It's delicious," Sara said, having finished at least one bite of the casserole. "We eat a lot of microwave dinners, so this is nice."

"I didn't get much warning you were coming for dinner." Jared's mother looked at him reproachfully.

"Sorry, mom," he said.

The conversation was pleasant. Jared's mother asked her a few pointed questions, but seemed satisfied by her answers. Kristi put her on the spot asking where her father was, so Sara explained about the divorce and his remarriage. Jared's mother moved the topic away to Sara's favorite subjects.

When dinner was over, Sara offered to help clean up, but Jared's mother said, "You're our guest, so we'll handle that. It was lovely to meet you. You and Jared can go sit on the porch for a bit."

Jared's father laughed. "But it's a school night, so not for long."

Outside on the porch it was already chilly, and Sara put on her jacket. The sky was still light enough in the west to outline the trees down the street. They sat on the wicker loveseat and talked about everything and nothing.

The door opened and Jared's father stuck his head out. "Time's up," he said. "So nice to have met you, Sara."

Jared stood up and offered his hand to help Sara up. "Let me show you around back."

Sara let him lead her around the side of the house to a less visible spot.

"So what do you think of us?" Jared said, turning back to face her and putting his arms around her. She melted into him and hugged him back.

"They seem very nice. You seem very—nice," she said, her voice muffled by his shirt. This is where I belong. Already she could not imagine how she had withstood the bleakness of the world before him.

"'Nice.' I guess I'll take it." Jared squeezed her tighter and kissed her ear. Then he was kissing her for real. It wasn't her first time, but it was the best. She felt safe in his arms and all the fears she carried dissolved in his warmth. He moved his hands down to the small of her back and pulled her in closer.

"I need to take you home," he said at last, giving her one more kiss on her neck.

As they walked back to the front of the house, they could hear his parents talking from the kitchen window above.

"—not one of us," Jared's mother was saying.

"You were the one worried about him," his father replied. The clatter of a pan being put away interrupted. "—could be the one. Give her a chance."

"Well, I don't know. The eternal family…" His mother's voice was drowned out by the sound of the garbage disposer.

Jared sighed. "That—*bullshit*," he whispered. "Sorry you had to hear that." He pulled her along toward his car. "I'll explain that to you later. I'm sure we have a seminary unit on it."

Jared dropped her off with a kiss in the parking lot of her apartments. Her mother was watching TV but turned it off when she came in.

"Just waiting up. I'm not sure I care which girl the bachelor picks. I'm more interested in your bachelor—how was he?"

"He's—awesome. Now I'm glad we moved!" Sara fought the impulse to hide her feelings. She had given her mother a lot of grief in the last few years, so sharing something that felt good for once was freeing. "His family is so normal."

"How do they feel about people from New York?"

"You mean Jews, Mom. They were very polite. His mother has doubts." Sara felt a sharp pang remembering what she had overheard.

"You're just seeing each other, not getting married. You'll meet your real guy in college." Sara's mother started up the stairs.

"I suppose," Sara said. But while she knew that was probably realistic, that was not what her heart told her.

❖　　❖　　❖　　❖　　❖

Sara went to bed and drifted into sleep. She tried to bring back the feeling of being surrounded and cared for that she had felt in Jared's strong arms.

Much later she noticed a shadow from the window, but it wasn't dawn. It was darkness absorbing all light. It was a growing absence swallowing up the normal glow of streetlights and moonlight. The velvet shadows gathered before her still-closed eyes and coalesced into the shape of a woman, with long chestnut hair cascading over her breasts and flowing down to cover her body. Her eyes were pools of deeper darkness in the dark, and when she spoke her voice was a contralto that sent waves of warmth through Sara's body.

"My child," said the voice, "you have been chosen."

Sara tried to wake up, but she was paralyzed. "Who are you?"

"I am Lailah, the bringer of souls to new life. You are destined to bear the child of God with the soul of the Blessed One, the Ender of Days, the Savior of Man."

Sara tried to laugh but it ended as a cough. "What? That's a worn-out old story."

Lailah's darkness expanded to fill the room. "Your doubts will all be ended. You will feel the power of His presence soon."

Deep bass notes rippled through Sara's body as she felt tendrils forcing their way into her mind. The searing pain lasted for a few seconds, but then she began to go limp as the tendrils took away her pain. She no longer felt like resisting.

"His seed will grow within you, and you will prepare His way in the world. You will seek allies to protect Him and smooth His path to rule. You will be honored and cherished, and saved before others, to stand at His side for Judgment Day." The angel's arms enclosed her and she felt safe.

"Why me?" She no longer protested, but she still had the idea that some … mistake had been made.

"You are the virgin vessel, bearing the line of King David to the present day. You will be the mother of the New Dawn of

Mankind."

Overpowered by Lailah's will, Sara Believed. A world of doubts and fears evaporated in the gust of unnatural certainty.

○　○　○　○　○

When her phone alarm woke her, Sara turned it off and fell back to stretch. She felt really great, actually. The birds singing outside and the first rays of the rising sun coming through the window of her room seemed more real than they ever had—everything was shining and new. Her dreams must have been fantastic, but as she tried to remember, it all slipped away. And then she returned to thinking about Jared while she showered and dressed.

Randy Wright usually used the drive-through at the coffee chain to pick up his early morning coffee on the way to school, but today he had left the house early enough to drop in to the donut shop. As he waited for his order he spotted Roger Spendlove looking at his phone while sitting at a table alone.

When his order was ready, Randy picked it up and took it back to the police chief's table. "Morning, Chief. Want to be alone?"

Roger looked up. "No, sit down. I'm finished but I was enjoying the peace and quiet to catch up on news before going in." He was in uniform, his hat on the table next to him, discarded wrappers and protein drink container piled on one side.

Randy sat down and sipped his coffee before starting on his muffin. "What's the latest on the search parties?"

"We've called off official search. Every area has been gone over many times. Maybe they got further east, but we can only do so much. The family and volunteers are still going out every day, but there's no chance they're still alive if they were injured. It's been almost a month."

"Sad. How many people disappear and we never find out what happened to them?" Randy remembered a troubled girl he had tried to help a few years earlier. One day she stopped coming to school, and when he called her family, her father had lashed out at him—She's no good. She's dead to me. Randy hoped she had found a new life somewhere where people cared about her. He had reported the family to Child Protective Services, who had found no cause to intervene.

Roger looked weary. "There are more disappearances than we want to know. It's hard to tell when so many kids run away to Las Vegas or LA. Usually they turn up again, but we've lost dozens just from this town. Our dirty little secret. Maybe they turn up in porn videos, maybe they vanish from the face of the Earth. We send a Missing Persons report to the BCI—Bureau of Criminal Identification—but we don't have the resources to track them down."

"The Interstate is always there, they can get on it and be hundreds of miles away before anyone knows they're gone. Or buy a bus ticket with cash and leave no trace." Randy imagined that's how his troubled student had left town. Hoped, anyway.

"Get on the Interstate going north, you end up in Salt Lake at Temple Square. Go south, and you end up in Hell." Roger shrugged. "Or at least it can be the next best thing to hell. Hollywood or whorehouses. Either way, selling flesh."

Randy chuckled. "Lots of upstanding, moral people live down there. They just have more temptation to deal with."

"True, true. If you bring your kids up right, they won't fall into those traps. I'd just rather keep those dangers away from my kids until they're grown up enough to resist." Roger's phone pinged. "Oops. Looks like my time is up."

"Well, good to see you. I'm enjoying having your son in my history class. He's very bright." Randy finished the muffin and crumpled the wrapper into a ball.

"He's scary smart. I just wish he'd try harder to make something of himself. He's been seeing a new girl, Sara." Roger put on his hat and got up to leave.

"They're both in my American History class. I've been watching them together. Gives me new hope for humanity—I forgot what young love felt like."

Roger's expression was neutral. "They're cute together. I like her, but my wife is not so thrilled—she wanted a Mormon daughter-in-law and a lot of grandchildren. Our older son is talking about going on to business school back East, so he's not having our grandchildren soon, either. Sharon had her hopes up for Jared."

"I don't think we get to decide these things for them." Randy understood how hard it was for people brought up with one model for living to accept that other models might take away their children. Enough stayed, but so many were lost to the faraway cities and their attractions.

"No, we don't," Roger agreed, his eyes looking on some far horizon. "We bring them up as best we can and let them go, hoping they fly right. Jared has his head on straight, I'm not worried. But Sharon is going to have trouble with it." His phone pinged again. "Now I really have to go."

❖   ❖   ❖   ❖   ❖

Randy's AP US History class was starting, and he started shuffling his notes as a signal he was about to begin. Jared and Sara had been sitting together in the second row for weeks, and Randy called upon one or the other frequently. When the two disagreed on something, it often sparked a general discussion that illuminated their cultural differences and drew in some of the more retiring students.

Randy went to the whiteboard and wrote, "ALBION'S SEED, by David Hackett Fischer."

"Has everyone read the excerpts I posted?" Randy looked

around and saw mostly nods, with the laggards studiously avoiding his glance. "His thesis is that the basic cultures of the US arose from four major British migrations to the early colonies, with later migrations from other parts of Europe, Asia, and Africa adding to the original mix."

He wrote, "Puritans - New England," and turned back to look at Jared. "We call the first group Pilgrims, and they settled New England to freely practice their Calvinist religion. They were dissenters from the Church of England, and many were jailed and persecuted before fleeing to Holland where there was more religious tolerance. But in Holland they were a small group and they feared being swallowed up and losing their culture. English authorities continued to pursue them and tried to extradite their leaders. Crossing the sea to the New World looked like an opportunity to create their own separate society. They landed in Massachusetts, far north of their original target. They found a depopulated land—we now know smallpox carried by earlier European traders had wiped out most of the native population, leaving abandoned villages and fertile fields ready for settlement."

A girl raised her hand. "But what about Pocahontas and Thanksgiving?"

Randy smiled. "The Pocahontas story is about a native princess and the Jamestown colony, in Virginia, which we'll get to. These stories have been simplified and retold to become our founding myths—it can be instructive to read the truth behind the children's stories you've been taught. The Thanksgiving story is a very useful myth, since it records the cooperation between natives and Pilgrims to live together in peace. When the US was absorbing millions of new immigrants from Europe in the 1800s, these stories were promoted to teach children the values of Americanism—that everyone could cooperate despite differing cultures by living side-by-side and peacefully trading.

"By our standards, though, the government of the Massachusetts Bay Colony was authoritarian and intolerant of other religions. The vote was given only to men who were members of the approved Puritan church, so called because it was a 'purified' version of the established Church of England, which they viewed as too corrupt and worldly. They were suspicious of anything pleasurable for its own sake, so sex was to be enjoyed only within marriage and for procreation, singing was for hymns to enhance the worship of God, and celebration of holidays like Christmas was forbidden. Idle time was the tool of the Devil and any unproductive activity was morally suspect. Is this sounding familiar?" He looked up to see nods and knowing laughter.

"That's right, there are some remnants of Puritan attitudes even today. Utah is not anything like as repressive as the Bay Colony was, but until recently it seemed to be dominated by men of the church. And it's true that the founders of the LDS church were from the area of the country influenced by Puritan culture. The Bay Colony's intense focus on hard work and large families allowed the initial twenty thousand settlers to grow to over half a million by 1776. By then the repressive Puritanism had eased as Enlightenment values spread.

"But in the hundred years when Puritanism ruled the Bay Colony, many still believed that demonic forces and witchcraft were ever-present dangers. Dozens of unfortunate citizens, mostly women, were convicted of witchcraft and hanged or crushed under heavy stones. In 1660, a Quaker, Mary Dyer, was hung in Boston Common for the crime of being a Quaker. That was so disturbing that King Charles II sent the colony an edict prohibiting such executions. In 1684 the English Parliament revoked the Massachusetts colony's charter, ending its near-theocratic local rule."

Jared raised his hand. "But Quakers were one of the other founding cultures, right?"

Randy turned to write, "Quakers - Pennsylvania" on the whiteboard and turned back to expand on the topic. "That's right. They believed every member of their church had a direct relationship with God and could experience communion with Christ without an established clergy as intermediaries. Clergy in England, and later in New England, found this threatening, so they prosecuted Quakers for blasphemy. Quakers settled in Pennsylvania and mid-Atlantic states, and they seeded the new country with ideals like equal rights for women and minorities and religious tolerance."

"Next, the original US Southern culture." Randy wrote on the whiteboard, "Cavaliers - Virginia."

"The southern seaboard of the US was settled by an upper class of relatively well-off Cavaliers from southern England and millions of indentured servants who paid for their passage with years of hard labor. They established the Southern model of plantations run by wealthy landowners and tended by indentured servants, and later on by black slaves traded from Africa. The first great cash crop was tobacco, then it became cotton. This model spread across the southern US and was only overturned by the Civil War, when the tension between Southern agriculturalists and Northern Abolitionists finally boiled over into war. But the legal support of slavery—state and local government enforcement of laws making slaves property and punishing slaves who escaped—was contrary to the Enlightenment values of most of the Founders, even those who owned slaves. It was only a matter of time before this conflict blew up. Any questions?"

Sara raised her hand then said, "When did Jews show up?"

"Quite early. Tens of thousands of Jews settled in the Colonies from earliest days. New Amsterdam, later to become New York, was welcoming. Even Massachusetts, where being the wrong kind of Protestant could get you into trouble, has no record of persecuting Jews." Randy shuffled through his notes. "Ah, there was a Jewish merchant from Holland who arrived in Boston in 1649 and found himself out-traded and penniless. The locals took pity on him and gave him an allowance from the public treasury until he could find passage back to Holland. Good thing he wasn't a Quaker!

"There's even a theory that Columbus himself was secretly a Sephardic Jew and undertook his voyages to the New World in part to find a safe place for Jews. Spain had expelled all Jews who refused to convert to Catholicism just days before his first expedition sailed in 1492. And later on, some speculated the Cherokees and other natives were descendants of the Lost Tribes of Israel, a belief that may have appeared again in the Book of Mormon in the form of the Nephites who also supposedly came from Israel to settle North America but died out before Columbus. There's no real evidence of any of that, though there are artifacts and genetic traces of pre-Columbian contact from the Old World.

"By the mid-Colonial period, Jews were settled in small numbers throughout the Colonies. Some Jews settled in the coastal cities, while others in the South moved inland and intermingled with the planters. Many intermarried and converted. By 1790, George Washington wrote to assure the Jews of Newport, Rhode Island that they would have an honored place in the new nation:

> Every one shall sit in safety under his own vine and figtree, and there shall be none to make him afraid… For happily the Government of the United States gives to bigotry no sanction, to persecution no assistance, requires only that they who live under its protection should demean themselves as good citizens, in giving it on all occasions their effectual support.[2]

"One of the respectable motivations for higher education was study of the Bible, and most Colonial colleges were set up to train the clergy. Study of the Old Testament required reading texts in the original Biblical Hebrew, and study of Hebrew was common, though not as important as Latin and Greek. Yale still has a Hebrew motto at the center of its official seal.

"And on to the last group, the hill people." Randy wrote on the board: "Scots-Irish - Backcountry."

"These people arrived in large numbers to settle the West, which first meant the Appalachians. They were poor, uneducated, suspicious of government, and tribal. They became the yeoman farmers of the South and Midwest as settlement spread west. Each founding group settled in streams flowing westward from their shore regions, joined later by immigrants from many other parts of Europe—Germans, Scandinavians, Italians, and Irish. Settlers would hop a few hundred miles to the west to clear and farm new land, until they reached the High Plains where farming became less practical without irrigation.

"The Hill People didn't like being told what to do, but their scrappiness and fighting spirit made them the backbone of US armed services. Even today, our ground forces owe a cultural debt to them, and volunteers are disproportionately from regions settled by them." Randy noticed Jared's raised hand and nodded toward him. "Jared?"

"So the Civil War was about the three other groups ganging up on the Southern plantation system and the Cavalier culture?"

"Interesting idea, but the war was about many things—trade protectionism, for example, had favored Northern manufacturers and hurt Southern agricultural exports. And the Hill People were evenly split, since they typically owned no slaves but ended up fighting in both armies. We'll get to that—but it's true that the near-feudal landowning aristocracy of the Old South, building on the original Virginia colony's tobacco plantation model, was the source of the South's resistance to change."

Sara looked thoughtful. "And there were Jews on both sides, too?"

"Yes," Randy replied. "Because the largest migration of Jews came later, from Eastern Europe into the Northeast cities, we now think of the US's Jews as urban, concentrated in New York City. But the South had a large Jewish population early on, and a few Jewish citizens traded slaves and ran cotton plantations. Even some black freemen owned and traded black slaves, demonstrating that the stain of slavery was broadly shared."

"So we're all guilty?" Jared said.

Randy paused to consider carefully what he might say. "None of us are guilty. That was long ago and no one alive today is responsible. But we study history to remember that what was once common and accepted may be seen as depraved and immoral by our descendants. Even in an evil system there are opportunities to do good—to free your slaves, metaphorically. Good human beings tend to do good for those around them no matter what the social or employment customs of the day, and likewise bad people will always find ways to do evil no matter how the system is set up."

9: Jared: Project with Sara

Jared got home from school and signed into the live seminary class just a few minutes ahead of the start time. This was the fourth live lecture with Lisa Atwater, a tiny powerhouse of a woman with short dark hair and a sweet face that could turn fierce in an instant when she detected a weak argument or a lazy mind. Her face was centered in the large window on the screen. Behind her was a bookcase full of leather-bound texts with gold-lettered titles, with a scattering of more colorful recent books below.

The right side of the screen showed her lecture slides. As she spoke the slide would change when she was about to start on the next topic. Students could type in questions in the chat feed in one of her windows, and if she chose to answer and clicked on the question, that student's face would appear in a small inset window and they could discuss the question live for the benefit of everyone on the call. This was not quite as good as a real classroom, but the structure prevented derailing questions, so they could cover more ground without giving up all of the benefits of immediate feedback. Jared had avoided asking questions and enjoyed being able to walk away from his desk while still listening to the lecture.

Prof. Atwater tapped her finger on her desk until the clock showed it was time to start. "Thirty-eight signed in, good enough." She chose a student to read a prayer, then after the prayer ended, turned to the notebook in front of her.

"I'll remind you again that you are a select group of students, chosen for capacity to go beyond our usual coursework. I'm working on a new curriculum for a new era, while our leaders—the General Authorities—are largely from an older generation that thought they could shepherd us away from temptation by keeping educational programs simplified and sanitized. Perhaps one of you will rise to leadership, and you are here to learn how to answer the most difficult questions of our members. I'm not one to shrink from tackling the dirty jobs, so we're going to look at our religion from both inside and out, and examine the areas of weakness to reinforce them with the strength of our faith. The video lectures and tests are from the standard curriculum, so I'll focus in my live lectures on the deeper stories behind your Sunday School tales and the corrosive effect of modern media saturation on our faith as well as others. What we need for survival is a more lion-hearted LDS, a muscular Mormonism for the battles to come, more able to defend itself from our intellectual enemies. We live in a bubble in Deseret where we are supported by our neighbors and friends, but we have successfully spread the faith around the world and we can expect more intense attacks because of our success. They will laugh at us, they will torment us, and they will try to overwhelm us with their Godless secular culture.

"We're covering historical material about Joseph Smith's discovery and translation of the Book of Mormon that is widely doubted outside the Church. It is one thing for Christians, for example, to be generally aware that their Bible consists of stories collected and translated by anonymous and flawed custodians over millennia, and quite another for our Book of Mormon to have been unearthed and translated by one man in the nineteenth century. Christians on the whole do not expect the Bible to be 'true' in the sense that everything written in it literally happened exactly as described in today's translations, and the same should be true for us—Joseph Smith received a revelation from God, and his translation of the writings on the golden plates was divinely inspired, but we cannot expect it to be perfect. And the plates themselves were the work of human beings in a distant past, and so like the Bible we can have faith that the writings are important and meaningful guides without requiring that every bit of them be literally true. Stories are often changed in the retelling to make their moral point more effectively.

"And then there is the record provided to us by archaeologists and historians. In the last century, it was fashionable to discount Biblical stories because there was little concrete evidence that any of the people and places cited in them actually existed—yet we now know almost every story has some foundation in truth, as references to ancient cities named in the Bible have been discovered in the records of other ancient peoples, and sites have been excavated and shown to have matched Biblical descriptions, for example Jericho. Even the oldest stories, like the Great Flood, have analogs in other cultures— the Flood is described in the Babylonian Epic of Gilgamesh, and recently it's suggested sudden flooding of the floor of the Black Sea or Persian Gulf post-Ice Age could be the source of the legends.

"As for the Book of Mormon, we'll review the evidence both from church scholars and outside linguists. It's important that you be able to defend it against criticisms. Church members will have read the works of skeptics and need answers to those criticisms to retain their faith—you have to be aware of and understand the arguments of the skeptics to do an honest job of refuting them. It is up to you to square the documents of our faith with the claims of secular researchers and historians in your own mind, then explain it to others."

She paused to read questions coming in, and apparently decided to take one. She looked to one side and clicked on it. An inset window appeared with a thin, pale boy's face.

"Wyatt. Repeat your question."

The boy glanced aside to read what he had typed. "My science teacher said there was no evidence of white people in the Americas, and that the Book of Mormon is racist for saying there were."

Prof. Atwater's lips set into a thin line and her eyes narrowed. "It's true there was a lot of wishful thinking about pre-Columbian contacts, with eccentrics claiming Phoenicians, Romans, Vikings, and other Europeans—as well as Chinese via the Pacific—traded and settled the Americas. Most but not all of the evidence supporting those theories has been discredited, though the Viking settlements in Newfoundland are now accepted. Your teacher is adopting the popular attitude that any questioning of the standard settlement model for the Americas is somehow insulting to Native American peoples. Yet anomalies remain, and recent analysis of the genetic records of Native Americans suggests there were a variety of groups migrating in waves, complex enough that some contributions from European and Mediterranean populations can't be ruled out. Your teacher may not be aware of this work, but scientists right now are trying out theories. One popular explanation has some of the populations coming across from East Asia partly composed of European tribes, a theory which allows the scientists to continue to believe only migrations across the Bering Strait are important. Another hypothesis has early populations arriving by boat via the Arctic sea routes—there may have been a circumpolar culture similar to the Inuit-Eskimo people of today."

Wyatt looked suitably chastened. "So you're saying my teacher doesn't know what she's talking about?"

"I wouldn't say that. She's just expressing the consensus of a few decades ago. And non-Mormons especially enjoy debunking what they see as our superstitions and obviously ridiculous beliefs. Learn her favored worldview, then repeat it back to her, but don't discount your faith because the current consensus conflicts with it. That consensus has changed and will change in the future, and our faith will not."

Jared remembered a history lesson from last year, and realized its similarity to what the Professor was talking about. He typed into the question window, "How did the Catholics deal with Galileo?"

Prof. Atwater's eyes flicked to one side. "Ah, Jared. Excellent question which is relevant to us today. Please repeat your question."

Jared saw himself live in the smaller inset onscreen. *I look so dorky.* He did his best to look serious but he still didn't like how he looked.

He licked his chapped lips and said, "What about Catholics and Galileo? How did they deal with science that contradicted their faith?"

Prof. Atwater said, "The popular legend is that Galileo was tried by the Catholic Inquisition and forced to recant his view that the Earth orbited the sun—the heliocentric hypothesis. True enough, but he was tried for publicly disputing the Church's authority more than his views. The Church was about to discover that its claim to authority over scientific knowledge would weaken its spiritual authority as scientific progress continued to discredit many of those views—if they were provably wrong about the solar system, why would they be right about the soul? Later on, the Church learned to tread more lightly and leave to scientists those aspects of natural law subject to empirical validation. Jesuit philosophers like Teilhard de Chardin built bridges between Catholic doctrine and science, and the Church wisely retreated from persecuting Catholic scientists when their work led them into issues the Church had previously deemed doctrinal.

"The reason why this is a very useful question is that the General Authorities of the church are having to face some of the same issues today, recognizing that some of our noncore doctrines may be less inspired by divine revelation than others. Our Prophets were, after all, only human beings. Even a message from God may have been misunderstood in the retelling, and some of the topics in the Doctrine and Covenants have been modified over the years by new revelations, the most famous one being the 1978 change that clarified that black men were fully able to participate in the church. The external pressure to change was, like the Church's ban on polygamy in 1890, a response to political problems that made church leaders examine the troublesome doctrines very closely. Revelations that adjust noncore doctrine to conform to new understandings in the real world have allowed the church to bring its benefits to many more countries and peoples."

Another question popped up and Jared felt relief when the inset picture changed to show a silver-haired girl instead of himself.

"What about gay people?" The girl had a purple stripe in her hair, so Jared wondered where she was from that the church ladies had let her get away with that.

"That's an active concern of our leaders right now. I am not speaking as a representative of the official curriculum on this, but the Church has clearly decided to soften its stance against gay people. By using Church resources to campaign against gay marriage in a California election, they came close to violating the law, which damaged their image and weakened their political position. They're getting more feedback from the community and families with gay children and trying hard now to emphasize the Christian love part of 'love the sinner, not the sin.' Core doctrine does not allow the Church to sanction gay marriages—yet." Prof. Atwater sighed deeply.

Prof. Atwater looked away from the screen, then said, "I see our time is almost up. Jared, stick around for a minute, I have a project for you." She clicked on something and the screen expanded to the one-on-one view. "You live in Mt. Hermon, close to the Zion Mine, right?"

"I can see the buildings from my house," he replied.

"It's a research topic for one of my grad students." Prof. Atwood opened a drawer and pulled out a thick stack of papers. "She's compiled a lot of material on the topic of real and false revelations, and how the Church has dealt with false prophets. The mine's promoter claimed to have had a revelation from the angel Moroni that the Nephi had left huge stores of gold and treasures—and a copy of the Book of Mormon—under the mountain for us to find in our time of need. A lot of the faithful wanted to believe him. They made the mine happen by buying stock in the mining company, financing the digging and construction of the buildings. The Church tried to ignore his popular support, but eventually they had to act against him—he was excommunicated and his mine pronounced a fraud."

"I've heard the story. Some people in town still believe it."

"And that was the danger—our people wanted to believe it, but the Church saw his revelations as threatening. If anyone can claim to have had a revelation, the Church would be beset by false prophets and split into a hundred competing sects. And if the mine was completed and nothing was found, it could undermine belief in Joseph Smith's revelation."

"I think most people understand that. They just wish it were true." Jared was nervous—even talking about false prophets seemed dangerous.

"The idea is attractive, which is why it was so insidious and hard to fight. We'd all like to find the gold plates and some concrete evidence the Book of Mormon is true. But it's a trap."

"So what would you like me to do?"

"Her thesis could easily be published as a book, but the chapter on the mine would really benefit from more recent photos of the site. I have permission from the company for you to enter the site for exterior photos—I understand they've had problems with vandalism and their insurance company won't allow site visits unaccompanied, but the caretaker is not responding to my calls. So if you'd hike around nearby without entering the fenced-off areas and take some pictures, we might be able to use them."

"My dad has a camera with a telephoto lens." Jared mimed taking a picture.

"That would be perfect. By the end of the month would be good. We'll give you a credit for it."

❋   ❋   ❋   ❋   ❋

After dinner Jared's mother left to call on an elderly shut-in as she did weekly, part of the church's efforts to support those in need. Jared and his father took over kitchen cleanup duty on those nights, and so tonight Jared was drying while his father washed the pots and pans and loaded the dishwasher.

His father handed him a washed pan to dry. "You know your mother and I only want what's best for you, right?"

Jared rolled his eyes. "I know. But it feels like pressure to me."

"You've been dropping the ball, avoiding the work of preparing to make a good living for yourself so you can start a family. It may be harder now than it was for us, I grant you that. But now you have a girl you care about who might be the one for you. We notice you're doing better in school."

Jared wanted to defend himself—the games were a kind of training for the battles of adult life, weren't they? But he had to concede his parents had a point. No one was going to hire him based on his game rankings. "I've been more interested, it's true. It's not that I can't, it's that I didn't care enough before."

"Well, I'm happy you've started to turn it around. It's kind of the secret of life—" His father paused to deliver the dollop of wisdom Jared knew was coming. "—You build your life out of what's real you have to start with, plus what you can build on top of that. If you don't understand what's real, you can't build on it—you have no foundation. Those people who say, 'If you can dream it, you can do it,' are just the most dangerous kind of wrong. No, you improve your world a little each day based on what and where you are that day. Maybe you look down the road and work toward a grander goal, but you have to be able to roll with the punches and be willing to accept what the world hands you. Fall down over and over again, fail and fail again, but always jump back up and start working again, and take the next step. If you stop trying you're dead."

"I know, Dad. I wasn't really sure what I wanted before." Jared took a serving platter to dry.

"So now you have a better idea. We don't work to get rich and famous. We work for our children, and our children's children, one step at a time. And if you keep at it, even if you have setbacks, you'll wake up one day realizing you made a good life for you and yours."

"And that's what you did for us?" Jared was struck by the incongruity of his father, elbows-deep in dishwater with his sleeves rolled up while giving him this pearl of wisdom.

"When I got out of the Army, I came back home and worked at a lot of things—insurance sales, auto mechanic. I met your mother and a few months later a friend helped me get on the police force. Not something I had dreamed of, but it came at just the right time, and I've been able to raise the three of you on my earnings while helping people every day. I'd say that is glory enough for one life."

"And we thank you, Dad. If sometimes we don't show it."

Jared's father closed the dishwasher and started it, drying his hands on the towel he took from Jared. "Happy to help, son. We just want to see you heading down the right path."

◊   ◊   ◊   ◊   ◊

After dinner Jared called Sara.

"Hey, want to go hiking with me Saturday? I'm supposed to take some photos of the mine." There was a long pause.

"Isn't that supposed to be dangerous? Missing kids and all?"

"The mine isn't deep in the mountains. The disappeared kids were on back trails miles to the east." Jared wasn't too worried about hiking on the slope of the mountain facing town, and his dad had given him the go-ahead.

"Well, okay. That's in cell phone range, right?"

"Sure. You can see the main road from there. We can't get lost."

So it was planned. They talked about bringing a picnic lunch and making a day of it.

❖   ❖   ❖   ❖   ❖

Jared spent a little time playing Morpheum Online, then went to bed.

He had been good for a whole month—no fapping. He was falling asleep without it, and he thought he had more energy. He noticed he was more interested in real people, and he could look at the curve of Sara's neck and feel a lightning bolt of the desire that had been absent when he had spent hours watching porn. He felt like he was winning the contest with his sinful urges and using the energy to get his work done.

As his body relaxed in bed, he could see Sara vividly in his mind's eye. Sometimes she appeared blended with her Morpheum Online avatar, with elf ears and a glowing sword, but with her real-life face and hair. He was imagining himself older, more muscular, more like his avatar Starclaw. He felt strength coursing through him, and his muscles rippled as he flexed his upper body and swung his axe side to side. He gathered Sara in his arms and began kissing her neck.

Sometime later he awoke to see the figure of Raphael floating above him, attended by a halo of emerald green light.

"Jared," Raphael said, his voice resonant. "I have been watching you, and I am pleased with your progress."

Jared tried to speak but couldn't. Finally he was able to say, "Thank you."

"Watch over your Sara. She is in danger. Dark spirits surround her. You must stay by her side."

"Dark spirits?" Jared wondered. "Who? What kind of danger?"

"The dark angels. The angels who rebelled against God and came to Earth. They mated with the daughters of Cain and created the race of Nephilim, the giants. When God released the Flood to cleanse the Earth of the evil, he allowed a tenth of their number to descend into the Earth to survive as demons, cursed to live in darkness and tempt Man. They live as spirits in the Underworld and trouble Mankind with visions and dreams."

Jared's thoughts were slowed. "But this is a dream. You are not one of them?"

"I speak to you the same way, but it is up to you to decide whether I am Good or Evil, whether I lie or speak truth."

Jared felt calm and goodness radiating from Raphael. "I think you speak truth."

"But Satan, who was Lucifer, is a silver-tongued devil who can trick anyone into believing. I give you the choice. A demon will leave you with no doubt. Sara is their target. They will turn her to their use if they can. Know that she will have been deceived, and do not lose faith in her, no matter what she does."

Jared fell back into darkness and slept.

10: Sara: Mine Hike

And it came to pass when the children of men began to multiply on the face of the earth and daughters were born unto them, that the angels of God saw ... that they were beautiful to look upon; and [the angels] took themselves wives of all whom they chose, and they bare unto them sons and they were giants. And lawlessness increased on the earth and all flesh corrupted its way... And God looked upon the earth, and behold it was corrupt... And He said: "I shall destroy man and all flesh upon the face of the earth which I have created." And against the angels whom He had sent upon the earth, He was exceedingly wroth, and He gave commandment to root them out of all their dominion, and He bade us to bind them in the depths of the earth, and behold they are bound in the midst of them, and are (kept) separate....

And as for all those who corrupted their ways and their thoughts before the Flood, no man's person was accepted save that of Noah alone; for his person was accepted in behalf of his sons, whom (God) saved from the waters of the flood on his account.... — Jubilees 5:1-19

Saturday dawned cold and clear. Sara was ready by ten and Jared knocked at the door a few minutes later. Sara's mother got the door. Jared was dressed in jeans, hiking boots, and a Carhartt jacket.

"Good morning, Jared," Sara's mother said. "Can I get you something? Need any supplies for your hike?"

"I've packed plenty, Mrs. Horowitz."

"Call me Rachel," she said. "You make me feel old."

"Okay, uh, Rachel. I think we have enough for a two-hour hike. Water, picnic lunch packed by my mother, cell phone fully charged."

Rachel looked at Sara and wagged her finger. "Now you text

me all along the way."

Sara rolled her eyes. "I will, Mom. Nothing will happen. It's only a short hike and a long way from where those kids disappeared."

❖   ❖   ❖   ❖   ❖

They parked along the road next to the gate barring access to the old mine road. Jared got his backpack out of the trunk and put it on, then picked up the big black Canon camera and began taking photos—posing Sara next to the car, then holding the picnic basket, then looking up toward the mountain. Some of the scrubbier trees were already bare, but the mine itself was still hidden by leaves.

"This is just an excuse to get me to model for you, isn't it?" she said, sticking out her tongue as he snapped the shutter again.

"Partly. I figure you'll get used to it and we can go back to my studio…" He grinned and waggled his eyebrows.

"I think artist's models get paid. I had a friend who made a lot of money modeling."

"Well, you're striking enough to be a model." He sounded sincere.

"Make me an offer. With or without nudity." She posed with one hand behind her head, pushing her bust out. The effect was mostly lost because of the bulky sweatshirt she wore.

The gate was chained shut but it was easy to step over the chain through the gap where the fencepost had pulled away from it. The rutted mine road had been graveled sometime long ago, but grass was growing along most of it so it seemed more like a wide trail than a road. Water had carved gullies across it hidden by weeds, so they had to watch their steps walking. But it was a beautiful day, birds were singing, and the sun was warm enough that Sara quickly stripped off her sweatshirt, pausing to stuff it into Jared's backpack.

There were several switchbacks, and as they rounded the last, the view of the town below opened up. Sara could see the highway, the high school, and the white classical Mormon Temple with its tiny gold trumpeter atop the central spire.

"Can you see my apartment?" Sara said.

"It's behind those trees." Jared pointed. "Main Street and the park are there. My house is over there," and he pointed toward a smudge of houses further out. "We can see the mine from there, but we're still not that high up." Jared took more pictures. "I can stitch these together later to make a panorama."

They climbed for another half hour before the mine buildings were visible, suddenly looming above them. They were white, in some 1920s modern style, stepped down the side of the mountain toward them. Windows on the upper floors made it look like an industrial version of the Mormon Temple down below, and a small golden trumpeter topped the spire on the top building.

"Looks like it needs a new coat of paint," Sara observed. This close they could see white paint peeling along one side, revealing gray concrete underneath.

"And you notice how much it was supposed to remind you of a temple," Jared added. "You can't really see the spire from town, but I can see why the Church was unhappy. The mining company was borrowing their trademarks." Jared snapped more pictures, pausing to adjust the telephoto lens each time.

"How close can we get?" Sara asked.

"There's a fence around the mine itself. We're not supposed to cross it."

They rounded another bend, and the parking lot below the mine came into view with the chain-link fence beyond it. Jared took more pictures. It was obvious the fence was not really a barrier—holes were cut in it and the fencing peeled back next to the gate. It would be easy to go in. Beyond the fence they could see trash and a spot where an old car had been burned. Scattered pieces of metal and glass glinted in the sun. Beyond the buildings, a dark tunnel into the side of the mountain had rusting ventilation ducts leading into it.

"We don't have permission to enter," Jared said, taking more pictures from different angles. "I have to get what shots I can get from outside the fence."

Sara pointed to the end of the parking lot, where the fence ended and a steep dirt slope began. "We can climb up a bit beyond the fence without actually crossing it."

"I think they wouldn't like that." Jared walked that way anyway. He got Sara to pose for a few shots with the mine buildings as background. "Probably can't allow people closer because of insurance."

After taking pictures from every angle, Jared pulled a folded tarp out from his backpack and spread it out on a cleared spot. The lunch came next, wrapped in brown paper. Jared asked his phone to play some Mozart.

"Voila! Classy, isn't it?" He motioned for Sara to sit down.

"I was hoping for crystal stemware and silver." Sara unwrapped a sandwich—peanut butter and jelly.

"I'm sorry if we're not up to your snobby Eastern standards,"

Jared said, shrugging. "We are who we are. At least we've up-graded to whole wheat bread."

Sara looked down at the town below. Behind the tinny phone rendition of Mozart, she could hear the distant roar of traffic from the Interstate. "I really am liking it here. All joking aside. People have been really kind to me. And I met you."

"And I'm happy to have met you. I didn't have to leave to meet someone... interesting."

They finished the food, and Jared put the trash in his back-pack before sitting down close to her. He put his arm around her and held her close—the wind was picking up and the sun had gone behind a cloud.

Sara moved to lay back with her head against Jared's chest. "You told me about Melissa, but you haven't asked me about my old boyfriends." She looked up at him questioningly, and he looked down into her eyes.

"Okay, I'll ask. Tell me about your old boyfriends." He squeezed her a bit harder.

"Not too much to tell. I went out with some boys, nothing serious. A few clumsy kisses. But mostly I was alone—I didn't really fit with the crowd in my school. I guess I need to tell you about Mr. Blank."

"Okay. Mr. Blank?"

"Teacher at my high school. I had him for English. He asked me to come by after class one day to discuss my journal. He said he was concerned—I had hinted at some drama with my father and he said he wanted to make sure I was not being abused. Which made me laugh, like my father would ever show that much emotion! Anyway, he stood behind me and started mas-saging my back and shoulders. It felt good but he started to creep me out when his hands started wandering."

"Did you find him attractive?"

"At first. Then I found out about his wife and kids. Handsome, but out of shape. Spreading around the middle." And she had felt Mr. Blank's hardness as he squeezed her against his pelvis from behind. Eww!

"So you weren't interested in…"

"No. Still, it was flattering to have him treat me like an adult and discuss my journal like it was important. I was enjoying the attention until it got creepy." Sara pulled his hand closer to her breast. "You are not the least bit creepy."

Jared squeezed her breast just a little. "Thanks, I guess. I have my creepy moments."

Sara shivered. "I'll let you know when to stop. It's not creepy if I want it."

Jared paused and got close to kissing her, but stopped to say, "I never had sex with Melissa. She wanted to reserve it for marriage. But she knew some loopholes. She had me do things for her…"

"Things? Like what?"

"Things like this." Jared moved his hand down to her stomach, then below. He stroked her inner thigh gently, from the knee upwards. She shivered as his ministrations began to excite her. "I can make you feel good." Then he kissed her in earnest.

❖   ❖   ❖   ❖   ❖

The wind grew colder and the skies began to cloud up. Jared reluctantly got up and retrieved the warm outerwear from his backpack. When they were ready to head back down, Sara looked over at the opening in the fence around the mine buildings.

Sara felt her curiosity take over. "It's only one o'clock and nobody's around. Why don't we take a quick look inside? I hear lots of kids have been in there."

"It'll take us an hour to get back to the car. We said we'd be back by three."

"So we have an hour to spare. I want to see inside!" Sara started toward the cut in the fence.

"But—" Jared gave up and followed her as she carefully made her way through the cut in the chain-link fence, avoiding the sharp ends of cut wires.

The plywood over the garage entrance had been pulled off and was rotting on the ground next to it. They walked into darkness and waited until their eyes had adjusted—the floor was concrete, covered with broken glass and twisted strips of metal. There was the remains of a fire surrounded by more broken bottles and cigarette butts. An unseen dead animal still smelled bad enough to make Sara gag, and a moist metallic smell seemed to come up from a shaft beyond, which were covered with metal grates.

"What you heard was true—lots of kids have been here." Jared poked at a beer bottle with the toe of his boot.

"I didn't think the locals drank or smoked," Sara said.

"Hah. Well, the good kids don't. Usually."

Sara walked further toward the back of the building where the square void of a tunnel shaft showed as deeper darkness. They looked down a vertical shaft covered by a metal grate, with heavy iron chains from the dimness above hanging down into the center. Other galleries led away to each side, back into the mountain.

"I don't see any gold or silver. Or jewels or gold plates covered with ancient writing." Jared explained the revelation that had led thousands to invest in the mine works. "So," he finished, "they never discovered anything. There was no promising ore, even. The church finally excommunicated the guy and the mining company went into hibernation. But still some people believe, and the story now is that the mine will reopen in the end times before Christ returns, and the people who've had faith will have enough treasure to tide them over while the world burns. They still have the annual stockholder's meeting."

"Kind of sad," Sara sighed.

Jared tried to take some pictures. "These aren't going to be any good since I didn't bring a flash. But might as well see what I can get."

Sara noticed a blank wall of rock behind Jared. She stared at it for a moment before seeing afterimages, outlines of light throbbing with her pulse, oozing around the edges. As she stepped back she stumbled over some debris in the dark.

Jared caught her before she fell. "We should get going. It's dangerous to move around in here without lights." He pulled out his cellphone and turned on its flashlight setting. "This will help."

They made their way back toward the light. Sara was shaking, and Jared wrapped his coat around her and held her hand as they walked. Outside, the sun was back out and everything seemed normal.

Behind them, the mine breathed, waiting. The watchers beneath exulted.

11: Jared: Study Session

Jared transferred the photos taken on the mine hike to his laptop. Then he began going through them, cropping and editing each photo as needed. He set aside the best exterior shots to send to Prof. Atwater, then looked through the mostly useless and dark shots from inside the mine.

He stopped when he noticed the fogged edges of some shots —but then there was no film since the camera was digital. Yet it looked like darkroom accidents. Ghostly blobs and streaks showed up in many of the photos.

One of the last showed an irregular shape against a black rock wall. He increased the contrast as much as he could. Against the rock face he thought he could make out the outline of a man, arms reaching out toward him.

Jared wondered if it was some kind of burn-in, the memory of a previous picture left in the electronic imaging chip. Or if it was a ghost—but he was sure all of those pictures of ghosts and the ghostchaser videos he had seen were fakes. He went back through the other inside shots, increasing the contrast to maximum, and found nothing but streaks and clouds, obviously artifacts. Still, he wanted to go back and explore more, this time with lights and tools.

◊　◊　◊　◊　◊

The next day was Sunday, but Jared skipped church, then drove over to Sara's after dinner for a study session. They were supposed to work on a term project covering some aspect of US history—Jared wanted to write about the Utah War, where the US Army fought Mormon forces to establish Federal authority over the semi-independent territory, while Sara wanted to work on a more current topic, like the Cold War. Sara led him up to her room.

"My mom's staying up in Salt Lake for a conference. I told her you were dropping in and she said that was fine, she trusts you." Sara pointed to her made bed. "Something about hoping we really study."

"I'm not sure whether that was a compliment or an insult." Jared opened his laptop on the desk next to Sara's computer. "I could have my way with you. No one's around to hear you scream."

"I probably wouldn't scream too loud." Sara laughed. "We could remake the bed after."

"If you're not going to struggle, it won't be much of a challenge." Jared pulled up a second chair and opened his photo app. "I wanted you to see this. It's one of the photos I took inside the mine, with the contrast all the way up."

Sara looked. "That looks like the outline of a person. Kind of scary."

"It might have been spray-painted on the rock by a visitor."

"I suppose. Or it might be a ghost."

"Did you hear any chains rattling, or feel a cold chill when we were there?" Jared turned to look into Sara's eyes.

"You know, I did have the oddest feeling just before we left. Like someone was watching us. First I wanted to see the inside, then I wanted to leave. Like something bad had happened there." Sara got goosebumps, remembering the feeling. She held Jared's hand tighter.

"As far as I know, no one was killed during the mining. I could do some more research. And I want to go back there with lights."

They started talking about which project to do for class. Then Jared paused—"Why don't we write about the mine? We've already got a head start, with photos, and we can use Prof. Atwater's student's thesis as a source."

"'The Zion Mine: Dream or Nightmare?'" Sara said. "Sounds like a fun topic, and easy enough."

"And there are still people living here who remember when it was in progress. If we can interview a few of them, we'll have it wrapped up." Jared wanted to know more anyway, so this way he could get credit for researching it.

"We should run it by Mr. Wright to see if it's an acceptable topic."

They sat side-by-side in front of the computers and wrote up a one-page description of their topic and the resources they would use for researching it. Jared inserted his best photo of the mine against the hillside at the top and clicked the option to make the text flow around it.

"Looks good," Sara said. "And we're done. My mom won't be back tonight."

"But I'm expected home." Jared checked the time. "In about two hours."

Sara lay down in her bed and beckoned. "That should be long enough."

Jared was torn. On the one hand, this was the moment he had been fantasizing about for a month. On the other hand, there was something off about the way Sara had set him up, and the look in her eyes as she invited him to sin. Her hunger scared him.

But he was prepared, and he had been carrying a rubber in the darkest corner of his wallet since he'd started seeing Melissa last year, just in case. He vowed to himself to remember to use it when the time came, and joined Sara on the bed. She held him close and they kissed.

12: Sara: Spellbound

Sara had been taken over by some kind of compulsion. Maybe she wanted to have sex with Jared—in fact, she knew she did. But she was not in control. She was in the grip of a lust and hunger not her own, her eager hands roaming his body, undoing his shirt. They kissed and she ripped open her shirt to let his hands reach her breasts, then his face was buried in them and he teased and licked her nipples. They were both breathing hard when he got up to take off his clothes and pulled hers off while she lay back. He jumped in next to her and kissed her in a frenzy, heading downward until he was sending waves of sensation through her with his tongue and fingers. She held his head and pushed him into her. Then he stopped and fumbled with his jeans to pull out a battered silver packet—he tore it open and put on the condom, hands shaking.

She gasped as he filled her. At first it was painful, but waves of sensation overcame any resistance and her world became his smell, his breathing, his thrusting. She held his pelvis and helped push him into her.

She found herself watching from outside while her body acted on its own. She felt wave after wave of orgasms and briefly blacked out. Her inner muscles clenched around him as she spasmed again, and she felt him expand inside her as he came.

He buried his face in her neck and shuddered, shouting. His sweat rolled down on her and he went limp. She lost consciousness.

Lailah was there, looking down on her, magnificent in

velvety black. The darkness around her breathed and flowed, and Sara was pierced by her voice.

"And so it begins. Jared's seed has already joined with your flesh and created a new life. My role is to prepare the way for the soul of the Messiah to come into your world for the final reckoning. Your child will be the new King of all Creation, Ender of Days, for Judgement Day is upon us."

Sara felt the new life within her. With all her heart she wanted this child, but the consequences.... She tried to speak.

"But—how? He—"

"Tried to interfere with my plan. That shield was no barrier, so old it was full of holes. It was no trouble at all to defeat it." Lailah laughed, and the darkness swelled.

"But I'm not sure I'm ready—" Sara stopped, paralyzed.

Lailah closed in, arms wrapping around her. Sara felt warmth spreading through her, then searing fire. "You are ready to serve our Master. You will follow my direction and prepare His way. Is that clear?" A shock wave went through her.

She heard herself speaking, again as if watching as someone used her body. "I will serve our Master, the Ender of Days. I will do everything to smooth His way into the world."

Sara opened her eyes. Her bedroom was dark, but she could feel Jared next to her, breathing slowly. She began to remember what they had done. She felt sick.

What time was it? She reached over to her phone on the nightstand. *Midnight! Jesus.* She shook Jared to wake him. "Wake up! It's really late."

Jared jerked awake and focused on her. "Hey. Sorry I fell asleep." He reached for her, and she turned to meet him.

She looked into his eyes and felt—love? Was that it? This was where she wanted to be, with him. And yet something nagged at her, something felt wrong. He was hers. She was happy, but it felt like she had cheated somehow and it would all be snatched away if she were found out.

Her tears welled up as they hugged and kissed again. She buried her face in his shoulder. His smell was—just right.

He squeezed her and said, "That was a surprise." His voice was low and she could feel his chest rumbling as he spoke. "I mean, it was great, don't get me wrong—"

Sara mumbled, "I'm sorry. I just wanted you so bad—"

"Are you crying?" Jared pulled back a little and looked at her face. "It's gonna be okay. We're good." He hugged her tighter. "I knew from the moment I saw you."

Sara sobbed out loud. "Me—*sob sob*—too." But she was scared and she didn't know why.

Minutes passed while they held each other and she felt better.

"You should get going," Sara said, getting out of bed and throwing on a top. "They'll wonder why you're so late."

"If I'm lucky nobody will be up to notice," he said.

Jared got up, showered, and dressed, and was out the door in minutes. Sara took a shower, too, and wondered why she wasn't happier. She was in love, right? Wasn't that supposed to make you happy?

13: Randy: Enlightenment

The classroom was darkened so the video screen could be read more easily. Randy Wright stood at the front, using his clicker to advance and point out items as he lectured.

"The Founding Fathers left an enormous quantity of written material documenting their deliberations and philosophy of government that led to the writing of the Declaration of Independence and later on the Constitution. Argument was often conducted in pamphlets or broadsides, which were single sheets of newsprint that could be produced cheaply and posted on public walls. Authors wrote under pseudonyms, especially before the Revolution when anyone opposing the King might be charged with sedition. You should have read a selection of them by now.

"Having thrown off a distant and abusive government, the Founders were especially interested in ensuring that a new government for the American states would not evolve into a similar oppressive form. The most prolific and far-seeing of the Founders, Hamilton and Jefferson, had differences of vision for the new country which, magnified, are still visible in today's politics. But both were grounded in the Enlightenment values of reason and recognition of the rightful government as the expression of the consent of the governed. Jefferson in particular was himself a scientist as well as a scholar, the kind of gentleman planter and independent thinker he envisioned as the ideal pillar of a free state. Jefferson wrote this letter in 1789." A new slide went up on the wall screen:

I have duly received your favor of the 5th. inst. with respect to the busts and pictures. I will put off till my return from America all of them except **Bacon, Locke and Newton**, whose pictures I will trouble you to have copied for me: and as I consider them as the three greatest men that have ever lived, without any exception, and as having laid the foundation of those superstructures which have been raised in the Physical and Moral sciences....[3]

"Let's go over each of Jefferson's heroes individually to see what they contributed to the philosophies the Founders viewed as key. First, Sir Francis Bacon, who had been active almost two centuries earlier. He not only was instrumental in founding the colony of Virginia and probably helped write the charter of the colony there in 1610, he was a pioneer in the scientific method. His writings in both science and government were enormously influential. The application of reason and empirical knowledge to the structuring of a new government was a radical notion, undermining the authority of both King and Church.

"Next, John Locke. His treatises on government were foundational."

The natural liberty of man is to be free from any superior power on earth, and not to be under the will or legislative authority of men but to be ruled only by the law of nature.

The liberty of man in society is to be under no legislative power except the one established by consent in the commonwealth; and not under the power of any will or under restraint from any law except what is enacted by the legislature in accordance with its mandate.

Freedom then is not what Sir Robert Filmer tells us (Observations on Hobbes, Milton, etc., page 55), namely a liberty for everyone to do what he wants, live as he pleases, and not be tied by any laws. Rather, freedom is one of two things: Freedom of nature is being under no restraint except the law of nature. Freedom of men under government is having a standing rule to live by, common to everyone in the society in question, and made by the legislative power that has been set up in it; a liberty to follow one's own will in anything that isn't forbidden by the rule, and not to be subject to the inconstant, uncertain, unknown, arbitrary will of another man.[4]

"The foundations of natural rights and contract theory—that every person began with natural rights to life, liberty, and property, and could freely enter into contracts to trade—had been established under English common law. The equality of citizens under law meant that no nobleman could rule by right or take the property of others, as had been the feudal rule. The English Civil War had established that Parliament, the people's legislature, ruled supreme, and the monarchy was restored thereafter as an ideal, with the monarch a figurehead representing good government in the people's interest, but in practice ruling only with the consent of the governed. The treatment of the English citizens of the Colonies as subjects without parliamentary representation had led to a series of taxes and impositions that the colonists found oppressive, imposed from thousands of miles across the Atlantic and designed to limit the colonist's trade with other nations. The radical notion of rebelling against British rule grew more attractive to the planters and merchants of the colonies, who were highly motivated to seek their own more responsive government closer to home. After a hundred years or more of benign neglect, the Colonies were already used to democratic self-government via their elected colonial legislatures.

"Next, Sir Isaac Newton. We think of him now as a scientist and mathematician, but he had many interests and spent the last part of his life as head of the Royal Mint and president of the Royal Society, the leading scientific society of its age. He was a father of calculus and the theory of gravity that still serves us in all but the most extreme circumstances. He also dabbled in alchemy and Bible interpretation, and was associated with the Deism of many of the Founders—a belief in a God who had created the Universe and its natural laws to be discovered by human beings using God's gift of reason. Adopting Deism allowed those raised in the religions of the day to privately reject the authority of churches, churchmen, and hierarchies in favor of applying the idea of scientific inquiry to God's laws, and ultimately to Man's laws for himself.

"So it was in that bubbling intellectual ferment that the Founders wrote new documents for a new nation. Different colonies had in some cases very different religious populations, and the framework for accommodating all beliefs in a great civil society was to separate church from state. The countries of Europe, including England, had suffered from centuries of warfare and oppression of religious minorities as governments meddled in religion for advantage or simply because the rulers of the day wished to impose their own beliefs on everyone. Sectarian violence was decreasing, but still a frequent occurrence, and the Founders wanted to create a new nation open to all ideas."

One of the boys on the back row raised his hand.

"Yes, Porter," Randy nodded at him.

"I saw a movie about how the Freemasons hid the treasure of the Knights Templar during the Revolution. Which is why all the Egyptian stuff like the pyramid and the eye on top on the dollar."

"That movie was fantasy with the tiniest kernel of truth, the true part being that many of the Founders were either Masons or quite familiar with their lore. Newton dabbled in it, and Franklin and Jefferson favored the metaphor of the Israelites escaping the Egyptian Pharoah as a legitimate rebellion against oppressive rulers. The Great Seal that appears on the dollar was designed in 1782, with Egyptian and Masonic symbolism mixed in. The eye is the eye of God, peeking through from Heaven on the unfinished pyramid beneath, and labelled by the slogan written on the pyramid below, '*Annuit cœptis*,' Latin for '[God] favors our undertakings." The Egyptians built their pyramids believing them to be pathways to Heaven. The motto '*Novus Ordo Seclorum*' on the back of the dollar, meaning 'New Order of the Ages,' shows that the Founders believed they were assisting God's plan by establishing freedom of thought to foster a flowering of science and philosophy in the new nation."

"What about the treasure?" Porter looked hopeful.

"Stories of lost treasure are almost always embellishments designed to entertain and attract the gullible. Templar gold, pieces of the True Cross Jesus was crucified on, relics of the saints—promoting the story could bring pilgrims and fortune-seekers to your bankrupt church or distant outpost."

Randy noticed Jared's hand up and nodded to him.

"There's supposed to be gold buried below the Zion Mine. But they gave up digging."

Randy thought his real opinion might seem too harsh, so softened his words. "That is a good example, and I'm looking forward to your project paper on the mine. An admirable Mormon man had a dream and enough people wanted to believe it was true that hundreds of thousands of dollars were spent building that dead end of a mine, in a time when most people had no money to spare. The idea of a fantasy jackpot that would change people's lives is compelling to some, which is why gambling addiction is a real problem. Utah outlaws all gambling, but the Internet and Las Vegas just a short drive away are taking a toll. Not to mention poker games and underground betting. The mine was the Mormon equivalent—a get-rich-quick scheme that seemed to come with God's blessing."

"I heard the mine guy was excommunicated. My father still has the stock," another student added.

"Can we interview your father?" Sara asked.

Randy broke in. "We're getting off-topic here. Take it up on your own time. Getting back to the concepts in the founding documents...."

After class, Sara and Jared stayed behind and approached Randy, who was ready.

"I'm okaying your project proposal. I've written a few suggestions in the margins, and one condition: no trespassing on the mine grounds." He tried to look stern as he handed back their proposal. "The school does not want you risking your safety."

Sara took the papers. "We'll stay out. We already took a look inside and there's nothing to see."

"Good. That said, it's a great subject right under our noses. If you do a good job you can turn it into a story for the Times. They haven't run a story on it for a few years at least, so I think I can interest the reporter."

That night, Randy dreamt again. He saw children sleepwalking through a cornfield. A rumbling noise, and then he could see as from above a giant harvesting machine moving slowly toward them. He shouted to warn them, but they could not hear him. He heard screams as the first children disappeared into the maw of the infernal machine.

14: Jared: Family Dinner

A week later, Jared was logged into the live session of the online seminary with Prof. Atwater.

"Let's get back to Joseph Smith and the Book of Mormon." Prof. Atwater clicked on something and a text appeared. "You should have already read through Joseph Smith's recounting of his discovery and translation of the gold plates inscribed with the Book of Mormon. Let's discuss these excerpts."

> He called me by name, and said unto me that he was a messenger sent from the presence of God to me, and that his name was Moroni; that God had a work for me to do; and that my name should be had for good and evil among all nations, kindreds, and tongues, or that it should be both good and evil spoken of among all people.

> He said there was a book deposited, written upon gold plates, giving an account of the former inhabitants of this continent, and the source from whence they sprang. He also said that the fulness of the everlasting Gospel was contained in it, as delivered by the Savior to the ancient inhabitants;

> Also, that there were two stones in silver bows—and these stones, fastened to a breastplate, constituted what is called the Urim and Thummim—deposited with the plates; and the possession and use of these stones were what constituted 'seers' in ancient or former times; and that God had prepared them for the purpose of translating the book. ...⁵

"So these stones were used as glasses, and he looked through them to read the inscriptions on the gold plates and translate the lost languages of the inscriptions into English. By the time he had translated much of the text, he had learned enough of those languages to do the translation without them.

Remember this was also the era of the Spiritualists, who claimed to be able to speak with the dead. To skeptics, supernatural artifacts like the seeing stones cast doubt on the story."

Jared typed, "What if the stones were advanced computers that could translate?"

Prof. Atwater laughed but didn't click on his question. "Jared asks if the stones could have been computers. This is an attempt to see them through modern glasses, so to speak—nothing in the text of the Book of Mormon suggests a high-tech civilization. The stones were either supernatural or of a technology so advanced we couldn't understand it. The *Urim and Thummim* referred to in the Jewish Talmud were channels to the Holy Spirit, and used by high priests to judge guilt or innocence in the absence of a recognized prophet. The Jewish versions were apparently lost when Jerusalem was looted by the Babylonians, so the stones left for Joseph Smith may have been different but similar channels to the Holy Spirit. In later writings Joseph Smith uses the idea of the stones as crystalline manifestations of God's order and suggests all will have the power to see through them. I don't think he meant that there will literally be billions of stones, but that they are a metaphor.

"Next slides: Joseph Smith's attempts to spread his vision to others."

> Owing to my continuing to assert that I had seen a vision, persecution still followed me, and my wife's father's family were very much opposed to our being married. I was, therefore, under the necessity of taking her elsewhere; so we went and were married at the house of Squire Tarbill, in South Bainbridge, Chenango county, New York. Immediately after my marriage, I left Mr. Stoal's, and went to my father's, and farmed with him that season....

I went to the city of New York, and presented the characters which had been translated, with the translation thereof, to Professor Charles Anthon, a gentleman celebrated for his literary attainments. Professor Anthon stated that the translation was correct, more so than any he had before seen translated from the Egyptian. I then showed him those which were not yet translated, and he said that they were Egyptian, Chaldaic, Assyriac, and Arabic; and he said they were true characters. He gave me a certificate, certifying to the people of Palmyra that they were true characters, and that the translation of such of them as had been translated was also correct. I took the certificate and put it into my pocket, and was just leaving the house, when Mr. Anthon called me back, and asked me how the young man found out that there were gold plates in the place where he found them. I answered that an angel of God had revealed it unto him.

He then said to me, 'Let me see that certificate.' I accordingly took it out of my pocket and gave it to him, when he took it and tore it to pieces, saying that there was no such thing now as ministering of angels, and that if I would bring the plates to him he would translate them. I informed him that part of the plates were sealed, and that I was forbidden to bring them. He replied, 'I cannot read a sealed book.'[6]

The class ended and Jared was logging out when he heard noises downstairs—his sister Kristi had just got home from school. He went downstairs and found her in the kitchen.

"What's up?" Jared said, pouring himself a glass of milk.

"Nothing much." Kristi was eating crackers at the table. "Walter Woods broke his arm falling out of a tree, so he has a big cast. I signed it."

"His brother isn't very lucky, either." Jared remembered a flag football game in gym where the unfortunate brother had managed to catch his foot in the only gopher hole on the field, spraining his ankle.

"Mrs. Hamilton announced she's pregnant." Kristi's eyes

widened as she remembered. "But her husband's stationed overseas!"

"I'm sure he's come back for visits." Jared tapped on the table and looked stern.

"It's more fun to think she's having an affair and this is her love child," Kristi said gleefully.

"You've been reading the wrong kind of stories." Jared dismissed the nonsense with a wave of his hand. "None of your business, anyway."

Kristi jumped to a new subject. "Is Sara coming over for dinner tonight?"

"Yes."

"Are you guys gonna get married?" Kristi had already asked that question too many times.

"You'll be the first to know if we decide. I ... maybe. That is also none of your business."

"I would like that. She's a lot more interesting than you."

Jared got up and rinsed out his glass before putting it in the dishwasher. "And I love you, too. And thank you for finally learning to hang your towel back up."

"Now if you could only learn to clean your shavings out of the sink. Disgusting!" Kristi mock-shuddered.

"I am but a work in progress. We both are—just ask mom."

When Sara rang the doorbell, Jared was upstairs. He could hear his father greeting her as he held the door open for her. He made it down the stairs in time to intercept his mother before Sara had to face her.

He helped his mother get the food on the table while Sara talked to his father.

In the kitchen, Jared whispered to his mother, "Now, be nice to her."

"I am nice to her," Sharon Spendlove said, too loudly. "I'm getting used to the idea. I like her well enough."

"But?" Jared said skeptically.

"No buts, I guess. If she makes you happy…"

"She does."

"Then I'm happy, too. I'll be fine."

The food went around the table. Roger Spendlove sat at the head of the table with Sara to his right. "So how is the mine project going?" His bushy eyebrows rose.

Sara paused in mid-bite. "Well. We've got two stockholders to interview, and the mine caretaker finally answered the message we left him, so we're supposed to interview him by phone Saturday afternoon."

Jared picked up from there. "And we have the draft of the thesis that covers the history. A few more sources and we can start writing."

Roger sat back in his chair. "I took a look at the state crime database. The rate of incidents on the mountain is unusually high—disappearances, the occasional dead body. Twenty years ago someone died falling down one of the mineshafts. Took days to fish the body out. The lower levels of the mine are flooded. Actually that's why they gave up on it—the pumps couldn't keep up and they hit rock too hard to drill. It hasn't been good luck for anybody."

"We're more interested in the history, and the Church's response to the claims of Nephi gold. Not to mention the gold plates." Jared laughed. "Touchy subjects. I'm supposed to see the Bishop again Monday, so I can get his statement on it. I think his father was one of the people who tried to discredit the mine promoters."

His mother looked worried. "I hope you'll be respectful. The Bishop has been a good friend to us."

"Of course, mom! He'll be happy I'm doing something useful." Jared was about to continue with *and I have a girlfriend and I'm cured of whacking off to porn,* but while true, there was no way he could say it, even to Sara. And besides, the Bishop would be forced to disapprove of what they had done, even though that sin was probably healthier than porn....

Jared's mother turned to Sara and said, "Sara, we so enjoy having you. You've been good for Jared. I can see the difference."

Jared blushed and stifled a groan.

Sara looked calmly back at her. "Thank you, Mrs. Spendlove. Your son has been good for me, too."

"Call me Sharon. I think we're going to be friends."

The conversation went on but Jared wasn't listening. He was looking at Sara while she talked, not hearing the words but soaking up how she moved and laughed. His father teased her and she blushed. So this really was how it would be. If he worked to make it happen. If he faced the world for Sara and started a family of his own. He looked ahead and could see his parents being wonderful grandparents, and suddenly understood they would grow old and die—he saw the gray in their hair and the wrinkles starting. And he was happy, because his part of the great project would be a success, and his children would carry it onward, into the distant future. He could almost reach out and touch it.

Dessert was a peach cobbler his mother had whipped up last night. She served it in the white china dessert bowls with spoons from the special silver set for guests only, silver plate that had to be hand-washed.

"This is wonderful, Mrs.—Sharon," Sara said after her first bite.

"Thank you." She looked proud. "I don't usually get such good peaches."

"Mom spoils us," Jared said. "Not that I'm complaining."

Kristi said, "May I be excused? I have some homework."

Jared's father nodded and she took her bowl to the sink before heading upstairs.

"Okay, now we can really talk," his mother said, looking to his father for his reaction.

Roger Spendlove straightened up in his chair. "Sharon," he warned, "isn't it a bit soon to talk seriously?"

"I just want them to know we support them. And what their plans are." She looked at Sara.

"What?" Jared said, his voice rising. "We appreciate your support. We're just getting started. We'll let you know if we're thinking of anything more than—"

"Leave the kids be, Sharon. The last thing they need is pressure from us."

"It's okay, Mrs. Spendlove, I mean Sharon," Sara said. "I know how you feel, my mom is always after me to go to a good college and meet the right boy, someday! Just not today. She thinks Jared is just the first of many tryout boyfriends I'll have before I meet the 'right' boy, that is, somebody upper-crust enough to meet her standards."

Roger Spendlove's face got red. "Let me get this straight.

Jared's not good enough?"

"That's my mother being—like she is! She doesn't know him like I do, and you don't really know me yet, either. I really really like your son."

Jared stepped in. "And I really really like you." He reached for her hand, and together they looked at his parents defiantly.

"Well, there you have it, Sharon. A good answer. Are you happy?" Jared's father laughed and reached out for his wife's hand. "Don't they remind you of us when we were young?"

Jared's mother smiled and squeezed her husband's hand. "I do remember. We had no idea what we were doing. But we made it work, and then the kids came along..."

"And by then we were too busy to have any doubts." Roger Spendlove put his arm around her for a moment.

Jared's mother sniffed and wiped her eyes with a napkin, then got up and cleared the table. Sara got up to help load the dishwasher. Jared looked at his father, who got up to hug him from behind and whispered, "Atta boy!" in his ear before heading back to his study.

15: Sara: Predator

Sara got home after dinner at Jared's, still feeling a glow. They were so unlike her family. Her mother was too busy to really pay attention to what Sara was feeling, and her father was distant in both senses. Even Jared's sister, who could be a little bratty, could also be charming, and she clearly loved her brother. It was hard to believe there were still people like that.

And most of all, Jared. Who made her feel safe, whose arms were like armor wrapped around her, whose body fitted into hers so well. She had stolen one of his dirty t-shirts so she could smell his smell whenever she wanted.

Her mother was drinking a glass of white wine and reading a report in front of the gas fireplace, which gave off a comforting warmth. It was getting very cold at night as October passed, and her mother had fallen into a habit. Since she had a lot of reading to do, she was either reading paper reports or on her laptop every night.

"Hi, Sweetie," she said. "I was just about to go to bed. How did it go?"

"They are incredibly nice. Even Jared's mother is warming up to me."

"Why don't we all go out to dinner somewhere soon?" Sara's mother didn't usually have time to cook anything that wasn't microwaved. "I'd like to meet them."

"I'll talk it over with Jared. You'd have to have a free night."

"Well, I'm free Friday or Saturday night! The backlog at work is finally getting down to merely staggering."

❂   ❂   ❂   ❂   ❂

Sara fell asleep that night unusually quickly. She awoke when the forced-air heat came on with a thump. She had just fallen back to sleep when she began to dream.

She was inside the mine, but bright light was coming from an open door up ahead. As she walked toward it, the view of what was beyond the door expanded—it showed blue sky above and sunny land of rolling hills and green grass covered with poppies receding into the distance. She stepped through the door and felt the soft grass on her bare feet.

"Welcome." The voice was coming from behind her, and she turned. A dark, bearded man dressed in white robes was watching her closely. "I am the angel of the Lord appointed to accompany you on your journey."

Sara noticed it was hard to look at him—she tried and her vision blurred out his face when she looked straight at it. She looked down at his cloth belt, and could then see his features indistinctly above.

"What kind of journey?" she asked. And then they were moving, somehow, over the landscape. In the distance green foothills rose in front of snow-capped mountains. It looked a lot like South Park.

"You are the chosen vessel to bear God's child. Much will be demanded of you, but your reward if you assist Him in His work will be an honored place in His household in Heaven." They were coming down to a gentle landing in front of an enormous white stone building, as tall as it was wide, with a great gold-framed doorway through which streamed brilliant golden light.

"What do I have to do?" Sara looked around and noticed other figures—angels?—going in and out. "Is this a temple?"

"It is *the* Temple, Sara. The template for those that were built on Earth." The angel looked up. "The Earth is nearing the End Days. Few believe, and you will be reviled and persecuted before the birth of the Messiah. It will be painful, and the envious and minions of Satan will do their best to stop you. You must build an army of believers to protect the Messiah in his infant form and help him grow into the man who will end evil and suffering forever."

"I did not believe," Sara said.

"But surely you do now. All that Torah study was not for nothing."

"This display would be convincing, but I still think I'm dreaming."

The angel stiffened. "That is the form our messages take. When we are stronger we can appear to your waking eye. But you will forget the dreams and carry out your duties unaware, which will be painful for you. I will bathe you in His light that you may feel our Presence when you need it, and use His powers of persuasion to assist you. Touch the person you need to convert and call upon me, and I will join with you to wash away their sins and bind them to you."

She must have looked skeptical, and the angel reached out to her and held her hands in his. "Like this," he said, and suddenly she Believed. It would all be worth it. A sense of wellbeing and goodness—and purpose—filled her.

"Now, return. You have a lot to do and not much time." The angel pushed her away and she flew backward along the path they had taken until she was again in the darkness of the mine.

❂   ❂   ❂   ❂   ❂

The next day Sara had overslept, so she had rushed through her shower and grabbed a muffin to eat in homeroom, which was against the rules but she planned to finish it before the bell rang. Brandy sat down next to her as she finished the muffin.

"A little rushed today?" Brandy said, helping clean up the crumbs from the desk.

"Bad night's sleep, so I overslept." Sara still felt woozy.

"Late night with Jared?" Brandy smiled knowingly.

"Not especially. I had dinner at his house but got home early."

"How is that going?"

"Well enough. His mom was really friendly for once. They were wanting to know where we're going. You know, like, are we serious?"

Brandy's eyes widened. "You're kidding! My parents wouldn't dare. Maybe because I'd never have my boyfriend over for questioning. If I had a boyfriend. Who would sit still for dinner with my parents…"

"It was really nice, actually. Just a surprise. I think they're on our side now." Sara realized the room had gone quiet. Mrs. Grimes was looking at them, waiting to call the roll.

❂   ❂   ❂   ❂   ❂

Gym went quickly. They were doing volleyball, which Sara enjoyed. She was only average in height, but she loved to jump to spike the ball over the net. The squealing of rubber-soled shoes on the varnished floor and the "uhs" and grunts of exertion were a reminder that they were physical creatures. The faint smell of old sweat in the lockerroom afterward reminded her again.

She had gotten used to showering in the gang shower, preferring a far corner where she could avoid the chatterers. She had trained herself not to look down or focus on the body parts of the other girls. Occasionally there was horseplay in the lockerroom, including the dreaded towel-snapping. Sara gave off a "don't touch me" vibe that no one so far had challenged.

The coach came through to check on them as they were still dressing. "Ladies, I shouldn't have to tell you to clean up your messes. If you get powder on the floor," she pointed at the offending white spot, "clean it up. If you must dispose of a tampon or pad, please please *please* use the bin provided for that purpose, not the regular trash—the staff has complained again, and if I catch the offender there will be hell to pay. And last but not least, one of you—" she looked directly at the only fat girl in the class—"has been wearing some kind of fragrance which at least two people have complained about. Knock it off, or at least cut back. We discourage heavy makeup and scents here." The coach nodded dismissal and went back to her glass-enclosed office.

Sara felt sorry for the target of that last, a heavy-set, moody girl who seemed to be trying too hard to make up for her size. But Sara had been bothered by the overpowering scent herself. After they were dressed, she caught up with the girl—Jaylyn, another one of those odd names a lot of girls here had—and put on her friendliest face.

"Jaylyn." Sara waited for recognition. Jaylyn looked back at her and stopped, wary. "That was mean to call you out in front of everybody."

"Thanks, Sara. That happens to me a lot." Other students passed them, and then they were alone in the hall.

"Well, I'm sorry. Coaches are thoughtless sometimes." Sara squeezed Jaylyn's forearm, and she visibly brightened. "But she does have a point. You have been overdoing it. This isn't the kind of crowd that appreciates, uh, unusual clothes or hairstyles."

"You're telling me. I'm planning to go to beauty school. I've always loved working on my look." She turned to display her hair. "What do you think?"

"It's nice. But that's a lot of work to keep up, isn't it?" Jaylyn's hair was woven into a thick braid which was wrapped around the top of her head like a cinnamon swirl.

"I like to mix it up. Try new things. Last year it was corn-rows, but they came out crooked. *That* was way too much work." Jaylyn shrugged. "It was good experience, though. I'm going to blow this town as quick as I can and go somewhere where people appreciate style. Like Salt Lake. Or LA."

Sara wondered how many other kids had interests and goals she would never dream of. She dimly understood that her concern and her touch had turned Jaylyn into a loyal ally, the first of an army to come.

◇   ◇   ◇   ◇   ◇

Chemistry class started as it usually did with the students at desks in front of the lab room. Mr. Edwards was deep into a discussion of molarity and how to mix up solutions with exact concentrations of ions for experimental use. He released them to work the lab exercise on the soapstone-topped benches that filled the back of the room. Sara joined her usual partner, Benjamin Rees, in measuring and mixing. Sara wrote the calculations down on paper and Benjie went to get the glassware they'd need from the storage cabinet.

Benjie was a quiet, kind boy, with glasses and a perpetually sleepy look. Sara liked him and he had a steady hand with the lab glassware, never dropping flasks as had happened to Sara several times. His family was poor and his clothes were cheap and unfashionable. He had asked her out once, to a movie, but Sara had let him down gently, explaining she already had a boyfriend, which he would have known if he were in the social loop.

The lab hummed with quiet conversations as the teams mixed and labeled solutions. Sara looked toward the front and could see Mr. Edwards smoking his pipe in his office. The storeroom behind the office was dark—it was normally used by the science teachers and their student assistants to prep equipment and animal specimens for labs.

They were nearly done with the lab part of the exercise, and Sara filled a page in her lab notebook with the answers to the exercise questions. When she was done she noted there were still fifteen minutes left in the period. Mr. Edwards came in to check on their work, passing all but one group, then left, Sara guessed, for the teacher's lunchroom.

Something clicked inside her, and Sara felt compelled to say, "Benjie, come back to the storeroom with me."

"I thought we were done," Benjie said, looking puzzled.

"I want to show you something. Something good."

Sara led Benjie by the hand, back through Mr. Edwards' office and into the darkened storeroom. Shelves filled with chemical bottles and reagents were above, and cabinets filled with fetal pigs in formaldehyde and other biological specimens were below.

Sara closed the door and turned to put her arms around Benjie, who stiffened in surprise.

"What are you doing?" he said, trying to pull away.

"I've been wanting you for a long time," she said, kissing him.

He relaxed into the kiss and began to respond. "But I thought...."

Sara pushed him up against the counter, kneeled in front of him, and started to unzip his fly.

16: Randy: Class

"The French and Indian War was the North American offshoot of the Seven Years' War between European coalitions, on one side Britain and Prussia, on the other France, Austria, Spain, and Sweden. The war actually began in North America when the British attacked French western forts and the French allied with the Iroquois Confederacy to try to halt British colonial expansion into territories west of the Appalachians. The need to coordinate the British North American response brought the largely self-governing colonies together, and the Colonial figures involved in the war, like George Washington, began to envision a unified response to external threats. Benjamin Franklin called on the colonies to "Join or Die," and when the British turned to imposing new taxes and enforcing mercantilist trade restrictions on the colonies, a small group of visionaries began to talk up a new nation. In 1773, the Boston Tea Party—a demonstration that destroyed a shipment of tea in defiance of a new tax—resulted in a British crackdown stripping the colony of Massachusetts of its traditional self-governance and imposing martial law. British troops occupied Boston and the powder keg of revolt was lit."

Randy looked up from the laptop running the slide presentation and noticed one girl in the back dozing off. He decided not to trouble the poor sleep-deprived thing. He plowed on through the rest of the lecture, pausing to crack jokes and make observations about how Colonial times compared to the current political environment.

Jared and Sara, as usual, sat in front, and as usual, they were intent on his words while still whispering asides to each other. This was mildly disruptive but not enough to justify reprimanding them. At least they were paying attention.

"Now remember, this was a time when the well-educated were steeped in the classics and wrote many letters a day, and letters were the only way to communicate with anyone distant. As a result, unlike the political leaders of today, the Founders were intensely literate and by today's standards overly verbose. A year before the Declaration of Independence, the Second Continental Congress issued a sort of precursor demand letter known as the Declaration of the Causes and Necessity of Taking Up Arms. I've had you read the original to get the full flavor of their mood. Going over the highlights...." Randy clicked to go on to the next slide:

> ...the commercial intercourse of whole Colonies with foreign countries, and with each other, was cut off by an act of Parliament; by another, several of them were entirely prohibited from the Fisheries in the seas near their coasts, on which they always depended for their sustenance; and large re-enforcements of ships and troops were immediately sent over to General Gage... Parliament adopted an insidious manœuvre, calculated to divide us, to establish a perpetual auction of taxations, where Colony should bid against Colony, all of them uninformed what ransom would redeem their lives; and thus to extort from us, at the point of the bayonet, the unknown sums ... Soon after intelligence of these proceedings arrived on this Continent, General Gage, who, in the course of the last year had taken possession of the Town of Boston... and still occupied it as a garrison, on the 19th day of April sent out from that place a large detachment of his army, who made an unprovoked assault on the inhabitants of the said Province, at the Town of Lexington... The inhabitants of Boston, being confined within that Town by the General... They accordingly delivered up their arms; but in open violation of honour, in defiance of the obligation of treaties... the Governour ordered the arms... to be seized by a body of soldiers;

[and] detained the greatest part of the inhabitants in the Town. ...
His troops have butchered our countrymen; have wantonly burnt
Charlestown, besides a considerable number of houses in other
places; our ships and vessels are seized; the necessary supplies of
provisions are intercepted, and he is exerting his utmost power to
spread destruction and devastation around him.

... We are reduced to the alternative of choosing an unconditional
submission to the tyranny of irritated Ministers, or resistance by
force. The latter is our choice.... Honour, justice, and humanity,
forbid us tamely to surrender that freedom which we received from
our gallant ancestors, and which our innocent posterity have a right
to receive from us. We cannot endure the infamy and guilt of resigning succeeding generations to that wretchedness which inevitably
awaits them, if we basely entail hereditary bondage upon them.[7]

"So they have petitioned Great Britain and announced they
will rebel, in hopes this petition will get a response—a few of
them still believed they could appeal to British politicians, and
they were right to think that some in Parliament were sympathetic. But not enough, and the war had already begun. A year
later when it was clear nothing would change, the Continental
Congress issued their Declaration of Independence, which
you're all familiar with. And the Revolutionary War was on in
earnest."

Sara spoke up. "What did more average people think? Was it
just the wealthiest and businessmen who wanted
independence?"

Randy set aside his notes and relaxed since they had finished the material with plenty of time remaining. "That's a good
question. The need to present a united front to bring public
opinion around to their side caused the Founders to paper over
a number of disagreements between themselves, notably over
the status of slavery. And it's misleading to suggest it was the

upper class who wanted independence—many wealthy people had assets and business interests that might be endangered by independence. Historians think about twenty percent of the colonial population opposed independence. Some fifty thousand of these Loyalists left for Canada, seeding that future country with a population more trusting of government generally, a cultural trait that is apparent even today."

The bell rang, and students started to move toward the door.

"Remember," Randy said, "the Declaration of Independence ends with the line, 'We mutually pledge to each other our Lives, our Fortunes and our sacred Honor.' Meaning they saw it as their duty to pay any price for the freedom of their children. Think about that when you're complaining about how tough you have it."

Sara and Jared waited until after the class had cleared to talk to him.

"We wanted to talk to you about our project—" Jared said.

Sara finished his sentence, "Mostly about audiovisual content. We were going to interview some of the local people we've found who worked on the mine or invested in it, but how would you feel about a short video instead of a written report?"

"Instead of?" Randy said, looking stern. "I need a written report so I can grade you on roughly similar presentations as other students. If you do a video I can give you a bit of extra credit, but it's outside the assignment."

The two exchanged glances. "We wanted to film the interviews anyway, since we have to record them to get good quotes," Randy said.

"There's your answer," Randy said. "Get the interviews on

video and write the report first. If you have extra time you can hand in a video version of your report. I don't want you spending time on video production you need to cover class material. It's a distraction and the report writing is more important."

"Okay," Sara said, looking at Jared. "You're the YouTube star, so you can do the video."

Jared smiled back at her. "While you're the on-camera talent." He turned back to Randy. "Thanks for letting us do this."

"Don't thank me until you see your grade," he replied. "You're ambitious, and this is more work than I would normally expect for the project. Just be sure you get it in on time."

⚙   ⚙   ⚙   ⚙   ⚙

Randy was at his office computer looking through the quiz results from another class. The quizzes were presented as multiple-choice forms on student tablets, so he didn't have to laboriously grade each one by hand the way he used to. But the report came with analytics showing how many students missed each question, and what students were weakest in what area, and he spent almost as much time looking through the report as he might have spent grading the test by hand.

One of the teachers he shared the office with, Suzette Handler, came in and paused in front of his desk until he looked up.

"Randy," she said, "you've got Sara Horowitz in your AP History class, right?" She looked troubled.

"Yes. One of my best students," he replied, tenting his hands and looking puzzled. "Something bothering you?"

She leaned down and whispered. "One of my students wrote about sex with another student in his private journal. He didn't name her but it was clearly her."

"The boy wasn't Jared?" Randy asked.

She shook her head. "No, another junior. This isn't the first report I've heard, either, just the most obvious. The kids are beginning to talk."

"Interesting. I haven't seen anything, but keep me posted. What are our responsibilities in this kind of case?" Randy knew, but wanted to be sure she knew.

"None. We'd be legally required to report to authorities if one of them were over twenty-one. Good thing or we'd be reporting half the students." She sighed. "I just felt better telling someone. She's one of my best students, too, and I don't want to see her get hurt."

"This is what you get for encouraging them to journal about their lives. Maybe you find out more than you want to know." Randy thought for a second. "And it could be made up. They're supposed to do creative writing, so maybe it is fictional. Besides, you told them it was confidential, right?"

"I did. And this boy is always very matter-of-fact, so I think it was a real event. But mum's the word. We never talked." She hummed tunelessly and went to her own desk.

A month after his last visit to Bishop Snow's office, Jared was back at the bank, waiting while sitting on the same couch and looking at magazines on the same coffee table. Only the magazine covers had changed, and the scene outside the window was gray-brown since the trees had shed most of their leaves.

But Jared felt the difference in himself—since Sara, he was different. Stronger, more confident, with a purpose. He no longer felt like a nobody with no place in the world.

The bishop ushered Jared into his office.

"I'm hearing lots of good things about you lately," he said. "Your mother came to me to seek guidance on your possible future wife. A bit premature, I suppose, but she was troubled. I encouraged her to accept the gifts of God no matter how presented. Marriage to a Gentile is not as unusual as all that, and as many are brought into the fold thereby as have left it."

"Thank you for that. Dad was fine, she was upset." Jared relaxed a little more as he realized the bishop was again more understanding than he expected.

"This isn't unusual. Mothers tend to obsess about their son's choice in partners. My mother was tough on all the girls I brought home to meet her. The one who became my wife was just barely good enough. It made me angry then, now I see it as typical. You don't want to tell them that their worrying does more harm than good."

"She started to warm up to Sara last week."

"Then my work is done." Bishop Snow looked down at the book opened in front of him and began to read. "This is from a piece written by Apostle Richards addressing the relationship between Jews and Mormons. 'You [Jews] have been driven, robbed, and ravished—so have we. You have been persecuted, mistreated, misunderstood—so have we. Why? We were driven from our homes to desolation beyond the boundaries of the United States. You, too, have been driven. Why? What a power we could be in the world if we [Mormons and Jews] were united.'

"I'm not suggesting you bring this up now," the Bishop added, "but if you continue with Sara and want to marry her, you should persuade her to bring up the children in the church. And Sara could convert if she wished so you could someday have a temple sealing. But she would also be accepted as a member of the community if she chooses not to convert."

Jared felt like blurting out that he wasn't sure he believed either, and no way was he going to talk Sara into converting, but then he also wanted his children to have the support of his friends and family and … or maybe they would just leave for somewhere where no one cared. He decided to smooth the way by saying, "It's too soon. I'll certainly keep that in mind, though."

Bishop Snow smiled and gave Jared a look that seemed to say he knew Jared was telling him what he wanted to hear. "In any case, you now have a serious girlfriend. How has that affected the problem you came to me about last month?"

"I stopped. I did pray a lot, but I think it was meeting Sara that made it easier. And thank you for the advice. I'm not sure I would have had the nerve to get anywhere with Sara if I'd been… using it up on porn."

"Reality is always more fulfilling. Now, you know premarital sex is a sin…" Bishop Snow raised an eyebrow and looked at him questioningly.

Jared just stared back. What was the bishop up to?

"…and I would advise you to repent of your sins. God is forgiving, and your path to ridding yourself of sin and addiction may not be smooth or ideal, but He will understand. He knows you are trying to be good. I think you are on the right path." The bishop sat back and sighed. "It's not my role to be your friend, so I will say no more. But you know you can come to me any time."

"I appreciate the support." Jared understood the bishop was unable to voice any approval of what he obviously suspected Jared was doing with Sara, but he felt warmed.

The bishop looked back to his screen, where his next appointment was highlighted. "You know we miss seeing you at church. I know you have a lot on your plate, but regular attendance keeps you centered. It's a reminder that you're a part of a larger community. Try to make it more often. Bring Sara."

"I'll work on it." Jared had stopped going after he started playing online games. First he made excuses, then when his parents stopped pressuring him to go, he just stopped. And now there was so little time to himself after school and Sara, he didn't expect to get back into the church habit. Maybe in some hazy future where he had a family and settled down.

"Anything else you'd like to discuss?" Bishop Snow's mind was apparently already moving on to his next appointment.

"There is something else—Sara and I are doing a school project on the Zion Mine. Prof. Atwater got us started looking at it, and we're going to write up interviews of people who were invested or who were involved when it was open."

Bishop Snow looked worried. "While that's an interesting subject, I have to warn you that my father became very unpopular in town when he came out against it. He thought it was a fraud and he opposed the reopening of the mine when he was a county commissioner. It was divisive, and half the town turned their back on him. So be careful. What are you going to say about it?"

"We're looking at it as an example of false prophecy. The question is, why do people keep believing in it after the church declared it a fraud?"

"I'd be interested in seeing your report. Just be careful not to call it a fraud with people you talk to. A lot of people still believe, and you won't get them to talk if they think you're going to make them look like fools." The bishop opened a file drawer and pulled out a folder. "Here's a position paper approved for distribution—I'll make you a copy. It avoids condemning supporters while making it clear the church does not wish to be affiliated with their claims in any way. Try to take the same stance."

"Oh, we will. Just going to write up what people tell us and let the reader judge. Our teacher says we might get it published in the paper."

"That's what worries me. We don't need to dredge up old controversies. No one has brought up the mine issue lately and I'd like to keep it that way." The bishop stood and opened the door. "It was good to see you, Jared."

◎   ◎   ◎   ◎   ◎

At dinner Jared's mother asked how his visit with Bishop Snow had gone. Jared put her off and quickly changed the subject. Kristi wanted to talk about the choral group she was in, and Jared was happy to turn the conversation toward her. His father teased Kristi about her apparent fixation on a boy one grade up from hers who had been chosen as a soloist for the holiday concert they were practicing for.

Sara was coming over after dinner, so his mother excused him from cleanup detail and shooed him out of the kitchen. He was noodling on his laptop up in his room when he heard his father letting Sara in downstairs.

"Hey," she said, sitting down on the bed across from him. "What's our plan?"

He moved to sit beside her and put his arm around her shoulders, then wiggled his eyebrows and an imaginary cigar. "What's always our plan?"

She giggled. "Not here, silly."

Right then Kristi passed by in the hall and stopped, looking in. "That doesn't look like homework!" She wagged her finger at them and made tut-tut sounds.

Jared shushed her and got up to close the door in Kristi's face.

"Much better," he said.

After Sara left, Jared went to bed. The dreams began again, and this time he was trying to cross a battlefield in Morpheum Online when Raphael appeared. Jared had just gutted an orc with his sword and was still covered in green ichor. Raphael waved his arm, and the game world disappeared. They were standing on a white plain under a blue sky.

"You must be prepared for the real battle," Raphael said. "You will be opposed at every turn. School, family, church—all will betray you. You must fight for what is right, and protect the ones you love."

Jared looked down and his sword had disappeared. "With what? I am disarmed."

"When the time comes, we will give you all the weapons you need. You will not go into the final battle alone."

Sara began to realize she wasn't entirely in control of her actions. She found slips of paper in her pockets with phone numbers written on them and had no idea where they came from; she found herself in conversations with no memory of how she got there. It was disturbing for a few seconds until she forgot why it was disturbing. Her mind absorbed the pebbles of disquiet like a pool of oil, disturbed for a moment by each troublesome thought but then placid again.

She had been talking to Owen Kimball, the homecoming king and star football player. Blandly handsome, blond, six-foot-one and muscular, boyfriend of Jessica Peterson, the queen bee of the Mean Girls. Sara got the impression they were a couple not because they liked each other but because Jessica wanted him as the trophy she needed to climb to prominence in Mt. Hermon's tiny country club set. Some kids reached their peak achievement in high school and never imagined they'd be tested again in the real world—they stayed close to home and ended up running a car dealership or being the town's best realtor. Owen got good grades by being agreeable and fulfilling all expectations, but would falter without someone to tell him what to do—and so Jessica had found in him the perfect mount for her ride to social prominence. Something in Sara took impish delight in leading him astray.

It was between classes and Sara had spotted him closing his locker.

"Did you get a chance to look at the casting call sheet?" Sara asked. The winter musical "White Christmas" had been announced and Sara intended to try out. She had seen Owen looking at the posted list outside the chorus room.

Owen turned to her and smiled in recognition. "Sure did. I'm not much of a dancer so I was worried, but Mr. Shumway said I can just sway."

"You're at least as good a dancer as anyone else here," Sara said, edging closer. "Mr. Shumway says there will be no tap dancing. And you'd be just right for Bob Wallace. Like he said, your basic decent guy with a good voice. I've heard you sing."

"I watched some clips on YouTube. I can do the Bing Crosby thing well enough." Owen burbled a few notes Crosby-style, "Buh buh buh BUH."

Sara got closer and looked up into his green eyes. Owen realized something was up and looked down at her with a puzzled expression. Sara squeezed his hand in hers and waited until his expression changed to a widening grin.

"So how about you show me how you can move?" The animal in Sara knew almost any line would do while she touched her prey.

Owen looked around to be sure no one was watching. "I have to go to class, but how about I meet you after school under the bleachers? We can go for a drive."

◊   ◊   ◊   ◊   ◊

Owen got more out of Sara in one afternoon than Jessica had allowed him in months, and begged her to see him again the next afternoon. When she met him at his house, he surprised her with the presence of his best friend and teammate Dean, who hurt her a bit in his enthusiasm.

After showering at home Sara realized she was very tired and she called Jared to postpone their date that evening. She fell into her bed and slept for two hours. When she woke up, she felt refreshed and the minimal chafing was the only sign she had been busy. The memory of what she had done was erased like all the others.

Sara's list of allies grew. The boys—it was mostly boys—had reason to come to her defense, as she dispensed sexual favors denied them by any girl they knew. What they didn't know was that their minds had been swayed by an unnatural force. They would rationalize that they had shared something special with Sara and that she was just a liberated girl from out of town, free of the social strictures that kept other girls from putting out.

19: Randy: Lost

"And so, by purchasing France's claim to the Louisiana territories from France, Jefferson doubled the size of the young United States and continued the process of removing European colonial powers from its future territories." Randy finished with a flourish. "After Thanksgiving we'll take up the War of 1812, the American part of the Napoleonic Wars in Europe. Try not to fall behind in the readings even though it's a holiday." Randy acknowledged a hand up in back—Chelsea Nichols, a studious mouse of a girl.

"Can we get an extension of the due date on the project updates? We need more time."

Randy tried not to show his anger. "Write up what you have done even if it's just to report you've been slacking off and made no progress. Better I find out now if you're going to blow it off."

Chelsea looked sullen. "Okay."

The bell rang and students filed out. Jared and Sara left, but Chelsea approached him.

"I know it sounds like special pleading, but I broke up with my boyfriend and I've been too upset to concentrate this week. So I was hoping—" she looked up at Randy with big brown eyes.

"I'm sorry you're having trouble, but I can't be making exceptions for everybody with a personal problem." Randy thought a little softening of his message would help. "Like I said, just write one page on what you have done, even if it's not much, and how you plan to catch up. If you're really distracted I'll work with you."

Her mouth worked, and then she began to sob, tears welling up. "It's just so hard. Dawson *lied* to me. We were *engaged*." The wailing grew louder.

Randy fought the urge to take Chelsea into his arms for comfort. The rule was no touching a student under any circumstances, no matter how much she needed a hug.

"And I just found out who he's seeing. Sara! That... *bitch*." It sounded tentative, like she had never used such a bad word before.

Randy was shocked. "Really? That's hard to believe. How do you know?"

"One of my friends saw them sneak off together this morning. Into a janitor's closet. They were in there ten minutes at least."

"That isn't possible. The maintenance staff keeps everything locked."

"Well, it opened for *her*." The sobbing had slowed and Randy got her a tissue from his desk.

"Have you talked to Dawson about it? Maybe there's an explanation."

Chelsea looked stricken. "I *tried*. He says it's none of my business."

"Well, I'm sorry your, uh, fiancé is not working out. You're better off knowing now than later. There are plenty of boys who won't do that to you."

Chelsea blew her nose and sniffed. "Thanks, Mr. Wright."

"Just hand in something by deadline. It's not a big factor in your grade as long as you get the project done." The first students for his next class came through the door. "Class is about to start."

Chelsea left, still sniffling.

✦   ✦   ✦   ✦   ✦

Chelsea's problem with Sara was the most serious of those Randy had heard of through the grapevine. He had chalked it up to gossip and jealousy, but it was starting to sound like Sara really might be out of control. He knew it was not his place to intervene, but he decided to go talk to the guidance counsellor, whose role it was; he would clue her in to a possible problem and get some advice on what he might do without overstepping his legal role. Student problems could be a minefield for teachers, with a well-meaning intervention leading to more trouble, while in other areas like bullying or abuse at home teachers were legally required to report the problem to authorities. The safest thing was to ask someone up the chain, which showed he saw a problem but passed the responsibility for dealing with it to someone else.

Randy found Mina Wilson in her office but on the phone. He waved at her from the doorway and she held up a finger, mouthing "one minute."

She hung up the phone and waved him in, saying, "That was interesting. Dixie State wanting to add time to their Recruiting Day slot."

"Our students are *just—that—good!*" he responded, mimicking the principal, who was known for his excessive belief in the power of positive thinking.

"Really! But Dixie State is a good backup school for our students when they've blown their grades and can't get into BYU."

Randy closed the door and sat in the chair in front of her desk. "Today's pressing issue: I have to report a social problem with one of my students. Sara Horowitz."

Mina's face went blank. "What have you heard?"

"One of my students wanted me to know she was behind in her work on a project because Sara had seduced her boyfriend. Or fiancé, it was that kind of short-term eternal love. Anyway, she's distraught. And I've had hints of similar behavior, but only hearsay." Randy gripped the chair arms tightly.

"Okay, that's another data point to add to things I have heard. As you know, we don't police student social activity unless it becomes disruptive. This is sounding borderline— should I be concerned about Sara? I could talk to her…"

Randy sighed in relief. "Would you? She seems fine. Her boyfriend Jared seems placidly unaware. I'm reluctant to talk to either of them since I have them both in a class."

"You're quite right to keep your distance. Let me talk to her and I'll give you a heads-up if there's anything you need to be concerned about."

Randy continued to think about it after he left Mina's office. The professional thing to do would be to forget about it—not his problem, and only trouble could come of his getting in-volved. What he didn't know couldn't hurt him, but a student complaint could. Being a male teacher in the modern era was hazardous; he couldn't afford to be accused of anything, so he had made it a habit to be sure he was never alone with a student, male or female. This wasn't an urban school district where the teacher's union would protect him and at worst he'd have to change schools; there were no other high schools nearby.

But he felt for Jared and Sara. If Sara was acting out and slutting around, there was surely something under the surface motivating her—maybe trauma in her past, some abuse that had happened to her back East, her absent father's doing? If Jared had no idea what she had been doing, it was going to hurt when he finally found out. Maybe he could get Jared into a conversation tangential to the topic and warn him indirectly?

He was still thinking about it when he rounded a corner in the hall and nearly ran into Sara coming out of the girl's bathroom.

"Mr. Wright! Sorry, I didn't see you," she said as they narrowly missed colliding.

"That's okay, I was lost in thought." He stood there, paralyzed. Then Sara reached out to steady him, her hand on his forearm. He felt warmth flow through him.

"I'm so clumsy," Sara said, her green eyes wide and long lashes fluttering.

Randy felt his thoughts lining up into dangerous sentences and tried to stop himself from speaking. Failing, and the words flowed out: "Are you in some sort of trouble? Let me help you..." He was conscious of a voice inside him screaming at him to get away from her. But he couldn't move, and even began to reach out for her. Who was operating his arms? It was bad enough he was endangering his job, his career, and his marriage—more frightening still was his inability to control his own body.

Sara led him down the hall into the next empty classroom and closed the door. "We shouldn't be here," Randy managed to say.

"You're my favorite teacher," Sara said, "and I want you to teach me about love." She undid the buttons of his shirt and ran her hands across his hairy chest. Then she started to unbuckle his belt. Randy looked on from somewhere outside himself, unable to push her away.

Randy stumbled into his office in a numbed state and slumped into his chair. At the other end of the office, Suzette Handler looked up from her screen, but said nothing and went back to her grading.

Randy was turning over the sex with Sara in his mind, trying to make sense of it. What had just happened? He felt guilty for fantasizing about Sara and Jared together a few weeks ago; just a fleeting fantasy while he was making love to his wife, which was routine enough after twenty years to require a boost from visualizing hotter, younger bodies in motion if he wanted to get off. Harmless! Until suddenly he had fallen into the trap Sara had set for him. She had left him with a desire to do her bidding and help her in any way possible, but set against that new compulsion was his anger at having been so manipulated and inexplicably out of control. Something *wrong* had happened, and away from Sara's influence he fought hard to remember his anger at how his will had been defeated and cowered in a dark corner of his mind while she had her way with him.

20: Jared: Thanksgiving

Thanksgiving morning dawned cold and crisp. Jared offered to help his mother in the kitchen, but she asked him to take out the trash—which was already full of potato peelings. His dad had started up the TV to watch sports, and Kristi was bouncing around the kitchen both getting in the way and learning how to prepare the turkey.

Jared's brother Connor was supposed to come down from BYU before dinner, and Sara and her mother were due to arrive around the same time. For the first time in his life Jared looked at their home as if seeing it as a guest, and hurriedly straightened slipcovers and put away the clutter of books, magazines, and DVDs in the family room. His mother noticed his activity from the kitchen and smiled at him.

"Oh, so *now* you care how things look," she said, laughing. "*Important* people are coming!"

"I just want to make a good impression. There's so much dust on the shelves...."

"If you start dusting, you'll have to dust all of them—a clean spot makes the dirty spots obvious. Welcome to my world!"

Jared turned back toward her. "Good point, Mom. Guess I shouldn't start."

"Don't let me discourage you, but it's a little late to turn into a neatnik. Sara and her mother will be here any minute. Maybe you should clean up your room instead? That's a little more do-able and I'm sure they'll want the tour."

Everyone sat around the table, lengthened with the two

leaves and covered with the fancy linen tablecloth and silver plate only brought out for special occasions. Jared's father carved the turkey while everyone else started filling their plates, the mashed potatoes steaming as they were uncovered. Kristi managed to drip gravy from the edge of the gravy boat onto the tablecloth, earning a hard look from her mother.

connor had heard that Jared had a girlfriend, but still seemed surprised that she was real. Connor had had a respectable high school football career and several serious girlfriends before leaving for BYU, and his overall success in both school and social life made Jared feel overshadowed. Jared was proud to have Connor see how well he was doing.

Jared took a drumstick and two slabs of breast meat before passing the platter on.

"...So I'm planning to apply to B-schools at Stanford and MIT. I want to get into technology management," Connor was saying as Sara nodded intently. "That's where the action is now."

Jared had heard this plan many times. Connor was a very successful bullshitter, but he did apply himself and had the high grades and recommendations to get into most any school he wanted. Jared wondered how well his brother would do once he had to deliver more concrete work than papers and multiple-choice quizzes, but if looking good on paper was the criteria, he'd be a winner.

"I thought BYU had a great B-school," Sara said.

"Marriott School of Business. I'm applying, but I want to get to where the networking is good. Utah is a backwater, and Marriott is more like a Mormon finishing school—"

"Connor," their mother said reproachfully, "you know we're happy to support your goals, but do you have to look down on your own people that way?"

"Sorry, Mom. But it's true. I need experience *outside Utah* to be taken seriously in finance."

Jared's mother winced and almost said something, but then caught herself as she looked at Sara and her mother listening intently. Starting again, she said, "If you think so, dear. But I'm sure you'd do very well staying here. There's plenty of finance and high tech jobs in Salt Lake."

Jared broke in. "*I* won't be leaving, Mom."

"And that's another thing," she said. "Connor, tell your brother he needs to go to a good college."

Connor rolled his eyes. "I think Jared can plan his life for himself, Mom. He's doing better than I am in some ways." He turned to Sara. "What's your plan, Sara? College?"

Sara's mother said, "She's going to a good school. Her father will help her with that. Maybe back East."

Sara turned to her mother with a look of exasperation. "That's far from settled. I'll apply, but I want to be near where Jared is."

Sara's mother was silent. Jared's mother took over. "Sara, don't get ahead of yourself. Plenty of time for that later. Just keep your options open."

Jared decided to calm things down. "Mom, I'm going to apply to BYU and a backup school. Like you said, keeping my options open. And there's always the military—"

Roger Spendlove spoke from the head of the table. "Always a good option, son. Did wonders for me."

Connor pulled his brother aside after dessert, when their father had gone back to watching football. Crowd noise from the game drowned out the clatter from the kitchen where cleanup was in progress.

"Sara's quite something," he said. "You did good, bro."

"Thanks. All my clean living and hard work has been rewarded."

Connor laughed. "Ah, funny. Hard work! If only you could get credit for playing games."

"Well, where's *your* girlfriend?" Jared asked. "The last one was kind of weird."

"Shana was a little too princess-y. I got tired of her trying to control my every move." He sighed, remembering. "Great sex, though."

Jared checked the kitchen—their mother couldn't hear. "What's that thing about hot versus crazy?"

"The hot-crazy matrix. The ones that look hot are often crazy. Sara seems fine and hot at the same time."

"So far. She's great to be with. And sexy."

"You, uh, doing it?" Connor raised his eyebrows.

Jared blushed. "Yes. I—"

"Oh, brother. Do be careful. Using protection?"

"Yes. Do I look stupid?"

"Yes. But use protection anyway."

After board games and another round of pie, Jared's mother went to the kitchen to prepare leftovers for Sara and her mother to take home. Connor, Jared, and Kristi were unpacking the boxes of Christmas ornaments from the garage, with Connor explaining the family lore about some of the older decorations.

"Mom made the stockings out of felt while she was pregnant with you," Connor said, speaking to Jared and holding up the one with "Jared" written in silver glitter across the top. "She made yours with the name she had already decided on."

"What if Jared had been a girl?" Kristi asked.

"She made the one with your name on it then, too, just in case. I figure when she finally had you she didn't want to make another stocking, so Kristi you became."

"Any more stockings in the box?" Jared said, laughing. "Is there something she's not telling us?"

"No," Connor said, "I think we were all she could handle."

Jared's father had been out on the porch sitting, and had been joined by Sara, who later came back in and rejoined her mother on the couch in front of the fireplace.

Jared's father came back in a few minutes later, a look of concern on his face.

"Jared, you want to come help me get the tree out of the garage?" he said.

"Sure, Dad." Jared followed his dad to the garage.

His dad closed the door. It was cold enough to see his breath as he said, "Is Sara okay? I just had the strangest talk with her."

"She's fine, though we're all getting tired. It's late." Jared was trying to think of a way to get her up to his room for a few minutes before they left.

"She put her hand on my leg and squeezed," Jared's father said. "If I were younger and prettier I'd have thought she was coming on to me."

"They're touchy-feely people. Her mom comes up behind me and rubs my neck sometimes."

"Maybe. I moved away and she stopped. But she was also— hard to explain, something about her voice changed. Uh, sexier."

"You must have been imagining it. She likes you, that I know."

"Well, of course. But it was like she was a different person. Not shy at all." Jared's father sighed and looked away. "I suppose I was just spooked by the touch."

"She's used to us now, so she's more comfortable being herself. I'm sure it was nothing." Jared dismissed this red flag as he had all the others.

Randy did his best not to think about what had happened with Sara, but his wife Stephanie could tell he was preoccupied during the Thanksgiving break. After the relatives had left and their daughter had gone to bed Thanksgiving night, she cornered him on the couch.

"Okay, what's bothering you?" she said. "It's like you're somewhere else. Everyone noticed."

Randy considered his options. He did need to talk to someone, but he couldn't risk telling anyone the full truth—even Stephanie, who he trusted with everything both good and bad about himself. This was one case where he might not be able to rely on her understanding—he didn't even trust himself to know. He wished he could forget, but he needed her support.

"I'm worried about Sara Horowitz. The gossip is she's having sex with every boy in school, and I got confirmation of that from a student who said Sara seduced her boyfriend."

"Since when did you start worrying about student's sex lives?" Stephanie looked skeptical. "This happens every year, and most of the time it's just gossip started by jealous kids."

"Something's different about this. There's a lot more smoke and there really is a fire this time, and it's going to cause trouble for her and other people. And maybe me." Randy let a little of his real worry show.

"How could it cause you problems?"

"Once the witch hunt starts, everyone's looking for witches. I'm a man with a sixteen-year-old student in my class who's becoming notorious for sleeping with any male around. Imagine how it'd go if she names me—or anyone else starts a rumor about me, for that matter. How can I defend myself? The school would fire me just to avoid the publicity."

"Surely they wouldn't." Stephanie frowned as his worry started to spread to her.

"You remember Eldon Sutter? He had to move to Salt Lake to get a job. At least that never hit the news." There had been a complaint from a student, covered up. They had both tried to help him at the time, but couldn't risk being publicly supportive. Sutter had been erased from the school. Randy had been surprised the old copies of the yearbook in the school library still had his picture—if they could, the administration would have cut those photos out.

"Let's hope that doesn't happen. Is there any clue as to why Sara might be acting out?" Stephanie usually looked for reasons rather than jumping to the conclusion anyone was actively bad. As a nurse she saw a lot of bad behavior under stress, but preferred to believe those in pain were not intentionally hurting others.

"I looked at her transfer records. There's a hint that she may have been treated for depression a few years ago, a gap in her attendance. And those scars on her wrists—I'm guessing there was an episode of cutting. She might be acting out of low self-esteem, borderline personality disorder, something to do with her father's exit from her life. Of course I can't just ask her." Randy knew his role as teacher drastically limited what he could do as a human being to reach out to students in need. Normally he didn't let that stop him from trying to help, but the hazards in this situation were too great to just go with his instincts to come to the rescue. No good deed went unpunished. It was safer not to care.

Sunday night he couldn't get to sleep, so he got up and went downstairs to read and have a glass of warm milk thinking that might relax him. His mind was busy exploring every scenario, ending up with his disgrace and exile. Would Stephanie stick with him if he had to leave the state? Would Mt. Hermon still be the cozy home town he had grown comfortable with when all of the Mormons and most of the rest of the town shunned him? They were his wife's people and she wouldn't want to leave.

He again wondered why he had been unable to get away from Sara when she came onto him. Was he that weak? He had fantasized about Sara as well as other female students in past years, but never, ever, ever would have acted on his interest. He had parried many attempts to seduce him and gently discouraged many girls—and a few boys—who had had crushes on him. The more he thought about it, the more impossible it seemed. Unless—somehow he had been drugged? Roofied? He hadn't had anything to drink. There was the moment Sara held his arm—hadn't someone been poisoned by skin contact a few years ago?

Monday morning he was exhausted from lack of sleep. By afternoon he had recovered somewhat. He got through his US History class by studiously ignoring Jared and Sara, though he knew he'd have to get over that before it became obvious, since he usually called on them often.

Mina Wilson had sent him an email asking him to drop by her office, so he waited until his free period and found her in.

"Mina. What's up?" He sat down in the guest chair.

"You wanted me to talk to Sara about her recent behavior. I had her come in this morning on the pretext of discussing her college plans. She seemed quite normal." Mina brought up Sara's record on her screen.

"I've since discovered there's a lot of truth to the rumors." Randy pushed away the intrusive memory of the delicate curve of Sara's neck and her moaning in ecstasy. "More reports."

"And I've been asking my student spies what they've heard. It's not good. The tip of the iceberg, I'm suspecting—she's been a busy girl."

Randy considered his strategy. "One of the reasons I brought this up with you is the danger to my reputation—I wanted you to know I'm not in any way involved with her. In case there's a rumor or something."

"I figured that out—a wise choice. Your report is on the record now and so you're protected against an allegation that you were somehow complicit." She opened a desk drawer, took out a notepad, and began writing.

"What did she say?" Randy relaxed a little and sat back in the chair.

"Sara denied having done anything with anyone but Jared. She seemed offended by the idea, so either she's a really good actress or she's dissociating—not remembering. Multiple personality disorder is rare, but would explain something like this. The dirty deeds are done by another persona, then forgotten."

"Is there anything we can do to head off trouble?"

"Formally? No, not until someone files a complaint. We can discipline a student for 'creating a disturbance,' but until a fight breaks out or someone goes on the record there's no cause to intervene. We can't act on rumors alone."

"What should I be doing?" Randy knew asking for advice was one way to gain Mina's sympathy and support for any future struggle.

"Just act normally and stay out of it. When the time comes I'll make sure you don't get dragged into it."

◊   ◊   ◊   ◊   ◊

When he got home that evening, Randy went to his computer and started doing research on MPD-multiple personality disorder, date rape drugs, and everything he could think of to explain the strange compulsion that had overcome his will. He read Wikipedia entries and followed a trail of links to sites on exorcism and possession by demons, the pre-psychiatry explanation for MPD. In between the crackpots and the Catholics, he stumbled upon a cool, rational paper on spirit possession by a BYU professor, Tomo Kovac, who had credentials as a physicist but appeared to have achieved notoriety for his physical explanations for paranormal phenomena like ghosts and zombies.

Randy found Kovac's listing as a consultant on the web site for a popular show about ancient aliens, where his wild hair and obvious obsession made for bravura video interviews. Kovac seemed to have stopped working with them a decade ago, though, and stopped publishing his work at the same time. There had been a widely-read article in the Salt Lake City

Tribune, which often printed stories that embarrassed the LDS authorities. The story suggested Kovac was trading on his affiliation with BYU to promote his media presence. The Church PR spokesman denied that any endorsement of Kovac was implied by his position at BYU—but Kovac had nearly disappeared from the public record after that.

Still, Kovac was still listed in BYU's faculty web pages, with a phone number. Randy picked up the phone and dialed.

22: Jared: Betrayal

Jared had added more red flags about Sara to his collection. She was distant at times, and she had started to put him off when he was hoping to get together at her house. At school he noticed he was getting odd looks, and more than once he walked by a group of kids talking and they stopped to stare at him before resuming their conversation. Still, he dismissed it as the consequence of his changed image—no longer a fade-into-the-background kid, but a member of a couple that people noticed.

He was putting books into his locker when Tiffany Harding touched his elbow to get his attention.

"Jared, how's it going," she said, smiling sympathetically.

Tiffany was one of the cool girls, cheerleader and enforcer of the social hierarchy. Mean-Girl-adjacent.

"Doing okay, Tiffany. What's up?"

"I wanted to talk to you about Sara." Tiffany waited for his reaction.

"What about her?" Jared was on guard now.

"She's making a fool of you," she said. "Everyone's talking about it. She's thrown herself at every boy in school."

"Oh, really? How would you know that?" Jared was starting to turn red.

"My boyfriend Jason. He confessed. He told me a lot of the boys have compared notes. She's either had sex with or tried to come on to nearly every boy in school. Nobody wants to tell you, but I thought you should know. She's probably infecting people—" She looked shocked as he slammed his locker hard enough to rattle the whole row of them.

"Look, Tiffany, I appreciate that you want to help, okay, but I don't need help. It's none of your business. Why don't you take it up with Sara if you have a beef with her?"

"I just—"

"I'm late for class," Jared said, and turned his back on her before she could see his expression.

❖   ❖   ❖   ❖   ❖

Mr. Wright was holding forth on the political issues of slavery as the Civil War approached. He had put up a slide:

> I admit that we find among the Jews, as well as other nations, cases where men sold themselves; but clearly they sold themselves only into drudgery, not slavery. It is evident that the person who was sold wasn't thereby put at the mercy of an absolute, arbitrary, despotic power; for the master was obliged at a certain time to let the other go free from his service, and so he couldn't at any time have the power to kill him. Indeed the master of this kind of servant was so far from having an arbitrary power over his life that he couldn't arbitrarily even maim him: the loss of an eye or a tooth set him free,[8]

"Slavery has existed since the dawn of history, but the slavery of antiquity was a social status quite different from the plantation system of the Old South, as Locke noted. Among the old Virginian plantation-owning class it was considered immoral to treat the black slave as of little value, and a proper Christian slaveowner would always take care of the needs of the slave and free them when possible. Benevolent masters were common in Southern fiction.

"Notice the children born to slaves were automatically deemed slaves in the US, which was abhorrent to the moralists of even pre-Enlightenment days. One had to consider black slaves to be subhuman to rationalize Southern-style slavery, with the comforting notion that slaves were 'better off' in slavery. The fact that for some this might be true, and that some slaves could not imagine being free and didn't want to be, does not change the fundamental immorality of what had grown up in the South. The US institution of slavery began to be enforced by law in the Colonies in 1640, when black men who had arrived to work under indenture were declared permanent slaves under the law. In 1662, the colonial government of Virginia decided that newborn children in the colony would inherit the status of their mother, so any child having a slave mother would automatically be considered a slave. This set up the pernicious system which treated black slaves as similar to domestic animals, with a similar incentive to breed them for profit. Importation of slaves was made illegal in 1808, and only 350,000 had been imported before then—the growth to the four million slaves shown in the 1860 Census was natural increase, and by the Civil War, almost all slaves were many generations removed from their African origins."

Jared raised his hand and asked, "Does that mean slaves were better off in the South than they would have been had they been left in Africa?"

Mr. Wright paused. "That argument was made by slave state politicians. It might well be true in a material sense, but even if better-fed and safer than they would have been in the West African territories of their ancestors, they were still slaves. They had no choice in where they lived, what work they would do, or even whether their children would stay with them or not. Families were broken up and cruel owners could work their slaves to death, perpetuating a system which prevented most slaves from winning the dignity of independence through their own labor. They had no property, no vote, and authorities would catch and punish them if they tried to leave. Choice is the foundation of freedom and human dignity, and they were allowed none."

Mr. Wright started into the Abolitionists and the religious foundation of the anti-slavery movement. Jared thought about his freedom to choose—he could leave town and get a job somewhere else, and take Sara with him. That would be a choice, and get them far away from the gossips. He wanted to ask Sara if the rumors were true, but he was afraid they might be. All of his plans and dreams for their future together were in danger of being exposed as the naïve fantasies of a failure.

After class, Jared parted from Sara at the corner where she usually took a left turn toward her next class, and returned in time to catch Mr. Wright in his classroom.

Jared explained what he had been hearing about Sara. Mr. Wright's face was expressionless but he nodded encouragement. It was awhile before Jared slowed down so Mr. Wright could respond.

"Jared, I know this is hard to hear, but I've heard similar talk, and I've discussed my concerns with the counselling staff. You have to be prepared for some bad news." Just then a group of students entered the classroom, talking loudly. Mr. Wright looked unhappy. "Can you come by my office after school? We need to talk. Don't worry too much, you're not alone in this."

Jared left as more students came in. He would be late for class.

❀   ❀   ❀   ❀   ❀

Jared found Mr. Wright waiting for him in his office. Two other teachers were there working on paperwork, so he invited Jared to take a walk with him outside.

They walked toward the back of the school. Shouts and grunts from the football field and music from the band room guaranteed no one would overhear them. The sky was gray and the wind was cold. Some of the highest peaks in the distance already were white with snow.

"Jared, you should know I'm taking a risk in speaking to you about this. As a teacher I'm supposed to leave the counselling to professionals. Do you promise to keep this discussion confidential?"

"Of course! I would really appreciate your advice. I don't know what to do."

"Do you love her?" Randy had never looked more serious.

"I do. Or at least I think I do—" Jared stopped, confused. What did he feel? Did he really know her, or had he been fooling himself these last few months?

"Don't equivocate—you may be called upon to help her. You have to be strong and believe in her if you're going to stand up for her. If what I suspect is true, she's suffering from some kind of mental illness. She's acting out unconsciously, maybe because of early childhood abuse, who knows. But it's not that she set out to hurt you or make you look bad. She's probably not even aware of most of what she's doing."

Jared looked away. The crimson shorts of the cheerleaders drew his eye—he was drawn to the curves but repulsed by his desire. The girls screamed in unison as something good happened on the field. He swallowed a sob.

"All right. I know she is not trying to hurt me. She wouldn't." Jared looked back to Mr. Wright. "What do I have to do?"

"That's the spirit. As for what we need to do, I don't know yet. But I'm going to try to find out. We'll get her some help." Mr. Wright defied his usual rules against touching and hugged Jared, hard. Jared buried his face in his teacher's shoulder and started to feel less alone.

❖   ❖   ❖   ❖   ❖

It was live seminary day again, and he got home in time to log into the class a few minutes early. Prof. Atwater was already in the side window on his computer screen, sipping something from a mug. It was unlikely to be coffee or tea, which were taboo (or close to it—Jared understood that the prohibition was not as absolute as everybody seemed to think.) Then he noticed an open carton on the other table—lemonade.

He was still worrying about Sara when Prof. Atwater turned on her microphone and the lecture began.

"What parts of Mormon culture are core doctrine? Historically what we think of as the distinctive rules that we are required to follow have changed over time. Can you say you are following the faith while drinking alcoholic beverages, for example?" She clicked and a new slide came up. "Valley Tan whiskey was made and sold under the authority of Brigham Young himself. While this was excused because whiskey had medicinal and trade uses, some of the seminal figures of the first Deseret settlement drank it. Famous visitors like Mark Twain wrote about it—and there's the charming story of William Francis Burton, famous African explorer and linguist, who visited the settlement in 1860 and met with Brigham Young and other leaders. Before leaving he spent an evening drinking Valley Tan with Orrin Porter Rockwell.' So at that time *moderate* consumption of alcohol was not forbidden. The full story is in your readings, but I want to point out this high-light." The next slides went up.

> Nearly a fortnight later, as the Briton prepared to take his leave of the city, he had the opportunity to visit Timpanogos Canyon and its cataracts with a couple of Army officers from Camp Floyd. They chanced to meet Orrin Porter Rockwell at American Fork. Burton had heard of Rockwell and his reputation as "an old Danite," one of a secret group that doled out church justice to apostates and unbeliev-ers. Again, Burton was in his element. He was naturally attracted to adventure and derring-do. Porter Rockwell was right down his line of sight. Two "hombres" who spoke the same language.... Rockwell, after a bit of business about a stolen horse, pulled out a dollar and sent to "the neighboring distillery for a bottle of Valley Tan." Burton writes, "We were asked to join him in a 'square' drink,' which means spirits without water. Of these, we had at least four, which, however, did not shake Mr. Rockwell's nerve, and then he sent out for more, meanwhile telling us of his last adventure. When he heard I was preparing for California, he gave me abundant good advice—to carry a double-barreled gun loaded with buckshot; to keep my eyes skinned,' especially in canyons and ravines; to make at times a dark camp--that is to say, unhitching for supper and then hitching up and turning a few miles off the road--ever to be ready for attack when the animals were being inspanned and outspanned, and never to trust to appearances in an Indian country." Burton later would send the "old Mormon Danite" a bottle of brandy for his kindness to a passing stranger and for his excellent trail advice.[10]

"You've read the part of the D&C known as the 'Word of

Wisdom,' which set forth what we would now call 'best prac-
tices' for clean and healthy living. Let's look at the full text, since
snippets out of context have been misconstrued." She clicked
and a new set of slides began.

1 A Word of Wisdom, for the benefit of the council of high priests,
assembled in Kirtland, and the church, and also the saints in Zion—

2 To be sent greeting; not by commandment or constraint, but by
revelation and the word of wisdom, showing forth the order and will
of God in the temporal salvation of all saints in the last days—

3 Given for a principle with promise, adapted to the capacity of the
weak and the weakest of all saints, who are or can be called saints.

4 Behold, verily, thus saith the Lord unto you: In consequence of evils
and designs which do and will exist in the hearts of conspiring men
in the last days, I have warned you, and forewarn you, by giving unto
you this word of wisdom by revelation—

5 That inasmuch as any man drinketh wine or strong drink among
you, behold it is not good, neither meet in the sight of your Father,
only in assembling yourselves together to offer up your sacraments
before him.

6 And, behold, this should be wine, yea, pure wine of the grape of the
vine, of your own make.

7 And, again, strong drinks are not for the belly, but for the washing
of your bodies.

8 And again, tobacco is not for the body, neither for the belly, and is
not good for man, but is an herb for bruises and all sick cattle, to be
used with judgment and skill.

9 And again, hot drinks are not for the body or belly.

10 And again, verily I say unto you, all wholesome herbs God hath
ordained for the constitution, nature, and use of man—

11 Every herb in the season thereof, and every fruit in the season thereof; all these to be used with prudence and thanksgiving.

12 Yea, flesh also of beasts and of the fowls of the air, I, the Lord, have ordained for the use of man with thanksgiving; nevertheless they are to be used sparingly;

13 And it is pleasing unto me that they should not be used, only in times of winter, or of cold, or famine.

14 All grain is ordained for the use of man and of beasts, to be the staff of life, not only for man but for the beasts of the field, and the fowls of heaven, and all wild animals that run or creep on the earth;

15 And these hath God made for the use of man only in times of famine and excess of hunger.

16 All grain is good for the food of man; as also the fruit of the vine; that which yieldeth fruit, whether in the ground or above the ground —

17 Nevertheless, wheat for man, and corn for the ox, and oats for the horse, and rye for the fowls and for swine, and for all beasts of the field, and barley for all useful animals, and for mild drinks, as also other grain.

18 And all saints who remember to keep and do these sayings, walking in obedience to the commandments, shall receive health in their navel and marrow to their bones;

19 And shall find wisdom and great treasures of knowledge, even hidden treasures;

20 And shall run and not be weary, and shall walk and not faint.

21 And I, the Lord, give unto them a promise, that the destroying angel shall pass by them, as the children of Israel, and not slay them. Amen."

"Read Verse 2 carefully. It's written in modern English, not Hebrew or Greek, so there is little ambiguity about what it means. It states the purpose of the Words of Wisdom is to be friendly advice or *guidance,* not commands, and Brigham Young himself did not believe it was to be rigidly enforced. Verse 3 makes it clear the intent is to provide simple rules even the 'weakest of all saints' can follow. The reward if the rules are followed is a long and healthy life on this earth, or 'temporal salvation.'

"There is an analogy to the Biblical rules found in Leviticus, guidelines for the earliest tribes of Israel—which were obviated by Christ in the New Testament, at least for Christians. Culturally, some Jews still hew to them as a mark of distinction, though the practical reasons for some of them may be long past.

"And so, too, our attachment to strict adherence to the Words of Wisdom is a signifier of our will as a community. Rational analysis shows inconsistencies. Looked at objectively, Verse 13 seems to require vegetarianism except in winter or time of great need. Yet the General Authorities do not promote vegetarian diets with the same enthusiasm as they prohibit alcoholic beverages. And beer or ale are surely what is intended by the approval of 'mild drinks' made from grains mentioned in Verse 17, yet we avoid those as well. In fact, the conversion of the Word of Wisdom from sound advice to an absolute requirement for fellowship only occurred in 1921 when Heber Grant, who supported the nationwide temperance movement that eventually brought in Prohibition, made it so."

Prof. Atwater stopped to field questions. "Brittany, please read your question."

In a side window, a redheaded girl appeared. "My father says the rules are about mind-altering substances, since they impair your ability to think."

Prof. Atwater responded, "Your father is correct to an extent. Despite the fact marijuana is a natural herb, the ingestion or smoking of it is also prohibited for that reason—we can generalize from the explicit prohibitions and extend them to cover anything that is mind-altering, will-sapping, or bad for long-term health. Conversely, we recognize some of these substances are legitimately useful and aid in fighting disease or injuries. For example, using caffeine or other stimulants to stay alert on a military mission would not be prohibited. Taking opioid drugs or marijuana for relief of pain is acceptable. But none of us need those things for normal, healthy living.

"The generalized rule is more about the distinction between productive and unproductive use. Addictions rule *you*, while your choice to *use* a drug as a tool for a short-term productive purpose is under your control. Caffeine for staying awake for an important task, say night driving, vs an *addiction* to caffeine that requires daily consumption. Your free choice oriented toward production and healthy living vs mindless compulsion. Healthy living through wise choices, not loss of control."

She clicked again and a new slide appeared.

The Latter-day Saints believe not only in the gospel of spiritual salvation, but also in the gospel of temporal salvation. We have to look after the cattle, ... the gardens and the farms, ... and other necessary things for the maintenance of ourselves and our families in the earth. ... We do not feel that it is possible for men to be really good and faithful Christian people unless they can also be good, faithful, honest and industrious people. Therefore, we preach the gospel of industry, the gospel of economy, the gospel of sobriety. —

Joseph F. Smith[12]

"'Honest, and industrious.' These are the virtues we seek—truth and abundance through hard work. Our community built something from nothing and grew despite persecution through our effort and faith. We rely on each other for strength and assistance in times of trouble, so we take care of each other and watch out for each other.

"But because we want these rules to be followed by the weakest among us, we look to the left, and then look to the right, and check to be sure no one we know sees us step outside the envelope of what is clearly godly. We seem to believe the scriptures set down these rules, but many are more shared cultural than scriptural prohibitions. Is it a sin to have one glass of wine before bed? Probably not. Is it a sin to neglect your work and family to drink to excess, night after night, or to get hooked on sleeping pills or Oxycontin? Yes, it is. There is a good argument that the bright-line simplicity of our prohibitions makes it easier for even the weakest of us to understand, and the social pressure to conform keeps many of us out of trouble when we might otherwise be tempted into addiction."

She clicked and a new slide appeared. In large letters it said, "Why, you simple creatures, the weakest of all weak things is a virtue which has not been tested in the fire. —Mark Twain, 'The Man That Corrupted Hadleyburg.'"

"Or as some have argued, 'You have to go into the valley to fight your way back out of it.' Yet our community's guardrails keep our weakest links from being permanently damaged to the extent they can't recover. 'What doesn't kill you makes you stronger.' True for some trials, not for others—some trials just

weaken you and set you up to succumb to the next you en-
counter. Gradually increasing challenges, designed to teach a
lesson but doing no permanent damage, are how children learn
to defend themselves in a world of dangers. And it's true that
bringing children up in a bubble where all danger has been
vanquished only guarantees they will have no defenses when
they venture beyond the bubble.

"But. Our children can learn from examples. We are surrounded by a godless and crassly hedonistic gentile culture that
provides plenty of object lessons for the observant. We send our
young people on missions not just to promote the faith, but also
so they can see the rest of the world in all its cruelty, sin, and
degradation."

Brittany was still on the line. "Does it ever happen that a
missionary ends up going over to the other side? Joining the
people they were sent to convert?" She seemed spooked by the
idea.

"Of course that happens. Not often, but it does. Those people are still carrying their upbringing in Christ, and there are
many examples of people who leave the fold who eventually
turn around and recognize how much they owe to their religious background. No one in this country is forced to stay with
the people of their birth, and it's part of a healthy nation to have
free movement geographically and culturally. What missionary
work does for most is confirm their beliefs and solidify their
commitment. And when they return, they know the grass is not
greener on the other side of the fence. It's just different."

23: Randy: The Noumenal Foundation

Randy used his GPS to guide his car to the address Kovac had given him. The GPS said he had arrived but there was no house to be seen, just a gate between two brick pillars. The bronze plaque above the address read "The Noumenal Foundation." He drove up and rolled down his window to push the button on the call box below to it.

"Yes?" a male voice said.

"Randy Wright, here to see Prof. Kovac." Randy could see the road beyond, narrow but paved, leading up the hill.

"Proceed up to the house. Park in the side lot," the voice said. There was a click and the gates opened. Randy drove slowly. Views of the valley were opening up to one side, and the road switched back and continued up the hill.

Three switchbacks later, the road straightened and reached a plateau. A massive house—really a castle or a chateau, with stone towers at either end and two stories of glass above a story of exposed concrete foundation—was centered in front of a formal garden. To the left was a series of low buildings that looked like a modern motel, and to the right a barn and some other steel prefab structures.

The drive looped in front of the house and he drove into the *porte-cochère* in front of the double entry doors. He could see the parking lot beyond, and drove on to park his car. There were two other cars, both luxury imports, and a battered pickup truck.

As Randy gathered his briefcase and got out of the car, he heard someone approaching. He turned to see a tall man, scarecrow-like, with an explosion of gray hair and a patriarch's beard. His cornflower-blue eyes were the most colorful thing about him—his pants were gray, his shirt faded green flannel.

Tomo Kovac's voice was deep and faintly accented. "Mr. Wright, so glad you could come," he said, holding out his hand.

"Quite a place you have here," Randy observed, looking up at the stone tower beyond. Were those gun ports near the top?

"Thank you, I've been working on it since I moved to Utah thirty years ago. Bought the land and started building as money allowed. But first—" he held out a clipboard with a pen. "Before we go any further, I will need you to sign this NDA. You swear by the blood of your ancestors not to disclose any of what I will tell you, or we will sue you into the ground. And make fun of you. Take a minute to read it and sign."

Randy was thankful the print was large since his reading glasses were in his briefcase. It seemed straightforward, so he signed and handed it back.

"That's better," Kovac said. "Let me give you the tour." He led Randy along the walkway to the north side of the house and around the corner.

"These are my workshops. We build instruments here, tools for exploring. Sensors for all spectra. We sell them so we can buy more off-the-shelf hardware—have you seen the infrared cam you can attach to your phone? It's a wonder. The computers are mostly on the office floor of the main house. We are wired to the world, and we have microwave and satellite links for backup."

"Why do you need all this? I thought you were a physicist..."

"I *am,* sir. But many more things as well, notably a *meta-*

physicist. You were looking for an expert in the paranormal. I am *the* expert, at least for Utah. I teach physics partly to find young people with the right cast of mind for my *real* work. Which is to respond when people need help with a spiritual infestation. We are like the Ghostbusters, but real. No routine hauntings for us—they are almost always fakes. What we see most often is people ridden by demons, possessed."

"So you're exorcists?"

"The Catholics can sometimes succeed with their procedures, I think by the power of suggestion when the host is a believer—the demons are a kind of parasite that use the host's own spiritual beliefs and symbols to control them. But we use science to break the demon's hold on its victim and disrupt it for good."

"And how do you keep that a secret?" Randy was wondering if Kovac was just a wealthy man with an insane hobby.

"Our clients are usually worried family members. They are so *grateful*. And they sign NDAs. They also hope no one will find out their child or spouse has been possessed by a demon. So much safer to pretend nothing happened, or that they went to rehab for a few weeks. A drug problem is practically normal these days."

"How often does this happen?"

"We send out a team every few days, more when the moon is full or after elections. We have sites in Europe and Asia now to cover their needs. I'm ashamed to admit that we have no way of knowing how many victims are committed to asylums or come to a bad end with authorities while they are possessed— surely thousands every year. The lucky ones have concerned people who find us. And we charge a sliding scale, so everyone who comes to us gets our best efforts."

"But you don't take insurance, I take it?" Randy imagined calling his health insurance claim center to ask if he were covered in case of possession.

"Our treatment is, shall we say, *experimental*. The government quietly tolerates us under certain protocols—and they kick in money to keep us on call for 'consulting.' Security agencies have tried to approach us to use our tools on selected ... foreign personages, but we have resisted their pressure. We are legally treated like faith healers—we promise nothing, and we're a nonprofit religious foundation. Grateful clients continue to support us."

"I'm surprised that BYU allows that kind of activity for a professor." Randy assumed the Mormons looked askance on anything that smacked of the supernatural that wasn't laid out by their prophets.

Kovac gave him a hard look. "One of the first people we saved was high in the LDS leadership. I shouldn't say *how* high, but important enough that my way was smoothed. I moved the Foundation here when he offered me his support. And I'm an *adjunct* professor at BYU, so I don't have to be too respectable, just teach the occasional course. It's just a nice title that helps reassure people that I am legit."

Kovac led him around the back of the manor. "And behind we have training fields, and over on that side dormitories for visiting team members. It's quiet now, but next week there will be dozens of new trainees from around the world living here. Our local team has their own housing in town."

"Impressive. But my students aren't possessed. No pea-soup-vomiting or levitating."

"But they are acting in ways that harm themselves and others," Kovac said. "While seeming to be blind to what they have done. Could be garden-variety *psychopaths*. Do you think so?"

"No. They're sweet kids." Randy thought back. "Something changed a few weeks ago."

Kovac led him to a side entrance; the door unlocked itself. The cameras posted above the doors apparently did facial recognition.

Kovac walked him up the stairs and then down a terrazzo-floored hall, opening a glass-and-steel door to reveal a meeting room with Aeron chairs and a walnut table. He motioned Randy to take the chair looking out.

"Great view, eh?" Kovac filled two glasses with water and sat down to face Randy.

And it was a great view. Through the floor-to-ceiling windows Randy could see south to the buildings of BYU on a terrace above distant Provo. Straight west, the town of Orem spread out into the far haze, with the thin sea-green line of Utah Lake below the horizon of low mountains on the other side of the valley.

"Quite a view," Randy agreed, and took a sip of the water. "Now, about my students...."

"I would not normally diagnose without interviewing. We get deluded parents coming to us about standard rebellious *teens*, drug habits, and so forth—we try to refer them to local agencies. But I did some checking when you called, and there's a hotspot down in your area. The ley lines intersect in your mountain—the entities have an easier time acting up there. Which is why I'm guessing your students are under malignant influence."

"Ley lines?" Randy had heard the term somewhere but assumed it was mumbo-jumbo.

"The strongest flows of underworld force can come to the surface along lines called ley lines. People have speculated that 'sacred' sites tend to be along great circle lines, but it's really not that simple. Our maps show hot spots along major faults or where ore bodies channel magnetic fields. The entities are complex, self-sustaining vortices in the fields—they can travel most easily and project their forces through metallic veins of good conductors like copper, or silver, or gold. Your mountain is underlain by such. The legendary Nephi gold may not be there, but something is."

"I thought metal grounded electromagnetic waves. Like, those shielded boxes—"

"Faraday cages. Yes, a conducting enclosure shields the inside from higher-frequency electromagnetic waves like radio and microwaves. That's the origin of the tinfoil hat myth, but they need to be grounded to work well. And the entities can work through them since the entities are primarily magnetic and low-frequency—in fact, they love conductors. To keep them out requires much heavier shielding made of a ferromagnetic alloy called mu-metal, which has a composition similar to the metallic core of the earth. Our labs are shielded with mu-metal, but it was very expensive. So far the entities haven't figured out how to interfere with digital devices, but we fear they will learn, so we've taken precautions."

"So what do you know about these, uh, entities?" Randy was taking notes on his legal pad.

"That is the focus of my research. Blocking them and freeing their victims pays the bills, but I want to know what makes them *tick*, if they are *intelligent* or just creatures of instinct like psychic *tapeworms*, how we can *communicate* with them. They use their minute control over electrical forces to influence the electrochemical brains of their hosts—for what purpose we don't know. They have their strongest influence in *dreams*, where they can use the victim's memories and subconscious building-blocks to recast narratives—spin stories and plant ideas and suggestions, like a hypnotist would."

"My understanding is hypnotists can't make you do something you wouldn't normally do."

Kovac tented his fingers and sighed. "Not *directly*, no. But for the suggestible, they can create a false story that gives the victim a motive for acting as the hypnotist wishes. For example, one of our clients was completely *convinced* she had worms crawling under her skin. She was so desperate to get them out she cut her arms to ribbons with a razor blade, which she wouldn't have done if directly instructed to do so by a hypnotist. But the *illusion* was so strong it overrode self-preservation."

"That's horrible. What happened to her?"

"We got to her just in time. Wrapped her arms with pressure bandages and took her to the ER in our mobile unit, which has a mu-metal holding cell in back. The entity fled, so we were unable to use the *disruptor* on it." Kovac arched a brow, apparently expecting a question.

"Disruptor? What's that?" Randy underlined the word three times on his pad.

Kovac looked proud. "Our high-tech weapon. We tried a lot of things on them, and nothing worked. Our scanners were too slow to catch their movement—the vortices are like the point where scissors cut, they move much faster along the intersection of field lines than the underlying fields themselves. A few years ago the wonders of portable electronics caught up, so our magnetic field sensors can pass back a lot more data a lot faster, and we can map the entity in real-time. And fast microprocessors—we use multicore graphics processors—can adaptively predict their next movements and calculate counter-fields, which are generated by the timed firing of capacitor-charged coils."

"So, kind of like the Ghostbuster's guns?" Randy said, thinking this would get a laugh.

Kovac rolled his eyes and looked annoyed instead. "Not at all. Those were particle accelerators. Not really feasible to carry around, and not very effective. Our disruptor doesn't look like a gun—it's a box with a wand you can aim at the target. Well, that attachment does look something like a gun, with a small targeting display."

"So what happens to the entity when you use your disruptor on it?"

"It leaves or it dies. Or we think it does—there's no pretty plasma display or satisfying ectoplasmic death scene. Just a series of pops, the smell of ozone from the discharge, and the entity is neutralized. We think the strongest are spread through a large area underground and send up a pseudopod to occupy the victim, so it may be we're just burning off one of their hands. But they don't come back to occupy the victim again."

Someone knocked on the door and came in with a tray of sandwiches. The young Asian woman had purple streaks in her short hair and spoke softly to Kovac: "Tomo, you have a conference call in twenty minutes."

Kovac nodded to her and the woman bowed and left.

"My assistant, Kumiko. I had a *devil* of a time finding someone reliable after my wife died—she handled all the details for me. I never realized how much she did until she went in for treatment. I was *lost.*" His face was bleak, then he took a deep breath and brightened. "But the work goes on."

"I'm sorry," Randy said. "I can't imagine."

"No one can, until it's you ... As I was saying, we've tried to understand what these entities want. Sifting through world folklore, a common thread is an underground world—an *underworld*—where souls go after death. The Greeks had their Hades, the Christians their Hell, the Jews, Sheol; Hindus called it Patala. This idea of an Underworld below, the Earth between, and a Heaven or high place where the gods live is so commonly shared that it must have some basis in fact. I have looked—" again he was deadly serious—"for my wife's *soul* in our scans of the entities, trying to match her patterns to theirs. Surely she would try to contact me if she *could*. But the myths often suggest *forgetfulness* is a feature—souls entering the world as newborns had their past memories erased, and souls after death could choose to forget—in the Greek Hades, by drinking from the River Lethe."

Randy looked up from his note-taking. "Souls are recycled?"

"In many religions, yes. Jews certainly thought so, and Christians retain some of that belief. I have no evidence of that, but as a scientist I am open to all possibilities until there's some empirical evidence disproving it. Christians, Jews, Muslims, and Hindus all believe in spirits from above and below: angels and demons of various kinds. The entities we're called to expel seem to be malevolent, but perhaps there are good ones, too—if a spirit is helping you make more moral choices, then perhaps no one wonders why you are suddenly acting like a *good* person."

Randy pondered that. "Sara is acting out self-destructively, while Jared is seemingly helping her when it makes no sense for him to do so. Is it possible they are being driven by different entities?"

Kovac sat back in his chair and turned to look out the window. "There have been hints of that in some of our cases, but there's only one I can recall where there was not some other explanation—the father of the possessed victim, who had been calmly focused on getting her help, completely changed personality after he joined her inside the mu-metal box. He returned to his formerly dismissive personality and asked to be dropped off at his favorite bar. It was *astonishing*, and hard to explain any other way—his protective stance must have been coming from some benign *possession*, which the box blocked."

"So what should I do? How can we get them out of this trap?" Randy was dubious about Kovac's work, but even if it wasn't a crackpot idea, how he would get the kids to a secure place where he could have Kovac's demon-disrupting gun ready to use on them? And no way could he bring it into the school. Lockdown was the least that would happen. He had a brief vision of a future where SWAT team members stood over his bullet-riddled body.

"As I said, I wouldn't be able to help without personally diagnosing them. That would require legal authorization. You may be *in loco parentis*, but it's usually the parents who call us. I can't do much without their permission. But you are free to persuade them. And keep us posted on developments—so far nothing you've reported rises to the level of danger that would allow us to intervene."

A knock, and the door opened a crack. "Five minutes," Kumiko's delicate voice said.

Randy gathered his notes. "Thank you very much, Prof. Kovac. It was deeply informative." And perhaps the ravings of a madman, though Kovac's story was convincing once Randy admitted to himself that there were forces in motion that couldn't be explained in mundane terms. "I'll try to persuade their parents to bring you in to investigate. Before it gets worse."

24: Sara: Lunchroom Fight

Sara worked through the lunch line picking up her usual—sandwich in plastic wrap, apple, milk. After paying she looked around for a suitable table. She spotted two likely boys sitting at the end of an empty table and smiled at them as she approached. It was almost too easy, once she stopped caring what anyone thought.

As she passed the table where the Mean Girls always ate, she heard a hiss. Then another hiss, and she turned to see three girls and one boy staring at her as they hissed loudly. One of the girls —it was Jessica Peterson, homecoming queen and Owen Kimball's girlfriend—got up and blocked her path.

"Bitch. I know what you did," Jessica said, spitting.

Sara knew she had somehow made an enemy, and her mind went on high alert as the background personality to handle threats took over.

"I have no idea what you're talking about." Sara was calm but ready to throw her tray of food in Jessica's face if she got any closer.

Two other girls came up to back Jessica—it was a blonde tag-team. One was Tiffany Harding, who said, "How many guys do you think you can sleep with before everyone realizes what a slut you are?"

Jessica came closer and slapped Sara hard. "You're trash! You ought to have a biohazard tattoo on your forehead!" The other two were screaming insults.

Sara looked down at her tray. *Kill them. No, run away. No, hurt them and run away.* She used the tray to throw her food at

Jessica, then swung the tray as hard as she could, landing a blow to Jessica's jaw with the hard edge. Jessica looked stunned and crumpled backward. Her blood had spattered on the tile floor, bright red against white.

The other two girls looked on in horror, and Sara realized everyone in the lunchroom had stopped what they were doing and were watching her.

She picked her battered sandwich off the floor and turned to walk away. As she passed the two boys she had intended to seduce, she gave them a sideways smile and waltzed out the exit door.

Behind her, the frozen tableau broke as everyone began talking at once.

She left the school by the side exit and slowly ate the sandwich as she walked home. Everything seemed normal, though it was too early to be home. Why was she here? The sun was still high in the sky.

Somewhere in the back of her mind the knowledge of what she had been doing lurked. Her normal consciousness was being prevented from seeing it—but there was a small rebellion going on, as if a new Sara was growing inside who had seen everything Lailah had been making her do and was screaming to stop her. But for now that Sara was locked down tight while surface Sara remained placid under Lailah's control.

As she entered the apartment, the phone was ringing. She ignored it and it went to message. She finished the sandwich and got a glass of milk to drink with an apple from the fridge. Then her cell phone rang—Mom! No good could come of answering it. She finished eating, brushed her teeth, and had just started to do her chemistry homework when her cell phone rang again—Jared. She answered.

"Where are you?" He sounded upset.

"At home. Doing a chemistry lab report."

"You do know you're in trouble. Everyone's talking about it. They asked me if I knew anything." He sounded like he was trying not to talk loud enough to be overheard.

"'They?' Who are they? I'm fine."

Jared said nothing for a second. When he did speak, his voice was low and intense. "I can't leave until after next period. But I'll be right there as soon as I can. Don't go anywhere."

"Why would I do that?" But he had hung up.

The phone rang several more times, but she was upstairs in the bathroom peeing again. Something odd was going on with her body. She felt sick, and she vaguely remembered having felt that way for days. She brushed against the door and felt pain where her breasts were sensitive—and that, too, had been happening for days. A thought surfaced—pregnant? When had her last period happened? She couldn't remember. And then she forgot about it.

25: Jared: White Knight

Jared had been pulled out of class by the principal's office. The principal had been a star football player in high school, and his booming voice and optimistic slogans concealed his lack of knowledge of the school and its students. He was always good for a motivational speech, but seemed more concerned about the sports teams than academics.

Jared told the principal and Mina Wilson, the counsellor, that he knew nothing about what might have caused Sara to snap and assault Jessica Peterson. Of course he could guess. He wanted to get away as quickly as possible to talk to Sara. Their meeting was interrupted by a phone call from Jessica's parents. The principal took it on speaker.

The tinny female voice—Jessica's mom—said, "We were about to call the police to file a report. Her lip needed three stitches and she's badly shaken. We want to know how you're going to handle this."

The principal looked pained. "Of course we take this incident very seriously. We're interviewing students to find out more. Words were exchanged and it's not absolutely clear what happened. But I'd ask you not to report it to the police—their investigation would do more harm than good. We'll take disciplinary action—"

"See that you do. If you expel that awful girl we'd rather avoid getting the police involved."

"I think that would be best for everyone," the principal said, sounding relieved. "Involving the juvenile court should be a last resort."

Jessica's mother went on about the trauma her little girl had suffered. The principal made supportive sounds until she wound down. When the call ended, the principal sighed deeply.

"I wouldn't want any of mine to be involved in a juvenile court case. Even as the victim."

Mina Wilson nodded in agreement. "But the parents will want a definite punishment."

"Jared, would you wait outside for a bit? We have to talk in private."

Jared closed the door behind him and waited in the reception area. He called Sara's number and was surprised when she answered immediately. She seemed unaware of what she had done, and he went cold as he realized she might be seriously crazy—so he told her he'd been there as soon as he could.

Randy Wright rushed in from the outer hall.

"Jared! I just heard," Randy said, breathing hard. "Do you know where she is?"

"At home. I just talked to her on the phone. I was going to see her as soon as I can."

Randy stood over him, looking concerned. "I guess the shit has hit the fan. A fight is one thing, assault drawing blood and an ER visit is another. The school will have to take some action to punish her."

"Maybe it was an accident?" Jared doubted that. But who could prove otherwise?

"Maybe. She's never been in trouble before, so it's at least plausible she didn't mean to injure Jessica. That will be the only reason she avoids being expelled." The "good kids" usually got one strike free before any real punishment would be imposed. But you never knew—it would be political in the end. Jessica's parents were Important People, and they could pressure the administration more effectively than most parents.

Jared looked crushed. "I wish there was something I could have done."

"Whatever's wrong with her, you couldn't have fixed it. I've looked for help for her and found someone who might be able to. It's time for me to approach her mother and get her permission for treatment. Maybe you could help with that?"

"I'll try." Jared's face hardened. "Sara's a great person. I know this isn't her."

"You may be right," Randy said.

Just then the door opened and Mina Wilson motioned them in.

"Sara's mother is on her way. We'd like to have Sara evaluated by a psychologist before going any further," she said.

"That will help back up any decision we make on punishment," the principal added.

"Jared, you can go now unless you have anything you want to add," Mina said.

"I guess not." Jared was itching to leave—the period had ended and he could skip the next class without problems. He needed to be with Sara.

❖   ❖   ❖   ❖   ❖

Jared knocked on Sara's apartment door and she let him in, looking surprised to see him.

"Are you okay?" he said, hugging her.

She pulled away quickly. "I'm fine. What's all the noise about?"

"Hasn't your mother called?" Jared led her over to the couch and they sat next to each other. He put his arm around her. She was trembling.

"She tried. I didn't want to talk to her."

"Well, you have a problem. We have a problem." He strengthened his hold on her as he began to explain what had happened. "Now, I'm guessing you don't remember any of it."

"No." She looked far away.

"Your mom will be here any minute. She's going to take you to a psychologist who's going to try to assess whether there's something wrong with you." He used his other hand to turn her face toward him so he could look into her eyes. "You're going to tell him you got angry and wanted to toss your food at Jessica, but the tray slipped out of your hand. You didn't mean to hurt her.… Repeat after me, you didn't mean to hurt her."

"I didn't mean to hurt her." A tear spilled from one of her eyes.

"Just tell them you were angry, but you were so shocked when you realized you *accidentally* hurt her, you ran away. The idea is not to let them kick you out of school."

"I don't understand." She cried silently and turned away from him.

"There *is* something wrong with you, like a temporary mental illness, but we'll get it fixed. Mr. Wright is helping us. We can get you through this and you'll be fine. But we don't want you expelled, that would kill your chances for college. Okay? Can you just tell the story like I told you?"

She nodded, sniffling. "I'm sorry for whatever I did."

"That's just it, babe. That wasn't you."

Mina Wilson had informed Randy that he was expected to attend the meeting two days later in the principal's office. Normally disciplinary matters were decided by the principal alone, but in practice, if there was any chance of appeals or legal action, the principal sought informal input from the district's lawyer as well as interested staff.

Randy noted the incongruous Christmas tree and Santa cutouts in the waiting area. He found the principal's office already full of people—the district lawyer, Mina Wilson and the other guidance counsellor, the consulting psychologist they called in when there was trouble. Randy got another chair from the waiting area and brought it in.

The psychologist spoke at length, outlining his talk with Sara, and wrapped up by saying, "Her record shows some emotional instability, but I don't think she's a danger to others. She claims it was an accident, and witness statements are consistent with that. Jessica slapped her, so there was provocation. Unless there's another incident, I don't think expulsion is justifiable. Probation and counselling should be action enough."

Mina looked relieved. "Of course a second offense should result in a note on her permanent record and a suspension. But the term is almost over and a suspension this week would be very disruptive. Teachers would almost have to grade her down or incomplete."

This was Randy's cue to jump in. "I agree. She should get some punishment, but this is the worst possible time for a suspension. She should not be penalized academically for a brief lapse in judgement under provocation. It could effectively ruin her college chances."

The principal cleared his throat, then said, "She's a good student. I understand she's had some personal problems and gotten on the wrong side of some of the social cliques. And we have two additional mothers complaining that her indecent behavior has corrupted their innocent young boys. So I have to punish her visibly to pacify them, but not in any way that mars her permanent record. Sara's mother has agreed to the condition that she see a psychologist, so I'm going to give her six months on probation and an order she stay out of the lunchroom and drop out of the winter musical. Jessica's parents told me they are willing to accept that."

The meeting broke up. Randy lingered to catch the principal alone.

"I appreciate your going easy on her," Randy said. "She's a good kid."

The principal eyed him warily. "I'm caught between a rock and a hard place. Sara's been playing with fire—has she come on to you, too?"

Randy did his best not to react at all.

The principal continued, "Jessica's parents had to be placated, but Sara—" he began to whisper, "has dirt on enough staff and students to blow this school sky-high. We can't risk the kind of scandal she could create by talking. We can only hope she gets through to graduation with no further trouble. I don't want to lose my job."

Randy was stunned. He swallowed several times and finally got out, "I had no idea you knew anything about what's been going on."

The principal looked away, out the window, toward the mountain. "It's my job to smooth over the rough edges and inspire students and staff. I'm always paying attention, no matter how it might look to you. Making sure trouble doesn't come to the attention of the school board is my number one priority. If I could expel her, I would—but I can't."

"Oh," was all Randy felt safe to say. They stood together in silence for another minute watching the school buses line up outside.

27: Sara: The Stick

Sara weathered the storm of gossip and the humiliation of her probation. She saw the psychologist at his office twice a week—and noticed after the second visit he was much friendlier. Her sessions left her dazed and couldn't remember what they had talked about, but he seemed happy with her progress and began texting her during the day. He asked her to send photos of herself, and she obliged, but he kept asking.

At school, she came for classes and went home for lunch. The production of "White Christmas" went on without her, her role being small enough to easily replace. She stayed in touch by text messaging with some of the boys she had met doing the show. She knew everyone was watching her now, and whatever inner demons she carried were quieted for the duration, aware that they had endangered her by showing themselves too much.

Jared had been attentive as well. They were together more often than ever, and were close to finishing the project for Mr. Wright's class. It hadn't been too difficult to combine a summary of the thesis Jared had obtained from his seminary professor with documents from the web and interviews of the locals they had found who remembered the days of the mine and the controversies over the excommunication of its visionary founder, Freeman Kain.

She was editing the Dropbox shared file, adding another quote from contemporary accounts:

> The Securities Commission ordered a suit filed against the company for selling stock without permission. When the trial was held in the

latter part of 1933, it was readily dismissed because key witnesses for the state changed their testimonies. Instead of accusing him, they defended Kain and asked his forgiveness.

Over the years, ore of many kinds had been taken from the mine. Values had been found but none in sufficient quantity to merit the refining and processing of the ores which contained them. Kain maintained that theirs was a special ore that when heated by the current methods of processing, the precious metals contained therein disappeared in a black smoke. There was simply no plant that could handle it. So in July 1932, during the depths of the depression, he built and equipped a concrete flotation mill at a cost of over $60,000. The mill was paid for in full at the time of its building.

In this same year Kain felt that he should make preparations for the large grain bins which were to hold the millions of bushels of grain to be purchased with gold derived from the mine. Large tracts of land were surveyed, leveled, graded, and terraced; but although the plans were drawn up, the bins were never built. In 1937, visitors brought a new type of processing plant to the mine. The plant contained a solution which had the power of dissolving the metals contained in the ore. The metals previously reported to have disappeared in smoke could now be preserved. The plant was installed in the flotation mill which seemed to have been built to the exact specifications necessary to house it.

....On Thursday, April 7, 1948, Kain was excommunicated from the Latter Day Saint Church on charges of insubordination to the rules and authority of the Church. He was rather ill at the time and became much worse thereafter. This illness continued until May of 1949 when he was taken to the Mt. Hermon Hospital. On May 18, at the age of 85, Kain died.

Jared came by after school. He had dropped the idea of doing a video for YouTube since they were already way behind on the project. They had to get it wrapped up now to leave enough study time for their exams.

They worked together on the file for an hour to put the final touches on the project report. Jared had added some of the pictures they had taken at the mine, and after a bit more tweaking, they agreed it was good enough. Sara attached the file to an email, then sent it to Mr. Wright.

Jared put his arm around her, but it made it harder to type, so she pulled away. He kept touching her until she snapped at him—"Could you not do that? I'm not in the mood…."

"Sorry," Jared said, moving away. "It's just that I miss touching you."

Sara thought before reacting. He was right, she had been putting him off for weeks. But she didn't feel it, and that was that. Maybe after the trouble had settled down … she knew they had to talk about something else.

"I have to tell you something," she said, getting up to get something from her dresser drawer. She showed it to him; it was a pregnancy test strip.

"I've been feeling odd and missed my period, so I bought a test kit. The two red lines means I'm pregnant." She had dreaded telling him. It was just better to get it said.

Jared stared for a second.

"I wondered," he said. "You've been off lately. Any idea whose it is?" He looked like a trapped animal waiting for the trapper.

"Yours, silly." She just knew.

"There hasn't been anybody else?"

"No," she said, knowing in the back of her mind that it was not literally true, but sure that Jared had been the one, their first time together.

Jared's face smoothed. "That changes everything." He took her hand. "I can get a job and take care of you. After I graduate."

She looked at him in exasperation. "No, you won't. You're supposed to go to college. My mom will help me out."

"I think we should get married." He squeezed her hand tighter. "My kid is going to have a father."

"He'll have a father even if we don't get married." She had heard stories from friends about abortions and adoption as possibilities, but she wanted this child. And she did love Jared. They didn't have to get married immediately to be there for the kid. Maybe they could get married next year after she graduated and go to college somewhere together. That would be ideal.

"How are we going to tell my parents? And yours?" Jared got up and paced in the narrow space between her bed and her desk.

"We can tell my mom when she gets home, and you can tell your parents tonight. It's good news—I think." Or at least she hoped. Her reputation was already trashed, so getting pregnant by Jared was almost an improvement over being labelled the school slut.

Her mother got home shortly after Jared left, and she got angry when Sara told her she was pregnant.

"How could you? I know you like him, but how many times have I told you not to have sex without protection? We could have got you birth control…" She went on to list all the bad things in store for a young mother. "And college! You can't be toting a baby to a good school."

"I don't see why not. I can take care of it and go to school later anyway."

Her mother sighed. "This is just not the right time. Maybe in a few years, after you're graduated and married."

"What do you think I should do with this child? It's on the way. I'm not having an abortion."

"I know you're emotional. I know you think you love Jared. But you can't wreck your life just for one boy." Sara's mother was firm. "You need to see an obstetrician, stat. Then we'll talk about what you should do."

◊   ◊   ◊   ◊   ◊

Sara had difficulty concentrating enough to study for the finals, but she had built up plenty of points in most classes, and with the American History project in, she thought she was doing well. Jared was as attentive as he could be given his own studies. They gave each other token gifts before her mother took her to the airport in Salt Lake City to catch a flight to New York for her first visit back since they moved. Her father picked her up at JFK and took her back to his apartment in Fort Greene, near Brooklyn Heights and the Brooklyn Bridge to Lower Manhattan.

She hadn't been to his new highrise apartment. One side had a great view of the new World Trade Center, the river, and all of Lower Manhattan. She could watch it for hours ... but Dad immediately wanted to take her out to eat, so after she dropped her bags in the tiny alcove that held the foldout couch for guests, she cleaned herself up and they left. The sun had set and the cold wind made her shiver even with a heavy jacket on.

Her father had been an investment banker, and accustomed to the best clothes and grooming. But now he looked a little shaggy, and his graying hair had grown wild and flown up around his ears like wings. His clothes were mismatched, a button-down shirt with blue jeans. Since he'd joined a blockchain software startup and gone to court to reduce the child support payments to Sara's mother, how he looked seemed no longer to be that important to him.

When they'd been seated, her father started the difficult conversation.

"Your mother tells me you were doing very well with this new boy Jared until you got into trouble. Want to tell me what happened?" He looked over the top of his reading glasses at her.

"I just got overwhelmed. Maybe it was hormones. We used condoms, but I guess there was a leak." She had always felt under examination by her father. By the time she was twelve, her parents had stopped talking to each other, so busy in their work worlds that they were hardly present at all when they were home. Her mother had gone back to school to get credentials for a position as a hospital administrator before the divorce.

"A screaming fight from just hormones? Doesn't sound like your normal self at all." The server came by, so he gave up scanning the menu and ordered blackened seared ahi from memory.

Sara ordered a Caesar's salad.

"I know," she said. "I didn't mean to hurt anyone, I just snapped."

"I've done that a few times myself. Luckily for me it wasn't in front of witnesses." He reached over to take her hand. "Now you know you can tell me anything, right? It's hard to believe I have to pay for more therapy sessions for you, but I've agreed to split the cost with your mother. And I find it hard to believe my daughter would be so stupid as to get pregnant by some farm-boy."

"He's not a farmboy. He's bright and funny and…." She tried to think of what would impress her father. "His dad is a policeman, his mom is a nurse, and he's as smart as I am, maybe smarter. We're going to get married someday."

His eyebrows went up. "Well, well. Your mother said you were talking like that. She thinks you're too young to know what's good for you. I'm not so sure—if this boy is still who you want to be with in a few years, then so be it. But we have to be realistic about your having this child. You don't know what a burden it is to be a parent so young. It takes up all your time, maybe more. You've got a whole career ahead of you. Why don't you…" he paused, looking for a good way to say it.

"Kill it? Have an abortion? Not you, too." She looked away, disgusted. "We're keeping this baby." Now she was mad enough to just say what she felt. "I love Jared, he loves me, and we have a child. And we're not changing our minds."

Her father sat back a little and looked tired. "So be it, then. If you need help, you can count on me. I don't have much extra money since I'm already sending your mother two thousand a month in child support, but I can scrounge up more. It's hard to imagine myself being a grandpa, but I look forward to meeting the little bugger." Then his face relaxed into a rueful smile. "I could never tell you what to do."

"Not really," she said, remembering her stubborn days as a wild child. Maybe she had sensed something was wrong between her parents, so she had fought with them both as the only way to get their full attention. And when her father had moved out, she had collapsed into depression and began to cut herself to at least feel something. A cry for help that no one had answered. Finally she had realized no one was coming to help her and stopped, dried her eyes, and went on, knowing she was going to have to rescue herself.

Which was one of the reasons, she realized, she had fallen for Jared so hard. He had the companionate strength she had been looking for, and now that she was strong enough to make her way in the world without it, she was ready to lean on him. And laugh at his lame jokes, and relax into his warm embrace. She looked at her father and saw a glimpse of how Jared might look, older. They didn't look at all alike, but someday Jared too would have reading glasses, gray hair, and a distracted manner —Jared already had the scruffy clothes. This made her feel strangely happy.

When the week was over, her father put her on the plane back to Utah. Before she visited him, she had thought she missed New York, but on returning realized there was nothing there she needed as much as she needed Jared. The baby grew within her, just beginning to show a little—she would need new clothes soon. She would move heaven and earth to raise their child and protect it from harm.

She fell into the new routine at school—go to class, walk home for lunch, go back to class, spend the day avoiding the Mean Girls. She saw Jessica in the halls a few times, but turned and went the other way to avoid getting closer. Jared often came to her house for lunch, and they grew closer.

Sara also saw some of the boys (and men) she had converted to her cause, but the spirit riding her kept her from remembering those visits. Her converts began to acknowledge each other, and she had invited the most devoted to meet up to start planning for protection of her child. While Lailah was in control, she allowed them to touch her belly to worship the child who would rule them all. Her control over them strengthened with each touch.

28: Jared: Attacked

Jared was doing his best to hold everything together. He knew something was still not right with Sara, but she had returned from visiting her father calmer and happier. Preston and his other old friends kept asking him how he was doing as if they expected him to be troubled. He had stopped seeing them when he took up with Sara, using all his spare time to be with her, and they had noticed. But it didn't seem unusual.

Sara was sweet if a bit distracted, but their sex was less frequent—he had at first been troubled by the idea of sex while she was visibly enlarged with child, but got over it when she insisted. Still, he felt more tender toward her than lustful, and he didn't initiate it. It was her idea when it happened at all.

She seemed chastened and he hoped she had given up her campaign of seduction. He tried to ignore subtle hints that she had not, and he continued to defend her when kids called her a slut to his face. His angry face usually stopped such talk.

But then he was forced to face the reality.

He had delayed going to study hall to get a book out of his locker that he needed to study for a test later in the day. As he turned a corner toward his study hall room, he saw a darkened classroom door open and Sara and Owen Kimball came out, smiling and laughing.

Jared paused, then decided to confront them. When they saw him, Sara's face froze, then she laughed again, with an edge of hysteria.

"Jared! Come join us," she said, reaching out with her hand.

Jared pulled back and her hand grasped air. "I don't think

so," he said. "How could you? When you're on probation? And carrying our child?" He turned to Owen, his rage beginning to build. "And what the fuck do you think you're doing? Haven't you caused enough trouble?"

Owen stared back, impassive. "None of your business, little man. Sara can do what she wants."

Jared looked back at Sara. "And you—"

Sara *hissed* at him. The look on her face was chilling.

Owen stepped forward and shoved Jared in the chest.

Jared saw red and put all his strength into a wild swing that Owen sidestepped. Owen's answer was to punch him in the stomach from the side. Jared doubled over in agony, but sprung up to hit Owen back. Owen grappled with him and they fell to the floor, with Owen holding his shirt and trying to knee him in the groin while Jared continued to try to punch him out. They fought for a minute, with Jared focused on hurting Owen if he could and Owen defending his face.

Jared landed a punch on Owen's nose, which began to bleed. Jared's shirt tore, freeing his arm, so he hit Owen again. Owen's hold slipped, but he was able to knee Jared's groin. The pain blinded Jared, and Owen punched him twice more in the face.

Sara had disappeared. Then Jared realized they were surrounded by boys—Dawson, Jason, and others he suspected Sara had been meeting for sex.

A teacher shouted at them to stop and ran to get help.

The crowd grew and Jared felt blows from all sides pummel him. Someone kicked him hard in the stomach and he threw up. More blows to the face and head. A cut in his scalp bled, and the floor was smeared with his vomit and blood.

He felt hands pick him up and carry him as he struggled to

get free. He was carried down two flights of stairs. When he opened his eyes, he saw Mr. Steves, the janitor, standing by the door to the utility room in the basement. Mr. Steves traded glances with the boys and opened the steel door for them.

Jared was dumped on a steel table and beaten. "She's ours," Owen said. "Best get used to that. Don't get in the way."

Jared blacked out as the blows continued.

He was somewhere else. It felt like cartoon Hell, with flames and the groans of the damned surrounding him. He was strapped to a giant X made of rough wood, the splinters digging into his skin, the manacles holding him up cutting his wrists and ankles. A horned goat-man tormented him, claws reaching into Jared's open viscera and removing scoops of his flesh, his intestines smelling foul and hanging out. He dimly understood it was a hallucination. The monster turned him over somehow and he blacked out again. Nightmare followed nightmare, each ending in pain and degradation. Finally he was brought before Raphael, who looked down upon his battered and filthy body and said, "Jared, you disappoint me." But Raphael took him into his arms and Jared felt the pain and the shame lessen.

He woke to find himself outside, propped up against a cinderblock wall next to the dumpsters in back of the school. He ached everywhere he wasn't numb. Blood stained his shirt and his pants had been pulled down—he suspected that he had been violated. His underwear was stained and torn. The sun was still high in the sky, so school was still in session—he could hear a gym class in progress.

He assembled the fragments of his memory to try to make

sense of what had just happened. He struggled to pull up his pants, then tried to get on his feet. It took a minute to stand up —he was still shaky and had to lean on the wall for support. He looked toward the freight dock, but all the doors were closed.

He stumbled to the parking lot, ignoring the curious stares of the two students who saw him, and got into his car. He needed to get away from here to clean up and gather his strength for what he needed to do.

At home, he slowly showered and thoroughly cleaned himself. He threw away his shirt and put his jeans into the laundry hamper, hoping his mother wouldn't notice how stained they were. He dabbed alcohol on his cuts and bandaged the one on his face. He fell into his bed and thought.

When he got up, he pulled out his phone. Its glass face had been cracked sometime during the fight, but it still worked.

"I can't do this any longer. Your friends beat me up. I won't be back," he texted Sara.

He told his parents he had fallen on a hike after school. Every morning for a week he feigned illness and got his mother to call the school to excuse him. He tried to do his homework but couldn't concentrate. He started to spend all his time in the Morpheum Online world. Sara didn't reply.

29: Randy: Truant Officer

Randy noticed Jared's absence. He wanted to congratulate Jared on the A he had given them for their Zion Mine report and encourage them to submit an edited version to the town newspaper, but Jared had been out sick for days. Sara didn't seem to have any idea what was wrong with him, and her lack of concern seemed out of character.

Randy dropped by Mina Wilson's office to chat about it. Mina, it turned out, had already been asked to look into Jared's absences—it was uncharacteristic and the reasons given were vague.

"I'll see if I can reach him," Randy said. "He doesn't answer his phone, so maybe I could drop by his house after school."

Mina rolled her eyes. "I wouldn't recommend that," she said. "Let us speak to the parents first." He left her office agreeing to that, but his curiosity gnawed at him.

Which was why he drove north instead of south to his house when he drove away from the school at three o'clock.

❖　　❖　　❖　　❖　　❖

Jared answered the repeated knocks on his front door after a few minutes.

"Mr. Wright," he said dully. "I'm still sick." His eyes were sunken and he looked pale and drawn.

"So they told me. Can I come in? We need to talk." Randy pushed through the door and they sat facing each other in the living room.

"Now what the hell is wrong with you?" Randy said. "You're not sick. Something's bothering you and you're hiding from it."

Jared looked resentful. "I broke up with Sara. She just stood there while I was beaten up by her bullyboys. There's only so much I will put up with."

Randy had put his worries about Sara's seduction of him on the back burner. After all, he had lots of company and it looked like he would have the support of the school administration if it ever came up. And so he hadn't thought much more about it, because he could only stay worried for so long. But if Sara had attacked Jared and broken his heart, no one was safe.

"You think she approved?" Randy said.

"I know she did. She brought those guys over to hurt me."

Randy decided Jared needed to know what he had heard from Kovac. Even a crackpot explanation for Sara's treacherous behavior might give Jared a way out of his bewilderment and depression.

Randy had been hoping it would all blow over and he'd never have to act on what Kovac had told him. But the look on Jared's face tipped him toward believing Kovac's demonic possession theory, and so he decided to throw it to Jared as a lifeline.

"I may have found out what's wrong with her. She might be possessed."

"Possessed? Like, by the Devil?" Jared looked skeptical but alert.

"By *a* devil. A spirit, an entity." Randy pulled out his phone and brought up a photo of Kovac's castle, and went through the rest of the shots of the equipment and Kovac. "I met with this guy, Tomo Kovac. He says he's seeing a lot of this possession, and he's developed a way to cast the demons out. 'Demons' I guess is as good a name as any for ancient spirits living in the magnetic field of the earth and able to influence the weak-willed near their centers of power. Like the mountain."

"'Weak-willed.' That doesn't sound like Sara." Jared's voice had strengthened.

"No, it doesn't. But unless she's just crazy, it's the best explanation I can see for how she has been acting. She's under a malevolent something's control and isn't responsible for her actions."

"I'd like to believe that. I don't understand how she could be so ... *cold* to me." Jared looked angry. "I was planning to be with her—"

"So hold on to that thought. If we can cure her of this evil influence, she'll be back to her old self. Don't give up so easily." Randy realized he had convinced himself so he could convince Jared. If it wasn't true, at least it gave him hope.

Jared brightened. "You really think so? What can we do?"

"I'll work on Sara's mother and get her permission to bring in Kovac to treat her. Then we hope the treatment works. In the meantime, you need to come back to school. Hold your head up and get your work done, or you'll wreck your grades. Right now you've got an 'A' in my class, but miss more tests and it will start to drop."

"I don't care."

"Yes, you do. And you need to be there for Sara. When she's better she'll remember you stood by her when she needed you." Randy sincerely hoped that would be true.

Sara idly wondered why she wasn't seeing much of Jared. He had stopped visiting her house for lunch, and she missed his calls and texts. She was briefly saddened, but each time she felt his absence something in her mind shifted and she thought of something else.

She went to the quarterly school dance by herself. Her mother had helped her find loose dresses that disguised her increasing girth, and she wore a red dress that flattered her bosom while distracting the eye from the bulk below. When she entered the decorated gymnasium, girls nearby went silent while boys turned to look.

Dawson asked her to dance. They spent a few minutes dancing, others giving them lots of space. The crowd of single boys stayed on one side while a few girls dared to dance with each other, having given up on being asked.

As the night progressed, more boys started dancing near her no matter who she had started the dance with, crowding in until she was dancing surrounded by a cloud of boys, all turned toward her.

The music stopped for a moment. Sara looked around and noticed Jessica, Tiffany, and two more girls staring at her and whispering to each other. They decided something, and came toward her looking grimly determined.

"Sara," Jessica said, "You're not supposed to be here. You're supposed to stay at least a hundred feet away from me."

"I have as much right to be here as you do," Sara said. "Don't I, boys?" The boys she had been dancing with perked up and began to move toward Jessica.

Sensing danger, Jessica and her friends retreated. "I'll report you to the principal." They turned and moved away quickly. The music began again, and Sara saw Jessica talking to one of the teachers assigned to chaperone. The male teacher listened, then shrugged. Jessica looked angry and stormed off with her friends, leaving by the rear exit doors.

Sara made three more converts during the dance. It ended at ten, and she walked home by herself, satisfied and sore. But her thoughts turned again to Jared. She felt vaguely guilty about something she had done to him, but her memory was fuzzy. Oh well, she knew they belonged together and he would forgive her. Her new friend—the voice who reassured her and gave her useful instructions that had helped her come out of her shell and get what she wanted from people—would help her get him back.

As she crossed the street in front of her apartment building, she heard an engine rev and saw a red car coming toward her, accelerating rapidly, tires squealing. Jessica was driving, the look of hatred on her face shared by the two other girls in the car. Sara stopped in the middle of the street and just watched as the car roared toward her.

Moments before Sara would have been hit, Jessica shrieked and her face paled in terror. She was seeing a vision of a giant tusked and tailed monster reaching out for her through the windshield, and she reacted by veering to the right. Rubber burned and the tires squealed as the car went off the road, crossed the sidewalk, and rammed a tree, with the sound of glass breaking, metal crumpling, and the screams of the girls pleasing to the spirit guiding Sara.

Sara continued into her apartment complex. As she opened the door, the distant sirens were background to the cries of agony still coming from the car. She closed the door behind her and waited.

After the EMTs and the police came, Sara came back out to talk to the police, pretending she knew nothing about the accident. Two of the cops were already converts. A photographer took pictures of the scene and the tire tracks in the street where the car had veered off. Others picked up debris and looked through the car before it was towed away.

One girl was dead—Jessica. Sara watched her mangled body being loaded onto a stretcher and into the ambulance. The other two girls were rushed off to the hospital, still alive, saved by the airbags. For some reason Jessica's airbag had failed and her head had hit the windshield. *Served her right.*

The chief's car pulled up and parked up the street. Sara glimpsed Roger Spendlove getting out, and turned away to avoid being seen. She got away before Jared's father noticed her.

In the paper the next day, the tragedy was blamed on teen drinking.

31: Jared: Defender

Jared returned to school that Monday determined not to let Sara's temporary insanity deter him. His anger grew as he realized Sara had not betrayed him—she had been taken over by an evil spirit. Did it matter if she were possessed, as opposed to just mentally ill? It did to him. It gave him something to hate. And he would do anything to have the real Sara back.

His father had come back from the scene of the crash Saturday night—one dead, two seriously injured. No one had told his father yet that Sara had tangled with Jessica and her friends at the school dance earlier, but he knew that Sara and Jessica had fought earlier. Jared truthfully told him he hadn't heard anything from Sara and it was probably just a coincidence that Jessica had crashed into a tree less than a block from Sara's apartment.

But before school the kids were speculating, and many concluded Sara had somehow caused the crash.

"She's a witch!" one boy said, intending for Jared to hear. The hall was full of students headed for their homerooms.

"Really?" He got in the kid's face, bristling with anger. "You don't know her at all. Isn't it more likely Jessica was just drunk out of her mind?"

Dawson, one of Sara's recent "friends," came up behind Jared and glared at the kid. "You ragging on Sara again? Jessica was out of control. I saw her that night. She went crazy. So shut your trap about Sara."

Faced with two against one, the kid said, "There's something wrong with her. And how you guys defend her is part of it."

Then he turned and walked away.

"Thanks," Jared said, turning to Dawson.

"De nada," Dawson replied, waving it off. "That twerp bugs me."

Jared remembered that Dawson had been in the crowd that had beaten him up just over a week ago—did Dawson remember it at all? Apparently Dawson would attack anyone who threatened Sara. He had felt it, too, that desire to take Sara's side even if she was wrong, and it was not the same as his desire to help her out of love. It was—*unnatural*, a kind of push from outside. Dawson and some of the other boys seemed to be acting out as puppets, unaware that they were being influenced. This made it possible for him to go about his business at school without confronting his attackers since he realized they were just the instruments of whatever had Sara in its grip. His beating had just been collateral damage, and if he let it get to him, the enemy would have won. The best revenge was to find and kill that demon.

◊   ◊   ◊   ◊   ◊

Sara hadn't answered his texts for days, and he discovered when he got to History class that she was absent. Mr. Wright was lecturing about the Civil War, but Jared's mind was elsewhere. Mr. Wright watched him closely but didn't call on him. After class, Jared lingered to talk to him.

Jared said, "You heard about Jessica Peterson?"

"Yes. Terrible. Are you thinking what I'm thinking? Sara had something to do with it?" Mr. Wright looked worried.

"There really is something evil controlling Sara," Jared said, finally voicing what he had been concluding. "She would never hurt anyone. If something can influence her to do such bad things, maybe it could have influenced Jessica as well."

"We have to assume the two events are connected." Mr. Wright got his phone and started to look up a number. "I tried to call Sara's mother and left a message, but I didn't hear back. So maybe I can catch her at work." He showed Jared the hospital web page and phone link, which he clicked on.

After waiting a bit for a live human, they were put through to Sara's mother, who of course didn't answer. Randy left her a message asking her to call back as soon as possible.

"Well, there's not much we can do to get Kovac on the case until her mother gives her approval." Randy put his phone down and turned to Jared. "Why don't you see if Sara's home when you have a free period?"

"She doesn't want to see me. She doesn't answer my texts."

Randy challenged him. "Are you so easily put off? She's not herself. I know it's hard, but you need to be there for her."

❖   ❖   ❖   ❖   ❖

After Jared's next class he had study hall, so instead he snuck away to visit Sara. He knocked on her apartment door and heard rustling.

"Go away." Sara's voice was muffled behind the closed door.

"Come on," Jared said. "We have to talk." He steeled himself for another rejection, but he wasn't going to be dissuaded this time.

The door opened. "I'm leaving town," Sara said. A suitcase was waiting on the floor next to the door.

"Has my father been by to talk to you yet?" Jared noticed the bags under her eyes and her unkempt hair.

"No, and why would he want to?" Sara waved him inside.

He crossed his arms. "You had a public fight with Jessica the night she died. The police might want to hear your side of it." Jared closed the door and stared into her eyes.

"That's ridiculous." She turned away.

"Is it? You're not yourself. You slept with Owen and broke them up, so Jessica had every reason to be angry. You assaulted her and were supposed to stay away from school social functions. Why did you go to the dance?" Jared reached for Sara, but she backed away. Her face twisted with hate.

"That bitch was in my way. Let me go or I'll hurt you, too."

Jared knew it wasn't her talking, but got angry anyway, and shouted, "Is the child even mine?"

"It is," she said, voice icy. "And you'll never see it." She picked up the suitcase and started to leave.

Jared grabbed her arm and stopped her. "You can't. I—"

Pain shot up his arm and stunned him. Agony spread through his body and he started jerking with muscle spasms before he fell to the floor, unconscious.

32: Randy: Cracking Up

Randy's phone buzzed while he was in his office. It was Sara's mother.

"Mr. Wright," she said. "Sorry it took so long to get back to you. All-day meetings."

"I wanted to talk to you about getting professional help for Sara." He wanted to present Kovac as just another form of talk therapy.

"She's seeing the psychologist. She seems to be over whatever that was."

"There have been some new developments you may not be aware of." Randy outlined the events at the dance.

"Oh, my! Surely no one thinks Sara had anything to do with that awful crash. We have the girls here in intensive care."

"Of course not," he lied. "But I have a friend who has done wonders for troubled young people like Sara. And he's agreed to see her. But you have to sign a permission form."

"The psychologist she's seeing is under our insurance. Does this therapist take insurance?"

"He's doing research, so it's free as long as she fits his research profile." His lies were getting more creative. Randy would be happy to pay for it himself to stop the juggernaut of awfulness that was threatening his way of life.

"Well, I don't know…"

"We should meet to discuss it. And I'll have the forms to sign."

After making a date to meet with Mrs. Horowitz, Randy called Kovac and outlined the what had happened at the dance and Jessica's death.

"That sounds like an emergency to me, a much more serious infestation—I think we have to conclude a demon was able to kill through suggestion. I'll alert the team and we'll start preparing a mission." Kovac paused. "Get those parental permission forms signed, and keep me posted."

Kovac's assistant emailed him the forms and he was printing them out when his phone rang again. It was Mrs. Horowitz.

"Sara's not answering her phone. I called the school and she's listed as absent. I'm worried."

"If you want I could check on her."

"Would you? I'd appreciate it. I have two more meetings before I can leave today." She sounded relieved to hand the problem off to him.

Randy left the school building and walked across and up the street to Sara's apartment, but as he got closer he saw Sara leave, carrying a suitcase. He caught up with her on the sidewalk.

She was breathing hard and her face was a mask of anger. At the same time she was crying, streaks of tears running down her cheeks.

"Sara," Randy said, "I've been on the phone with your mother. She's worried about you."

Sara snarled at him. "Fuck her. I'm getting out of this shitty town."

Randy held her shoulders, and she tried to wriggle away, but he held on tight.

"I know you're pregnant. The whole school knows." Randy realized there was no one on the street, no one to see if he wrung her neck and walked away. Something made him want to end her and the threat she represented to his family and his job. For a moment he struggled with the impulse, then he pushed it away. "Is it mine?"

Sara laughed. "You wish. You didn't even get close, how could you with that tiny dick? I like *men*, and you don't measure up."

Randy resisted a renewed urge to choke her. "Whatever thing you have inside you that's making you do this, I'm going to do everything I can to see that it's evicted. Sara, if you're in there, I know this isn't you."

"You're funny." Sara reached up and squeezed his arm.

Randy blanked out. When he awoke, he was flat on his back on the ground, looking up at Jared, who gazed down at him blearily since he had just recovered consciousness himself.

Sara was gone.

33: Sara: Escape

Sara walked away from Randy's crumpled body and waited along the side of the road. She noticed the shrine of flowers and a white-painted cross up the street, under the scarred tree Jessica's car had hit. She felt nothing but a distant satisfaction.

A Range Rover SUV drove up, and she got in after stowing her suitcase on the back seat.

"Where to?" the driver asked. He was a local realtor she had converted a few weeks back, middle-aged and fit. He had been one of the easiest to turn, being divorced and having little ethical fiber. She idly wished for a better caliber of minion, imagining that when she was at the right hand of the Messiah they would put these weaklings down and replace them with the righteous. But for now, these flawed tools would have to do.

"To the Luxor in Las Vegas," she said, and he set up his GPS to guide them. Soon they were on I-15 going south. Her minion wanted to talk, but she squeezed his thigh and pushed pleasure into him with the order to be silent.

Lailah had picked the Luxor for her base because its diverse clientele would cover the kind of visitors she expected to have, and it was perversely satisfying to again have a pyramid of her own. The giant bronze glass pyramid looked smaller now, surrounded by much taller glass towers. They pulled up under the *porte-cochère* behind the Sphinx replica, and a doorman opened the car door for her. Instead of tipping him, she gifted him with a smile and a touch of her hand.

In the atrium lobby, she looked up at the mock Egyptian

temple façades and garish posters for magic shows. Near the registration counters she noticed a dark-suited muscular black man she identified as security—he looked like a bouncer dressed up, with a shaved head and roaming eyes. Smiling, she approached him and touched his arm.

"Could you help me? I need to see the manager."

His face changed from grim to a broad smile as he realized she was special, probably a Hollywood star.

"Sure, babe," he said, raising his cuff to speak into the microphone there.

The response he heard in his earpiece must have been satisfactory, because he led her to a side door where a smaller man waited. He was dapper, but more wiry than muscular, with a carefully-trimmed moustache. This one's mind was more complex, and his face was hard. She reached out to him but he evaded her hand.

"Miss. Can I help you?" The manager sounded like he had better things to do.

"I know you're busy," Sara said, batting her eyelashes. Until she could touch him, the more usual tricks would have to do. "But I've never been here and my uncle was supposed to meet me in the lobby. I'm all alone..." She dragged it out to make herself seem as waiflike as possible.

And it worked. His face relaxed and he smiled, and this time when she reached for his forearm he let her squeeze it. He suddenly became friendly.

"Come back to my office," the manager said. He turned to the security guy and said, "Thank you."

The black security guy looked disappointed. "Nice to have met you, Miss."

Sara smiled at him. "Thank you." She did like the look of him, and if there was any time later, having him up for a few intensive imprinting sessions might be rewarding.

In the manager's office, she made a point of examining the framed pictures and certificates on the walls. "Impressive," she said. "You've met a lot of important people." He had photos of himself with everyone from Bill Clinton to Lady Gaga. It looked like he had been working at Vegas hotels for a long time.

He stood close, and she felt his hand go around her waist. It was even easier when the prey jumped into the net! She turned and sought out his lips for a kiss.

When she left the manager's office she had a comp card giving her free access to everything—she was entered into their computer as a high-roller with a luxury penthouse suite. He assured her Accounting wouldn't notice anything so long as he reset her status every month. Good minion! Another hungry man willing to ignore principle for reinforcement. A pellet a week would hold him, so now she had a base of operations.

The suite had a well-stocked kitchen, and she snacked on mixed nuts and sparkling water. The penthouse lounge had a full-time attendant, so she went to convert him and order up dinner—only to discover it was a her. She tried anyway, and was rewarded—despite her feminine appearance, the attendant was a lesbian who was rather easily swayed. Someone would be up shortly with dinner, and she had another set of eyes to warn her of danger.

Back in her suite, she started researching escort services. She needed a discreet, high-end service that would deliver the wealthiest, most powerful men to her for conversion. At several a night, she would soon have minions in place all over the country—and the world—who could help her defend her child and hasten his coming dominion. But she'd have to convert the escort service manager to be sure only the best candidates were sent her way. She wasn't going to waste time fucking losers.

Jared and Randy were still standing on the sidewalk in front of Sara's place, piecing together what had happened, when Sara's mother drove up.

"Where's Sara?" she said, frantic.

Jared looked at Randy, who shrugged.

"She left. With a suitcase. Said she was leaving town." Jared was still numb from the spell Sara had cast on him.

This did not calm Rachel Horowitz. "Why didn't you stop her? We have to call the police—" She started dialing her phone.

Randy stopped her. "First let me explain what's going on. This is going to sound crazy, but…" He outlined the signs that Sara had been possessed. "She's not having an attack of adolescent angst, she's under the control of a demon."

Sara's mother looked at him in horror. "My God. Is everyone in this town a religious fruitcake? We have to catch her before she gets far. The bus station—"

"We don't have a station," Jared noted. "Just a bus shelter by the exit ramp."

Sara's mother turned back toward her car and resumed dialing her phone. "Yes, I want to report my daughter is missing. Maybe kidnapped," she added.

Randy followed her. "That's nonsense," he said. "She left on her own."

Rachel glared at him as she was connected to the local police. "Yes, I want to report my daughter is missing. May have been abducted. She's in grave danger." She listened for a minute, then gave the address. "Sara Horowitz. I'm her mother. Hurry, she's probably still in town."

Two squad cars pulled up a minute later, and Jared's father and two other officers got out.

"Sara's missing?" Chief Spendlove nodded to his son and Randy, but kept his attention on Sara's mother, the most agitated party.

She pointed at Randy and Jared. "These two say she left with a suitcase."

"Why doesn't someone explain what we know? Have you checked inside your apartment?" Chief Spendlove gestured to his officers toward the doorway. "In the meantime, I'll put out an APB to be on the lookout for her." He went back to his car and radioed the basic description. "…carrying a suitcase. Check the bus stop and the usual hitching spots by the exit."

That done, the chief returned to questioning. Jared followed Randy's lead and left out the part where Sara hexed them into unconsciousness. His father looked confused.

"And you just let her walk away?" His pen was poised above the notepad.

Randy took over. "She slipped out the door while we were talking. By the time we realized it, she was gone."

The chief wrote something down and then looked up at Randy. "Something does not add up. Why were you here? Maybe we should go to the station so you can make a full statement."

◎　　◎　　◎　　◎　　◎

It was dinnertime by the time they were done. The station

was small, with only one couch in the waiting area. Randy gave his statement in the Chief Spendlove's office, then sat with Rachel Horowitz while Jared went in for the grilling.

Randy tried to explain Sara's possession to her mother. He described his visit to Kovac's Noumenal Foundation and the successful application of magnetic field blockers to cases of possession.

She was still rejecting the idea but at least listening. The invocation of science and a researcher with academic ties bought a little respect for the possibility of possession.

"Kovac can force the demon out of her long enough to get her back," Randy concluded. "It either works quickly or it doesn't work at all, is my view. It can't hurt to try it."

"Wouldn't it be nice if it were that simple?" Sara's mother said. "But she's had troubles before, and it took lots of therapy to bring her out of it. Why would it be different this time?"

"It's certainly possible she was more susceptible to influence because of her earlier problems," Randy said. "My understanding is the demon can only persuade, not override. At first it's small things, one choice instead of another with the demon tipping the balance. Eventually the demon exerts more complete control as the host personality is trained to act under command."

Sara's mother looked thoughtful. "I suppose it's possible. She has been acting oddly for months." She signed the authorization forms. Jared finished his statement, and Chief Spendlove came out of his office to suggest they meet at his house for a late dinner and to discuss strategy. His officers had searched the apartment and scoured the town for Sara and found nothing, so he had sent out a statewide alert.

After dinner at the Spendlove's, Randy called Kovac on speakerphone and introduced him to the others, then told him about Sara's escape.

"We've put out the APB and triggered the Amber Alert system," Roger Spendlove said, "but so far without result."

"That's unfortunate," Kovac said. "We can't do anything unless we know where she is."

Sara's mother asked, "But why my daughter? Sara's never been in trouble. Oh, she's had problems, but never wanted to run away or get into trouble with the law. Why would these … spirits want to possess *her?*"

Kovac exhaled loudly. "I wish I could tell you, Mrs. Horowitz. It may be that she is more suggestible than most, or that she was especially valuable for some reason we can't see."

Jared's father was skeptical. "There's no way I can officially recognize your theory, Mr. Kovac. I've heard rumors, but for now we'll just assume Sara's like any other wayward child runaway, acting out. No need for any more explanation than that."

They heard Kovac rustling papers. "I could drop some names to convince you, but it's not really important that you believe. What's important is that you find her and get her back here. If my treatment doesn't work, you can call me a fraud. But it will."

They talked into the night. Jared's mother was quiet, but it was clear she took the news badly. When Rachel Horowitz left, Jared's father took his son aside.

"I didn't want to talk in front of her mother," his father said, "but Sara is probably long gone. If she caught a bus or hitched a ride on the Interstate, she could be in LA by now. The only way we'll find her is if she gets into trouble. Most likely she'll come home when she runs out of money. But you have to be prepared for her not to."

Sara surveyed her rapidly growing domain. Through the window looking north, she could see the skyline of casino hotel towers—Excalibur, Aria, Vdara, Cosmopolitan. Cleaners and decorators were finishing up her suite for tonight's function, bringing in trays of food, ice for the bar, and extra seating. Somewhere inside, Sara was still a shy, sensitive girl who only pretended to be tough. But that girl could never have imagined that, by repressing all her fears and persuading men to do what she wanted through wiles both natural and supernatural, she could win this kind of power. She resented Lailah's control, but she revelled in her new-found sense of what she could accomplish when she stopped being ashamed. It was exhilarating, and frightening.

Sara had converted Vinnie Licenziato, who ran the best escort service in Las Vegas, the Company Company. He didn't need to advertise—business came through concierges at the most expensive hotels, or by word-of-mouth. Vinnie offered the highest quality escorts at the highest rates, and he wasn't troubled by the attrition as his best girls were snapped up to become trophy wives or mistresses to the wealthiest men in world capitals. For that was part of the allure—these ladies (and a few men) were the crème de la crème, many with advanced degrees and the hottest gymnast bodies, able to converse knowledgeably about many topics at fashionable dinner parties and afterward outperform in the sheets. He turned away women who had modified themselves to extremes—no obvious boob jobs, no collagen lips. His satisfied clients knew better than to talk about his services matching the quality youth in need of wealth with the wealthy in need of quality young companions. Clients were grateful for his help and happy to keep their names out of the news, the twin motivations that protected his business from official notice.

It was typical for wealthy gentlemen to test drive one of his escorts while they were in town. His fees were high, but it was common for his escorts to end up getting a far greater payoff if they became society wives. Vinnie was happy to be the match-maker for many good partnerships. And he had immediately understood what Sara wanted, sending her a steady stream of clients who reported back how good she was.

In three months she had converted over a hundred men. Those men, in turn, referred others who could be useful to her, especially those who held important posts—CEOs, congress-men, generals.

Tonight she was hosting a party for Nevada Senator Hubert Hastings, who had been led to believe it was a fundraiser for his re-election campaign. Vinnie had rounded up the best girls and Sara's suite had been decorated and furnished for a crowd. Vinnie himself manned the door and made sure the Senator's entourage was distracted so Sara would have the opportunity to work her magic on him.

Two lithe young blondes worked Senator Hastings over as he sat between them on a red leather couch, laughing at his lame jokes and making sure he could glimpse their swelling nipples and inner thighs as their skimpy dresses allowed. Hast-ings had the styled silver hair and tan of a camera-minded politician. Sara noted that his assistant had been led away to another room before she approached him. It wouldn't do to be overheard when she talked to him.

She signalled Vinnie to make sure no one interfered, then approached Senator Hastings. Her obvious pregnancy repelled some men before she could get close enough to them to lay on her hands, so the subterfuge of having other girls set them up first had become necessary.

"I've been looking forward to meeting you," Sara said. The two girls attending him looked up, then saw Vinnie's signal and moved to give Sara room next to him.

"Been looking forward to meeting you, dear," Hastings said, eying her up and down. "I've heard a lot about you."

Sara sat down and leaned into him. "All good, I hope." She started to stroke his arm, then squeezed, and pushed her will into him. His eyes defocused. "You will want to work with me," she commanded.

He reached for her thigh. "What can I do for you, little lady? You seem to have everything you want."

Sara allowed his hand to progress upward. "I will call upon you when the time comes," she said. "My son will need your help. He is to be lifted up."

"Lifted up?" Hastings repeated. "You are certainly looking far ahead. You haven't had your baby yet—"

"Put your hand here. Feel Him." She took his hand and placed it on her belly. She felt her son move, and Hastings fell deeper under the spell.

"I see," he said. A series of expressions ran across his face, settling into placid acceptance. "You—he—can call on me when the time comes."

The child within was a powerful draw, and it was no longer necessary to have sex to complete the conversion—touching her distended belly was enough. But she had rigged the bedroom with recording equipment to store video of each convert for possible later use, since while it was unusual, some conversions had worn off when the subjects were back with those they truly loved. Using sex tapes for blackmail was a useful backup when the strong-willed or happily married managed to throw off the compulsion.

She got up and pulled Hastings into the bedroom and shut the door. This wouldn't take long. Senator Hastings' wife was undergoing treatment for breast cancer and Vinnie had provided him with willing escorts for years, so he would not have resisted even if she hadn't cast a spell on him.

Jared had gone from angry and pumped for action to depressed as weeks dragged on with no news about Sara. He daydreamed about going off alone to look for her—he'd take her picture to LA and ask everyone he met if they had seen her. He knew without a lead it would be a waste of time—if only the APB had brought in a single report of a sighting. His father told him they had checked out two reports, neither credible.

With Sara gone, the boys who had attacked him returned to ignoring him, apparently not remembering much about the time spent under her influence. Jared's schoolwork suffered because he remembered it clearly, and when his anger faded, he still felt like a loser who should have been able to do something more to stop them. He had given up trying to talk to Sara's mother, who seemed to blame him for her disappearance. His mother was not much better, having decided it had been a mistake to consider a non-Mormon girl good enough for him, and her worst fears had come true. The town gossips had assigned Jared much of the blame for Sara's transgressions, and Sharon Spendlove discovered that many of her 'friends' now avoided her—they were reluctant to be seen with her, afraid of contamination.

Roger Spendlove did his best to fight the gossips, but it was like there were two separate worlds—men agreed with him in private but stayed silent with their wives, unwilling to buck the matriarchy. If he couldn't sway his own wife, how could he expect them to sway theirs? Mindless piety and enforcement of group norms was the province of the women. Men only appeared to be in charge.

But gradually Jared started to forget. He had polished up the Zion Mine paper, and the local newspaper had published a condensed version, complete with his photos. That led to a number of inquiries, and Prof. Atwater was encouraging him to apply to BYU. His grades were the weakest link, but with her recommendation, he stood a chance of admission. Bishop Snow wrote him a letter of recommendation as well.

Jared's father had supported him and explained the situation with the town gossips.

"Those people don't matter, if you leave for college," he said. "No one there will know anything about this, and by the time you graduate, if you come back it will all have been forgotten. Just hold your head up and do your work, and you'll be fine."

"I'm trying." Jared looked down. "I miss Sara."

"Son, I know you miss her. And I think you're right that she was suffering some kind of multiple personality disorder, or maybe even Kovac's demonic possession—she wasn't that kind of girl, at all. We all saw her change from good to bad. So maybe she'll recover and come back. But maybe she won't. You have to let go and get on with your life."

"I'll do my best," Jared replied, sighing. "If I could just talk to her...."

◊   ◊   ◊   ◊   ◊

A few days later, Jared got a text message from a new number: "Sorry I haven't been in touch. I'm okay, living in Las Vegas. Come alone and we can talk. —S"

He texted back. "I can't get away until Saturday. Where are

you?"

Sara texted him a map. It showed a restaurant near the Strip. "7 PM Saturday. Tell no one, Come alone."

He responded but there was no answer. He decided not to tell anyone—his father would surely insist on accompanying him and might try to get law enforcement involved, since Sara was technically an underaged runaway who could be arrested and placed in protective custody for return to her mother. Saturday after lunch, he told his parents he was going to Preston's house for a long music session, then drove away. The Interstate south took him to the center of the Las Vegas strip five hours later.

The chain restaurant served bland food but had a constant stream of customers from the street. The orange counters and cushioned vinyl booth seating made for easy cleaning. Jared looked around and spotted Sara alone in a booth at the back. She looked good, almost glowing, visibly pregnant and dressed in a colorful print muumuu. She saw him and waved.

The booth to the right of hers was occupied by two big men in dark suits who were looking his way. They watched him as he approached, but as he closed on Sara's booth their eyes slid past him to watch the entrance again.

"It's so good to see you," he said, sliding into the bench seat across from her. "You scared everyone."

Sara frowned. "You didn't tell anyone you were coming, did you?"

"No. I could guess what would happen if I did." He cocked his head and looked at her appraisingly. "What are you doing? How are you getting along without money? What's with the

Secret Service?"

"They're keeping me safe. And money is not a problem," she said. "I've got everything I need."

"And you don't need me." He meant it as a statement of fact, and a rebuke.

"Not for anything as simple as money. But I do need your support." She reached across the table and took his hand.

Jared felt a wave of warmth course through him. He felt— but he rejected the feeling and pulled his hand away as if burned. "That isn't going to work on me. I know what you are! I loved you and you threw it all away. You—" he lowered his voice to a whisper and leaned closer, hissing at her, "—seduced half the boys in school! You made a fool out of me. Why should I ever help you again?"

"Because our son is on his way. Because you have a duty to him. And I love you, too. We can be good together. Our son will rule the world." She took his hand again, but this time he felt nothing but the warmth of her touch.

"You're crazy. Or possessed. Come back home and we'll get you the help you need," he said, surprised to see tears in her eyes.

"I can't. Join me here and we will rise together." Her face hardened and she dried her eyes. "I need you to be with me."

"I can't do that. I have to finish school and graduate. I can't ruin my life to run off with you."

The waitress came by and he ordered a hamburger. They talked about school and Sara's mother's TV interviews to get publicity in the search for her daughter.

"Can I at least tell her you're safe?" Jared asked.

"No. I sent a message to her not to worry right after I left. If you say anything, they'll lean on you to tell them where I am. So tell no one. I'll find an untraceable way to send her another message."

They went round and round until Jared's half-eaten burger was cold.

"Look, I have to get back before they miss me and decide to check with Preston. I warned him I'd used him as cover, but better it never comes up. It'll be midnight before I get back."

"If you leave I don't want you coming back."

"I won't. Not until I graduate. Only two months away."

"Our son will be due then. I'll come back to have him there with you." Sara's eyes closed as she communed with some Other. "Yes, that will be necessary."

Jared wondered what that might be about. But he took her intention to return as progress.

"Look," he said, "I really have to go or my cover will be blown." He slid out of the booth and went around to kiss her. She hugged him back, and it almost felt right again. But he knew that thing was still inside her.

After Jared left, Sara went to the restroom to pee again. She paused on the way out and searched her face in the mirror. *I told you he was immune. His love for you protects him. He won't help us.* She started crying, but the voice inside her said nothing more.

Jared drove back up I-15, pushing the speed limit, and got home at midnight. The house was dark, but his father was waiting up for him, reading at the kitchen table.

"How's Preston?" he said, eying Jared skeptically.

Jared poured himself a glass of milk and sat down across from him. "He's fine. You wouldn't wait up for me if you didn't suspect that wasn't where I was."

"Good instincts, son. So why don't you tell me where you've been? I did check with Preston's father and he said you weren't around. So why the lie?"

"I went to see Sara. But I swore not to tell anybody." Jared wanted to have his father on his side. He might be a cop, but he was also a good man. He explained why he had gone alone and what he and Sara had talked about.

Jared's father said, "If you know where she is, her mother should know. She needs to come home—"

"I know that, but I promised." Jared spread his hands out flat on the table. "She said she'd come back to have the baby in May. Until then she seems to be fine. I don't want her to hate me."

"If her mother finds out you knew where she was, she's going to string you up." Jared's father closed the book he was reading and stood up. "It's late and we should be in bed. Don't ever lie to me, son. If you had told me and explained what you were doing, we could have come up with a better strategy for persuading her to come back. You don't really know where she is or what danger she might be in."

"But you're a cop. You have to follow the law."

"When I'm on duty, sure. But I wouldn't put Sara in danger, or leave her in danger like you just did. I could have called in some favors and had her tailed."

"She texted me from a new phone number," Jared said, pulling out his phone to bring up the message.

His father jotted down the number. "I'll run this and see if anything turns up. Tomorrow—now it's time for bed."

His father went up the stairs, and Jared followed, stopping to hang his coat up in the closet. He checked the front pocket and felt a piece of paper. It was a napkin, with HELP ME written in pencil diagonally across it. He thought back to when he had left his coat on the table while he went to use the restroom —Sara must have slipped it into the pocket. He hadn't been imagining it—his Sara was still in there, trying to get back control.

He tapped out a text to the number she had called from. "Talk to me. Come home. I love you."

He went to bed with the phone next to him on the nightstand. He dreamt he heard the message chime, but when he checked his phone, there was nothing there.

As her due date approached, Sara's entourage took over the two floors at the top of the Luxor pyramid and part of the newer tower next door. Senator Hastings had brought her Warren Ribble, a DC-based political consultant who had set up a PAC and a nonprofit foundation to sprinkle grants and advertising to soften the way for her son's future political career. Billionaire donors caught a whiff of a new political machine forming and flooded them with donations. It didn't hurt that she had entertained some of the donors in her suite.

She had paid off her earliest supporters—the hotel got full-price bookings and increased traffic and Senator Hastings got more campaign funds to sprinkle around to less-funded junior members of his party. Like all political machines, hers started with a small investment of seed capital and snowballed as the wave of influence paid back earlier supporters. Corporations began to donate money as well, buying protection from whatever future power her bloc would wield. She no longer needed to convert people to get their money.

There was the inner circle who knew about the coming of the Messiah and believed they were riding a bandwagon to unimaginable riches and power when lesser humans would be cast down in the coming reckoning, and an outer circle who were just hedging their bets by being sure they had access to a new ruling faction. Somehow the Scientologists had been clued in to her activities, and they were beginning to spy on her—she had converted one of their spies into a double agent who now gave her useful intelligence. The Scientologists only had their dead prophet and false religion, though, while she had the Son of God within her. If she had time, she would convert the core leadership of that church, since they had useful international connections. But the calendar ruled—that would have to wait for the birth. She had already had more success with older religions.

The doctor recruited by Senator Hastings came by her suite to examine her. Dr. Robles was Latino, handsome, and fully converted after the initial exams turned into sexual imprintings. He had a slight stutter which disappeared when he went into doctor mode.

"Everything looks good," he said, looking up from between her legs. "Effacement is complete and your cervix is beginning to dilate. That means contractions could begin at any time, or up to a week from now. We can bring you in for induced delivery now."

"The child must be born in the place of power," Sara said. "On Spirit Mountain, in the Zion Mine. It will happen when we get there."

"Is that wise? What if I need equipment or there's an emergency?" Dr. Robles looked unhappy. "It's risky to be far from help during a birth."

"Don't worry. The outcome has been foretold. Nothing will go wrong." Sara struggled to sit up, and the doctor helped her.

"Your word is my command," the doctor said, making a joke of the truth. "I'll bring a kit."

Next she welcomed a group of the faithful who were visiting to receive the blessings of the child. This group was largely religious leaders—Buddhists, Jews, Sufis, and Mormons, as well as the older established Protestant and Catholic churches. She had been rebuffed by the current Mormon President, but had succeeded in converting three of the Twelve, younger apostles of the church, and collected a few Catholic bishops from Western cities.

The group—all but one male—crowded in to her bedroom, and one by one she summoned them forward to touch her bare belly and feel the power of the child within. Each went silent and their faces relaxed as they felt blissful communion.

"We've waited two thousand years for this," one older Catholic bishop said. "To be alive for His return!"

The young rabbi rolled his eyes. "Can you not *see*? This is the *real* Messiah. Not some retread."

Sara shushed them. "Gentlemen, please don't bring your old battles in here. The old world is about to be washed away by the birth of the new. Be silent. Empty your mind of noise and listen."

As they left, each one bowed, kissed her hand, and thanked her for the chance to serve.

Sara conferred with Vinnie and her head of security to plan the trip north. They efficiently planned a convoy of vehicles, hotel rooms, and security—highway patrols in both Nevada and Utah were informed and agreed to provide escorts for the VIP. An advance guard would go up to set up positions overlooking the mine's access road. Nothing would be left to chance and no one would be allowed near to disrupt the birth ceremony, when God's chosen spirit would enter her child and be sealed to its new physical body by Lailah's power at the moment of first breath.

One loose end remained—Sara wanted Jared to be present for the birth, but Lailah blocked her from telling him anything that might leak to opposition forces. She had sensed Lailah's control was weaker at times and she could think and even act on her own a little without her noticing. So she came up with a plan during one of those times Lailah seemed less attentive. She tried not to think about her hope that somehow Jared would be able to free her—Lailah could read her surface thoughts. Somehow she had to get him to the mine without his talking to anyone about it. She thought up a ruse....

38: Randy: Rumblings

Randy had sent Kovac the permission forms Sara's mother had signed, but since Sara could not be found Kovac could do nothing. Randy's AP American History class went on as usual, minus one of his star pupils. Jared was not contributing and seemed withdrawn, at least until he showed some interest in World War II.

Randy wanted to get Jared to talk about Sara, but Jared didn't stay after class to talk the way he used to, so there was little opportunity. Randy felt for the kid—he had let himself fall for Sara, only to have the worst happen.

But Randy was secretly relieved that she—and the threat she represented—was gone. Things were back to normal. But she was still out there, and it could all still come back to blow up his life.

But after his lecture on Reagan-Gorbachev and the end of the Cold War, Jared stayed after class to talk.

"I've been meaning to tell you," Jared said, "Sara told me a few months ago that she would come back when the baby's due. That would be soon, now."

Randy was wary. "Oh? You talked to her?"

Jared described the text and his visit to Las Vegas, as well as the clues that she was being supported by someone else. "I'm guessing she hooked up with a rich older man, rich enough to have a security detail. It was weird, like she had bodyguards."

"Did she seem—herself?" Randy tried not to use the bad word 'possessed.' Anyone hearing him talk about it assumed he was the crazy one, so he had not tried to bring it up with anyone since Sara had left.

"Some of the time. But what she said didn't always agree with her face. And she slipped a note into my pocket that asked for help. Like the guards might overhear if she said it aloud. So maybe she's trapped. But she could have left if she wanted to. I think. It was odd."

"If she's being supported, she might be staying there to avoid being on the street, which is a lot more dangerous. You asked her to come home?"

"Of course I did! But she refused. She's stubborn. She said she'd come back for the baby's birth. Something about wanting me to be there."

"So there's that, at least. Is there anything I can do to help? Kovac says he's ready to try to cure her. All we have to do is take her up to his lab or get her into a secure facility where it's safe for him to visit." Randy wished again he had gotten Sara to Kovac earlier—he knew he had delayed because he was afraid to talk to Sara's mother about it. By the time he finally had, it was too late and Sara was gone.

"When I hear from her again, I'll let you know. The number she texted me from turned out to be fake—my dad looked it up. So I have no way to reach her or find out where she is." Jared looked down at the floor. "There was nothing I could do."

❂   ❂   ❂   ❂   ❂

A few hours later, Randy finally got a chance to call Kovac when his officemates were all in class. He outlined what he had heard from Jared, and he could hear Kovac humming and typing in notes.

Kovac hit a final key, then said, "All of this comes while there are increasing levels of geomagnetic activity around your mountain. We put a sensor array around it when you first reported activity and the signals are increasing daily—something big is building. Meanwhile, our Internet dragnets are catching more chatter from cultists. Twitter and 4chan conspiracy theorists are guessing there's some new religion being born. Some of our usual cult sources have disappeared or gone silent —like an underground army is forming."

"And this has to do with Sara somehow?" Randy didn't want to be drawn further into crackpot ideas. He was willing to try Kovac's methods because they would either work or they wouldn't, but the rest of his theories seemed nutty. Spirits of the dead? Fallen angels? Souls entrapped in magnetic fields under the earth?

"Could be coincidence. But we have activity under your mountain, chatter about a Messiah, and her child about to be born. Connect the dots."

"Assuming those things are really connected, what should we do about it?" Randy had imagined he'd chauffeur Sara up to Kovac's lab for a quiet degaussing session. But now that seemed unlikely.

"Keep me posted," Kovac said. "I can be there on short notice. I have the permission to treat, so all we need is the opportunity. A place and a time where I can work on her for a few minutes without interference."

"All right. I'll let you know. Jared says it could be soon or as long as a month from now."

Jared expected to hear from Sara, but weeks went by with nothing from her. Finals came and went, and he did surprisingly well considering how down he was feeling. The graduation ceremony was held in the school gym since the auditorium wasn't large enough to hold both graduating students and well-wishers. A portable stage at one end of the gym held a podium and room for the faculty who came for the occasion, while students in their rented caps and gowns were seated in the front in rows of folding chairs, behind them family and friends.

Jared ended up sitting next to Brandy Hansen, one of the few friends who had stuck by Sara after the gossip campaign had made her *persona non grata*. Brandy smiled and took his hand without comment, holding it as the principal droned on about how well the year had gone and how high achievement and clean living went together. The principal noted the death of Jessica Peterson and pointed out how even the most virtuous could be brought down by alcohol and drugs. When the speech ended and the valedictorian was introduced, Brandy whispered, "I know you miss Sara. I wish she could have been here."

The valedictorian, a science geek girl he had always liked, showed a side of herself he'd never seen by being funny and subtly hinting that she'd be glad to move on to the greater world outside—she'd been admitted to Stanford, so her talk was a tactful "So long, suckers!" to most of the audience. Judging by the blank looks he saw around him, Jared thought she might have been too subtle. She built toward the finish of her speech with, "I'll always be grateful for my teachers, my friends, and my family." And who could take offense at that?

And then the students got their diplomas. One of the girls injured in the crash that killed Jessica Peterson was first, in a wheelchair, and the principal came down from the dais to give her the diploma. The rest of the line waited, and then the long process of reading the names and handing each graduate their diploma began. The list was alphabetical, so Jared was in the last third. The principal winced when he saw Jared was next, but hid it well, giving him a solid pat on the shoulder and a "Good job!" with a genuine smile.

And then it was over. They had been warned not to throw their caps in the air at the end, but one rebellious soul did anyway. No one paid attention, and the hubbub of families and students finding each other in the back of the gym drowned out the principal's instructions on how to exit.

Jared made his way back to where his family waited.

Kristi hugged him and said, "You made it! Can we go get ice cream now?"

Jared laughed. "We'll see. What do you say, Dad?"

His father took him into a bear hug. "Sounds like a plan. It's a thing to celebrate."

"I am so relieved!" his mother said. "I was afraid your, uh, problem—" she meant Sara but could not bear to speak her name, "—was going to haunt you. But all's well that ends well. You got into a good school anyway." BYU had put him on a wait list, then accepted him in April. Jared knew it was because Prof. Atwater had put in a recommendation which overcame his weaker grades. He was looking forward to it, but still, he felt hollow inside without Sara to share it with.

Jared spotted Mr. Wright in the front chatting with other

teachers who'd come for the ceremony.

He approached and waited for Mr. Wright to notice him.

"Jared!" Mr. Wright said, looking suddenly somber. "Congratulations."

"Thanks. I feel like a traitor for being here."

"When Sara is still gone. I understand. Her path will be more difficult. But the consensus of the faculty is that she can re-enter and make up the term whenever she applies to come back."

"I was expecting to hear from her. She said she'd come home for the birth."

"I hope she does. We'd all like to help her," Mr. Wright said, nodding to the principal, who was watching them. "The District has dealt with a number of similar cases over the years. She can finish at another high school if she wants to get a fresh start." They both knew the gossip would follow Sara wherever she went, but at least by going to a different school, she'd not have to face kids who already hated her.

Jared had set his phone on vibrate before the ceremony, and he felt it buzzing in his pocket. "I should check this," he said, pulling it out. "Excuse me." Mr. Wright nodded and Jared moved to one side.

The message was from an unknown number. "Congrats on your graduation. I'm waiting at the west door. I don't want anyone to see me."

Jared caught Mr. Wright's eye and pointed to his phone. Mouthing "Sara," Jared turned and hurried to the west fire exit, which opened when he pushed on the safety bar. He looked around outside—there were people leaving from the main doors to the south, but no one near him. As he looked around, he heard an engine rev nearby, and a black limo drove up and stopped abruptly in front of him. He could see Sara in the front passenger seat—she waved, and he started toward the car. The rear doors opened, and two men in black suits got out and rushed him.

Before he could react, one had pulled his legs out from under him and the other leaned down to stab his thigh with a needle. They picked him back up and hustled him into the back seat of the car as his vision faded and his face was ground into the carpeted floor. He could dimly hear the men talking, but it stopped meaning anything as he lost consciousness.

40: Randy: The Chase

Randy was chatting with Suzette Handler when he noticed Jared was trying to get his attention, pointing at his phone and mouthing "Sara." Suzette followed his eyes and cut off her sentence, then said, "Jared's on a mission!"

"I think you're right. Excuse me, will you? I should get his father involved."

Randy saw the Spendloves still talking by the back door. Roger Spendlove looked his way, so Randy waved and beckoned to get his attention. Randy made his way to the back.

"Roger? I am guessing Jared just got a message from Sara."

"And hightailed it out the exit door. Shall we go see what he's up to?"

Randy nodded, and Jared's father told the rest of the family to wait. They strode to the west exit door.

Outside, they saw a black car with dark-tinted glass drive off, leaving the parking lot and accelerating up the street. Randy thought he recognized Sara in the front passenger seat. The car slowed, then blew through the red light at the first cross street.

"I think Sara was in that car. She was the lure," Randy said. "Jared must have gone with them."

"We may have a crime in progress," Roger said. "Let's go." He led Randy to his car. "Get in and buckle up."

Roger pushed a button below the dash. "LED lights and siren, hidden in the front grill." The car took off down the street, the siren blaring. The black car ahead of them accelerated further and started pulling away. Roger floored it, and the intersections went by faster and faster as other cars pulled over to the right to let them pass.

The car ahead of them made it through another red. Randy gripped the dash as their car closed on the red light, and a car crossing from the side street slowed and stopped right in front of them. Roger braked and screeched around the stopped car. Randy glimpsed the shocked face of the old woman driving as they passed a foot or two in front of her car.

The black car had pulled far ahead, and turned right, toward the freeway entrance. Roger made the turn on two wheels. He called in to ask for backup and for someone to call in the information to the Highway Patrol in case they got on the Interstate.

Randy got his phone out and called Kovac's number. A recording answered, and he waited to record a message. Then it was Kovac live, breaking in,

"Randy, I'm at home. What's up?" He sounded sleepy.

"Jared got a message from Sara, it looks like it lured him out for a kidnapping. I'm with his father, we're a mile east of town, heading for the freeway. They're in a black car."

"Can you send your precise coordinates? I can follow along on the map."

Randy fiddled with the phone. Where was that app? He pulled up the mapping app and hit the button that would text his location. "Did you get that?"

He heard Kovac typing. "Yes. What would you like us to do?"

"When we find out where they're going, there's a good chance Sara will be there. Can you come down with your magic machines?"

"It would take two hours to get a team together and get down there. I'll get things started here. We have a helicopter—"

Randy had put the call on speaker, and Roger looked surprised at that. "—So we can be down there in twenty minutes once we know our target."

The car they were chasing turned again, away from the freeway ramp and toward the state highway that hugged the foothills of the mountains.

"Okay," Randy said. "It looks like they might be heading for the mine. I'll let you know as soon as we know." He hung up.

Roger cleared his throat. "Who was that? A team with a helicopter?"

Randy filled him in on Kovac's team of exorcists—and the quiet LDS and government support for Kovac's work.

Roger had trouble believing it. "But he's got a post at BYU because he saved a church leader?" He looked thoughtful. "I did ask around about him and got some odd answers. Kovac's theory would explain why Sara changed overnight."

The car in front of them pulled onto the two-lane state highway and increased its speed. Roger accelerated to keep it in sight. "And these guys tell me someone important is interested in Jared and Sara. These guys are pros."

Spirit Mountain loomed above them, snowcapped peaks above and forested below. The white Zion Mine buildings stepped up the side of the mountain, glimpsed between trees.

Soon they saw the car in front turn into the mine access road. An official car was parked next to the gate and two men in paramilitary getups guarded it. They waved the black car in. Roger pulled over to the shoulder as one of the men closed the gate, the black car speeding up the driveway to the first hairpin turn.

Roger conjured a gun from somewhere into his right hand.

"That's a Highway Patrol car," he said. "But those don't look like state troopers. I'm getting a bad feeling about this." He shifted into reverse and backed down the shoulder slowly until the gate was just out of sight behind some bushes. "They know we're here, but I want to get some backup before getting close." He got on the radio.

The tinny radio voice had bad news. "Highway Patrol says that vehicle is being escorted under national security orders; requests cooperation—their words were, 'Back off.' Our Unit 3 is on the way, but there are no other units available."

Roger looked disgusted. "Copy that." Turning to Randy, he said, "These guys have some pull with the Feds. Dispatch is sending Phil and Sandy. I'm supposed to just let them walk over us."

"But they took Jared," Randy said. "Surely the feds don't know that—"

"That might not matter," Roger said bleakly. "As a courtesy, we're supposed to give national security ops a wide berth. But they have no legal standing to prevent me from investigating a crime in progress. Trouble is, I can't be taking on those guys with two uniformed officers—God love'em, but those two are wimps—and we're handicapped by our limited equipment."

Randy looked up the hill—aside from thick grass and trees further on, the path straight up the hill to the mine was open, and shielded from view from the road entrance by a ridge.

"Any reason we can't just hike straight up?" he said, pointing.

Roger thought. "It'll be ten minutes before our guys can get here, and that's not enough to safely approach these guys." He picked up the radio handset again. "Proceeding on foot to the mine buildings. Unit 3 should watch and wait at our current location pending further backup. When we have more people, block the road and prevent anyone from leaving."

The acknowledgement came and Roger got out, checking again to be sure no one was visible on the road. Randy joined him as he opened the trunk and pulled out a rifle. "M-14, surplus. Not up to what those guys are carrying, I expect." He opened another case and pulled out a double-barrelled shotgun. "This is mine, good for hunting. You take it. Point in the direction of enemy and squeeze the trigger. I'll carry the shells. Just in case."

Randy took the gun. It wasn't the first time he'd held a shotgun, but it had been years. "Uh, are we really going to need weapons?"

"I'd say we might, looking at what we're up against. We'll sneak up and take a look. If there's something we can do without risking Jared or getting into a firefight with what might be a legal security company, we'll do it. If not, we'll consider our options and come back down if they look bad. They can't take him away without my guys seeing them."

They waded through the tall grass and weeds, burrs sticking to their pants legs. As they entered the thin forest, a dusting of snow covered the ground where the sun hadn't reached.

They came to an old barbed-wire fence and stepped carefully through the loose wires. The going got steeper and rockier, then they crossed the mine road. Looking down, the main road was hidden by trees and brush.

"Straight up?" Randy asked, and Roger nodded, jumping across the ditch on the uphill side of the road.

They climbed through another copse of trees. The buildings

of the mine were starting to show through the trees in front of them. They crossed the mine road again. As they cleared the last copse of trees, the mine parking area was visible behind a line of brush. Randy could see movement and the shimmer of light reflected from four cars and a black van.

"You want to call in your friend with the helicopter?" Roger said. "This is a good landing spot. If we can be sure they won't be fired on."

"I'll send the location and warn them not to get too close until we say so." Randy texted the message and sent their coordinates. The reply came quickly: UNDERSTOOD ETA 20 MIN.

"Wait here," Roger whispered. "I'm going to sneak a better look." Crouched, he crept forward, rifle held ready. Randy was surprised Roger was so graceful—at least fifty and paunchy, he moved like a stalking cat.

Randy saw more movement by the mine building's open garage doors. Two men in suits came out, blinking in the afternoon sunshine after being in the darker interior. They were talking quietly and he couldn't quite hear well enough to understand. The black one lit a cigarette and began to puff. The other had a bright red buzz cut. They chatted amiably, laughing.

Randy returned. "Got the plate numbers for two of the vehicles. The two guys talking are all I can see, the interior looks empty. The rest of them must be deeper inside."

"How are we going to make sure it's safe for the helicopter to land?" Randy felt like he had stepped into a bad cop show.

"Well, we can hope these guys go back in, then take positions at the door and make sure nobody comes back out."

"Does that involve shooting?"

Roger grinned. "It might. Do it right, we just tell them we're cops, yell some official-sounding orders, and fire at the ceiling if they come at us. They'll hide."

The minutes ticked down—ten minutes left, then five. The black guy finished his cigarette and ground it into the dirt with his foot. The two men went back inside, still talking and gesturing.

"This would be our chance," Roger said, waving Randy forward. They took up positions on either side of the door. Roger stuck his head out to check inside. "They're gone. Passages go way back. You can tell your helicopter guys it's a go."

Randy texted Kovac: CLEAR TO LAND.

Two minutes later, a mid-sized helicopter—painted a uniform gray, with the Noumenal Foundation symbol and numbers on the side—came up over the closest ridge where it had apparently been hovering out of sight. The noise increased and Randy looked back inside the mine in case anyone had come to investigate—no. Randy waved at Kovac sitting in the front passenger seat, and the helicopter settled to a landing in the center of the clearing. The side door slid open, and two men with rifles jumped out. They quickly surveyed the area and signalled okay.

Kovac himself came next, followed by his assistant, Kumiko, who wore the same tactical outfit as the men. The copter shut down, but the blades kept turning slowly.

"What's the situation?" Kovac yelled over the noise.

"At least two armed inside," Roger said. "Most likely more. Sara and Jared are probably with them."

"I rounded up the guys with military experience," Kovac said. "We're not set up for firefights. But something big is going down—the sensors are overloaded from all the activity. The spirits are restless. Good thing we had some trainees visiting." He opened a metal case and took out what looked like a Geiger counter, a small box with a handle. "Take this," he said, handing it to Randy. "The LEDs will light in the direction of the strongest signals. When we go in, tell us which way to go. My guys will take point, Kumiko the rear. Let's go."

The darkness inside the mine grew as they went further in. Old machinery loomed to one side, and tunnels split off in two directions. Randy looked down at the detector, and whispered, "Go left." The men in front walked slowly, scanning the path ahead and to the sides for danger.

Roger whispered, "Everyone stop. I think I hear something." When silence fell, they could hear a rustling and faint voices in the distance in front of them.

"I'll go look around the corner," Kumiko said. She crept forward warily to the next intersecting tunnel a hundred feet ahead. Crouching down and peeking around the corner, she looked back at them and shook her head, waving them forward. "They're even deeper," she whispered. "The rock walls reflect the sound."

They came to a jagged opening in the side wall. Roger sniffed. "Explosives," he said. "Recent." Through the jagged opening they could see another tunnel with smooth stone walls, quite unlike the mine tunnels.

"They're that way," Randy said. The LEDs were brighter, pointing toward the opening and down.

The front men stepped through, and the party walked another few hundred feet, subtly down, then the tunnel turned and they were going down more steeply, until the floor flattened and broadened out. Their flashlights revealed—an underground town? A wide concourse was lined with what looked like building fronts with cut-stone door and window openings. It reminded Randy of pictures of Petra, the "rose-red city half as old as time" in Jordan.

The group paused as the men aimed their lights into a side room. They could feel air moving, coming from what looked like a long tunnel at the other end. Disintegrating cloth and two mummified bodies were huddled against the side wall.

"Looks like there was another way in," Roger whispered. "I wonder how many hikers were lured in and never got out?"

Randy showed them the detector display. "We're going the wrong way. We need to get back to the main concourse."

"We can find out where this goes later," Roger said, leading them back. The concourse led further to a curve. When they rounded the curve, a light shone through a doorway at the far end.

"Strong signal from that direction," Randy whispered.

"Lights off," one of the men said. "We should approach from darkness."

41: Sara: Labor

The convoy up I-15 to Mt. Hermon had taken half a day, since they stopped for lunch in St. George. Sara was having contractions, but Dr. Robles timed them and pronounced everything in order for induced labor that evening. As the convoy approached Mt. Hermon, Sara felt herself losing direct control of her body —Lailah was growing stronger, and exulting in her power to see through Sara's eyes and feel as Sara felt. Lailah's animal joy reminded Sara of how lucky she was to be young and healthy. The cost was that she was now watching Lailah and her own body from a distance. She realized she should be angry and fight back, but she had lost the will to do so.

The rest of the convoy went on to the Zion Mine to set up security checkpoints around it, while her car drove to the high school where Jared would be attending his graduation ceremony. Sara had timed everything to lure him outside where she could talk him into coming with them. Lailah had other ideas— she heard herself ordering the doctor to prepare an anaesthetic for injection, the doctor instructing one of the goons on where to inject it. Lailah wanted a quick snatch without the risk of his refusing and calling for help. Sara struggled to object, screaming no inside, but Lailah ignored her.

Sara watched Jared taken down and knocked out. Sara-locked-inside melted when she saw the look of hope on Jared's face as he came out of the door in the blank brick wall of the gym and looked for her, then felt guilt as the goons threw him into the back seat. *My love, I will make this up to you someday if I can.*

The driver and security team were concerned when they heard a distant siren and noticed a car following them. "Unmarked cop car, special siren kit," one observed. They sped up and tried to lose it, but it was still behind them when they reached the mine road gate, which had been opened for them.

"It's stopped well back. Probably calling for backup," the driver said. "Won't they be surprised?" Since the leader of the state police had been suborned to their cause, no large force would be coming to this local cop's assistance. They would have time.

They found the rest of the convoy parked up by the mine buildings. The garage door yawned open and lights had been set up inside. Sara got out to direct the demolition team down to the spot of tunnel wall she knew blocked the way to the Nephi storehouse underneath—Lailah's master had influenced the original miners to prepare the way for the day he would be reborn by coming close to the buried chambers, but redirected them whenever they got close to breaking through. Funded by the gold and riches stored there, Sara's child would crush all opposition and remake the world for the rule of the spirits below.

The explosives opened up a wide hole in the rock that led to the upper galleries of the buried Nephi city. The tunnels were still filled with smoke and dust, so they had to wait a few minutes before returning. The doctor handed out dust masks and flashlights, and they went in.

Dust was thick on the floor. The stone of the halls and trim was beautifully worked, and where the doctor brushed the dust aside with his foot, the floor was black granite with inlays of iridescent opal. Lailah recognized the inlaid symbol—the Seal of Melchizedek, an eight-pointed star made of interlocking squares. Sara recognized it from somewhere but didn't know what it meant. But she could tell Lailah was afraid of its power, that it was from an age when wise men understood how dangerous the fallen angels were to humanity.

Lailah led them to the throne room (as Sara dubbed it), a long hall with a raised platform at the end with two massive golden chairs. It looked to her like some medieval king and queen's audience hall, minus the velvet drapery. Jared was brought in on a stretcher and moved to a low table where the doctor hooked him up to a drip IV.

"Doctor, it's time," Lailah said through Sara. "Induce labor." She stripped and lay down next to Jared, and the doctor injected her.

"This may take hours or days," he observed.

"I have my ways," Lailah responded. "The baby will arrive within the hour. I will it so."

"Do you want an epidural pain block?" the doctor asked, gesturing to his kit bag.

Lailah laughed. "We have no need for such things."

Sara felt another contraction beginning, and this time the pain was intense. She felt it ease as Lailah blocked it from her. *Thanks for that.* She felt Lailah's amusement in response.

Sara sensed a massive presence, a masculine power intruding into their consciousness. She could overhear the unvoiced conversation between Lailah and the presence.

"I AM READY," the presence thundered.

"All is well," Lailah thought back. "I will prepare your way into the newborn at birth, and seal your soul into the new flesh."

Sara felt the room shaking, but it was just a projection of the presence's power. "AND YOU SHALL BE MY QUEEN," it roared.

"Samyaza, my King!" Lailah replied.

And the next contraction began—Sara felt herself stretched beyond possibility. Her consciousness fled.

42: Jared: Submerged

Jared dreamed.

He found himself in a dark world. Everything was shades of dark, a rich tapestry of absence, threaded with deeper satin blacks. The one hint of color was the orange-red of flames on the horizon—his mind settled on the idea of Mordor, and what he saw then snapped into focus as a vast plain spread out before him, a darkling plain. He knew that was a literary reference he had seen, and the armies of darkness clashed below to the sound of pain and chaos.

He felt a presence and a cobalt blue glow beside him and turned to see a new angel, not dressed in simple robes like Raphael, but superhuman and armored in gleaming metal and carrying a sword. His face was rough with age and he was bearded. Scars marred his face, yet he was beautiful. He looked up, and his eyes bore into Jared's.

"You who are about to battle Darkness, greetings. I am Michael, brought in by Raphael to prepare you for battle."

"Where am I?" Jared said.

"You are in the Underworld. I was able to bring your spirit into the world down below. We don't have much time since your mortal form is being brought closer to the nexus—a place of power where the ancient spirits dwelling in the earth can most easily influence the outer world. Our power is increased here as well, but we are only able to shield you from the others for a little while longer. Soon they will break through and you will have to find a way to defeat them."

"How will I fight them? I mean, I have no weapons—" Jared

showed his empty hands.

"Everything here is a projection of the symbols and ideas the dwellers in darkness have stolen from humans over history. The demons are fields of energy locked in struggle to survive and dominate others. You bring your own memories and symbols in with you—and you must use your will to make them real in this realm." Michael reached out with both arms and held Jared's head between his hands. Jared felt strength flow into him. "The Nephilim—the fallen angels who were struck down by God and bound to endless pain here, far from the grace of His presence—are ever influencing men, trying to tempt them to sin. They saw in your union with Sara a chance to escape—to have Samyaza, their leader, reborn in your son's body, to prepare the way for the rest to be restored to flesh, to enjoy again the pleasures denied them, to defy God yet again and make mankind their slaves."

"Why us? Why now?"

"Your child will unite the bloodlines of Jesus Christ and the apostle Joseph Smith. Sara is descended from the families of Mary and Joseph, and you are a direct descendant of Joseph Smith's father. Your coming together so close to the nexus was an opportunity they could not resist." Michael withdrew his hands, leaving Jared feeling cold and alone.

Jared thought back. "But—they didn't push us together, did they? I mean, Sara wasn't voodooed into liking me, was she?"

"No, they only magnified an attraction that was already there. She truly loves you." Michael smiled. "It is a miracle when it happens. Even we who are awed by the power of God's love respect the new love of two humans. It is resonant with the natural order of Creation. It is, as your people say, what makes the world go 'round. That is why they are bringing you to be with her at the birth—there is power in your presence near her. It will ease the sealing of Samyaza's spirit with your newborn son. But you must stop that from happening, or the world as you know it will end—the Nephilim will enslave humanity, and God will again have to cleanse the Earth with fire and flood."

"But—who are you, really? There are good spirits? What's in it for you?"

Michael beckoned a figure in the distance, who approached. He was gray-haired and bearded, and wore armor gleaming with gold inlay.

"I bring you Moroni, a great general of your Nephi. He was human once, but was elevated after his death. We are both angels loyal to God—we can enter the Underworld with some difficulty, just as we can appear to human beings. As the Nephilim sway humans to sin, we work to influence men to work toward that union with God that they may achieve, with time and wisdom. To 'level up,' as you put it."

Moroni nodded. "It was I who wrote down your Book of Mormon, when I was alive, and stored it for your ancestor Joseph Smith to find. There is a copy in the library of the storehouse you are being taken to which we prepared for your people's time of need."

Without thinking, Jared blurted out, "But—that's why they excommunicated the guy that started it. He said there was gold —"

"There is. And precious stones, and books of lore. The treasures of our people, stored before our doom. Enough to sustain your people when the rest of the world is collapsing."

Michael nodded to Moroni, who began to recede, saluting.

"Good fighting, young man. You are of the blood of champions. I see it within you."

Michael watched as Moroni faded into the distance. "He was quite a man. A man of letters, but a fierce warrior as well. But now time's nearly up. You need to know what's about to happen."

"Tell me." Jared wished he had spent more time on the earliest texts of the Bible which mentioned the wicked giants. He had thought those parts foolish legends from prehistory, exaggerated in the retelling. "How can I fight them?"

"Their weapons are your fears and weaknesses. You defeat them when you transcend your own fears and face reality with courage and purpose. You cannot hurt them, but you can make them powerless to harm you and yours." Michael winced, and turned to look toward the red glow on the horizon. "Samyaza marshals his forces. Let me show you one more thing."

The plain faded and Jared found himself watching as a mob of angry men, faces blackened, flowed down a rough street to gather around the doors of a squarish two-story stone building. "The jail in Carthage, Illinois, where Joseph Smith and his brother Hyrum are being held on charges of sedition." Their viewpoint went through a wall and upstairs into the room of the jail where Smith—who Jared recognized from all the por-traits he had seen—and some other men tried to hold closed the wooden door against the men trying to push their way in through it. A shot was fired through the door, hitting one defender in the face. "That is Hyrum Smith, Joseph's brother," Michael commented. "He died quickly."

The door was pushed open and rifle barrels came through the opening, firing blindly. "Smith had a pistol that had been smuggled to him and tried to shoot back. But to no avail." Jared saw Smith empty his pistol then run for the window. Bullets hit him, once, twice, three times. He staggered back towards the window and fell through it.

Then they were back at street level, watching as jeering men dragged Smith to a wall, where they propped him up. The men stood back and three of them shot Smith a dozen times, until his blood pooled under him and ran over the ground to the gutter. "The killers were tried and acquitted, and the governor of Illinois later said the expulsion of the Mormons had been good for them and that Smith had been 'the most successful imposter in modern times.'"

And then they were back. "You should meet your forebear," Michael said, and out of the mists walked Joseph Smith, wearing the clothes Jared had just seen him in, but his face was placid and unmarked.

"It's gratifying to see my family has done well," Smith said. "You are a fine young man, about to be tested, as we were. I will be watching." Smith faded into smoke which dissipated.

Jared wondered. *All of this is a dream, and these people are just figments of my imagination.*

Michael laughed. "But your dreams are real, down here. And they can hurt you. Our time is up—they are pounding on the door to get in. You will have to defeat them yourself. We can lend you our strength, but you must be the one to use it."

Michael disappeared, and from somewhere a great wind howled, and clouds streamed toward him from the red-glowing horizon. The world dissolved and reformed.

Jared struggled against bonds—he was tied to a rack. In

front of him, a brazier glowed with hot coals and iron instruments. He heard laughter, and gagged at the overpowering smell—a rank, vile, animal smell, of rot and garbage and gangrene combined.

"Welcome to my kingdom," a low, gravelly voice said. A chiseled face like animated stone loomed in front of him, with the hairy body of a goat below—a satyr? The prominent phallus dangled between its legs, dark red and throbbing.

"Samyaza is one of my many names. I have been waiting for this moment for thousands of your years." The demon reached for the tongs in the brazier. The tips glowed red-hot. He brought them closer to Jared's face. He could feel the heat on his cheeks. "I could just burn out your eyes. But then you would not see what I have done to the rest of your delicate parts."

The monster brought the tongs down toward his crotch. "But not there, either," he said. "Best to save the best for last. We start with something you won't miss so much. All you have to do is bow to me and accept me as your master, and I won't have to damage you at all."

"Never," Jared sputtered. "None of this is real. You can't hurt me."

"Let's test your belief, shall we?" Samyaza held the tongs near his bare feet. "You sure you want to defy me?"

Jared tried to spit in his face, but his mouth was desert-dry.

Samyaza squeezed, and the ends of the tongs burned into Jared's big toe. He screamed as the pain blanked out all thought.

"See? It really does hurt. I tried to spare you. Any second thoughts?"

Jared's tears flowed and he struggled to catch his breath. *Wait, I don't need to breathe. None of this is real.* "I will never serve you. And you can't have our son."

"I have you, and soon your son. Might as well save yourself while you can. Your life will be easy under my rule. You can have Sara. You can have other brats with her." The demon took another tool from the brazier—the glowing end was a brand. He brought the glowing end close to Jared's chest. "Still time to get to yes. I'm told this kind of body marking is trendy in your world."

"Go to hell."

"Hah, you're funny. Where do you think we are?" The brand pressed into his flesh. The pain was staggering, and Jared smelled his flesh burning.

The agony clouded his thinking, but he clung to what Michael had told him. This world was all inside his head. If Samyaza was creating these hallucinations from his own nightmares, he could fight back if he could marshal his own thoughts. He settled on the idea of water to fight fire, imagining a great waterfall, all the pictures he had ever seen of Niagara Falls, plus the time they had visited Snoqualmie Falls in Washington. Water thundered over his head, the roar deafening him. And then he realized the water had washed away Samyaza and his brazier of hot implements. He was cool and the pain of the burns had vanished.

He could still hear the dripping of water runoff, and his imagination supplied a rain forest. But the sun came out and the clouds thinned, and soon he was kneeling on a sunbaked hillside. Looking up, he heard crowds jeering and saw three crosses, three crucified men bleeding and near death, and Roman soldiers taunting them as the crowd cheered the soldiers on. He recognized Samyaza as the soldier who was leading the others, and watched in horror as the soldier thrust his spear into the belly of one of the hanging men. He was sure he smelled the blood and viscera....

And then he was looking down from his cross at the up-raised faces, some jeering and some sad. He heard a sigh as the man hanging next to him expired, one last breath released into the wind.

And then it was his turn, as Samyaza jeered at him and plunged the spear into his belly.

He screamed in agony as the spear tore through his gut. It was a few seconds before he could focus enough to ignore the pain and concentrate on changing the scene.

He imagined himself growing as his anger filled him. His arms and legs grew muscular, veins popping, with a greenish tinge. His bonds broke and he jumped down from the cross as the nails lost their hold. He confronted Samyaza and attacked....

And then—his pulse raced and he was nowhere, in black-ness. He worked at conjuring up something, and thought of Sara.

Gradually he became aware of Sara by his side, and figures looking down on them.

The booming voice of Samyaza echoed in the room. "It is done!"

A doctor loomed over Sara, wearing a white mask and hat. He held up a pink, wet newborn. The baby gasped and began to cry.

Samyaza's voice was a loud whisper in his head. "You fought well, Jared, but your son is mine now, and your Sara is dead."

43: Randy: Standoff

As Randy, Roger, and Kovac's team approached the doorway to the lighted chamber in the dark, they could see further into the lighted room beyond. It was another large space, floored in granite tile and lit by lights along the walls like sconces. There were people at the other end of the room, gathered around a raised platform. Gold glinted from the altar and throne chairs set up on either side of a table where two bodies lay side-by-side.

The guards at the door must have heard them coming. One shouted, "Halt! Don't come any closer!" He fired his rifle over their heads and then returned to cover.

"Shit has hit the fan," Roger observed. They scattered to find cover in doorways on either side. It was a standoff; they couldn't rush the door without taking bullets, but they could stop anyone from leaving. The guards at the door were joined by others from across the room. One of them shouted, "We are FBI. Stand down. Throw your weapons down and come out with your hands in the air."

Randy and Kovac had taken cover in the same doorway. Opposite them, Roger peeked around the corner of his alcove. "These boys aren't any FBI I know," Roger shouted. "Is there anything we can do from here?"

Kovac was opening the case he had carried in, pulling out a metal box. "I can set up the field generator. It won't do much from this distance but give the demons a headache. But it's worth trying." He turned some knobs and the display came on. "Very high readings ahead. This—" he pushed a slider up to max, "—should make them squeal." He plugged in the gunlike attachment and aimed it around the corner toward the platform, then pressed the trigger. The box hummed and the graphs on the screen changed.

44: Sara: Crowning

Sara felt the contractions, but it was all some distance away. Lailah was exulting, orgasmic and panting with exertion as the baby pushed out a little more with each contraction. Sara felt more through Lailah than directly as Lailah had taken over her sensory inputs. Sara was locked away inside her own mind, but freer to think while Lailah was preoccupied with operating Sara's body.

Dr. Robles coached her to breathe. "The crowning has begun." The baby's head was squashed as it stretched her wide to push through. "An apropos term for this occasion, no?"

Lailah grunted in response. Sara sensed movement in her mind—the portal between the Underworld where Samyaza's pattern waited and the baby's brain was also opening wide, and Samyaza was beginning to slip through, tendrils of his spirit beginning to take root in the neural networks of the about-to-be-born.

Sara could feel Jared next to her. He convulsed and cried out.

45: Jared: Compulsion

Jared spun down through the dark, despairing. He had failed and all was lost.

But then he remembered his father's words. *Never give up. If they knock you down, get back up and keep fighting.*

This was no schoolyard fight. This was a fight for his life, his future, and his family.

None of this is real. That was Raphael's musical voice, and he could see the green glow of his goodness and the flowing red of his hair in his mind's eye.

We fight for the ones we love. That was Michael's strength he felt.

Satan is the father of lies. That was Bishop Snow's voice, and he sensed the bishop near, avuncular and solid.

Time to get back up.

Jared remembered when he had first met Sara, when she was an anime elf on his screen in Morpheum Online. He filled out the memory, made it real and solid. And he remembered how he had loved her. She couldn't be dead—he gave her some of his health points. Her cheeks turned rosy and her eyes opened.

Then he worked on himself.

He was again Starclaw, Thane of Falconhurst. He was heavily muscled, armored, and fast. He had his axe in one hand, and he conjured up the Sword of Righteousness in the other. He was coldly angry and ready to avenge his family.

The world around him filled in, and he was in Morpheum's version of the Underworld, colorful and full of hidden treasures and adventure. His sword edges sparked electric blue as currents of magic flowed through and around it.

He was at the head of his Army of Light, facing the Dark Lord Samyaza and his Army of Darkness. Lightning streaked across the sky and thunder roared as the facing armies began to run toward each other. The rains fell, and the field turned to mud, churned up by the battle, warhorses stumbling.

A hundred feet still separated the main bodies of the armies when a screeching from above caused his front men to look up. Enormous flying creatures with leathery wings—dragons!— were diving toward them, and his men screamed as they were picked off the ground and impaled by the talons of the scaly beasts. His line broke in confusion and the enemy cried out and ran faster toward them.

Jared knew these creatures—they were from a game he had played years ago and didn't belong in Morpheum. He thought back to remember how they were fought, and visualized another creature from memory—the giant basilisk, a serpent whose skin was impervious to dragon flame and whose gaze could stun a dragon and bring it to the ground where it could be attacked. His first basilisk was weak and blurred, but in his second effort he got it almost perfect, and that one hissed as it saw the dragons flying above and slithered toward where the dragons were coming in low for an attack.

He lost more men, and one of the dragons attacked him while he was trying to create a third basilisk. The dragon released a gout of flame toward him, singeing Starclaw's long hair, but before it got close enough for a killing strike, the new basilisk looked directly into its eyes and the dragon faltered and crashed to the ground in front of him, digging a furrow before coming to rest only a few feet away, its ruby eyes dimmed in shock.

Jared stepped forward and swung the heavy sword. The dragon's head bounced away, bluish blood spraying everywhere as it died. He turned his attention back to creating basilisks, and sent more off to fight for him.

The battle lines had crashed together and hand-to-hand fighting was spreading as the two armies intermingled. More dragons fell, and the basilisks were making quick work of them and any orcs who happened to be near.

Starclaw was injured—Jared sensed that the dragon's flame had badly burned his skin and his health and energy levels were dangerously low. One of the last dragons in the sky, the largest remaining, banked and dived toward him. No basilisk was near, and the dragon's flame seared him again as he dodged the talons. The dragon's spiked tail struck him a glancing blow, knocking him to the ground.

Jared's senses dimmed. He heard a great crash—one of the basilisks had circled back and downed the dragon who had attacked him. He opened his eyes and saw the basilisk and the dragon fighting, with the weakened dragon trying to push away from the basilisk's snakelike jaws and sharp fangs. The dragon clawed at the basilisk's head but the basilisk twisted away before bringing his jaws down on the dragon's neck. Jared could sense the venom being injected into the dragon's twitching body, and it was soon still.

Which didn't help his avatar. Jared knew he needed rest to recover.

As he thought, he noticed the elf representing Sara was nearby—had she just appeared, or had she been there all along?

She was suddenly by his side, and he felt her open his breast-plate to apply ointments and rub in magic herbs she had in her pouch. She waved a sprig of greenery over him, and he felt much better—stronger, and all pain was gone. She smiled, and it was like his Sara, warm and funny and calling him to adventures they would have…. She faded and suddenly he heard the noise of battle again.

A revived Starclaw stood up, picked up his weapons, and looked around. The sky was clear of dragons and the features of the battlefield had changed again. He made his way through his own forces toward the heaviest fighting.

And then the orcish forces of the enemy were on him.

He swung his axe and decapitated the first orc that charged him and stabbed the second with his sword. He spotted Samyaza's black armor and red-crested helmet across a gully full of orcs—it would be suicide to cross. He looked around and signalled some of his troops to follow, then jumped across, taking off another orc's head as he did.

On the other side, his fellows cleared an area around them, but that only attracted more orcs. They found themselves back-to-back, facing out to take on a continuous stream of attackers.

His people were tiring. They might each take out ten orcs in a row, but the orcs were fresh though clumsy, while his men were running on empty. He could sense their energy levels dropping, and the man to his left cried out as he was run through by a particularly large orc. Starclaw took the orc's head off with one swing of his sword, the green orc blood sizzling along the blue-glowing cutting edge. But they weren't going to last long surrounded like this.

He killed another orc, and then he found himself face to

face with Samyaza, who called for his fighters to stop. "It is time to take this one off the board," Samyaza said, "so leave him to me."

They faced each other as the soldiers near them backed away and watched. The silence near them expanded as word of the duel spread, until they could see every face turned toward them and silence fell, broken only by the cries and moans of the wounded.

"Come on, Hero," Samyaza taunted, "I'll let you have the first move."

Jared weighed his options. If he kept both axe and sword, he'd be slowed down. But his axe was more familiar. The Sword of Righteousness had more powerful magic. Drop one? He decided.

Jared ran at Samyaza, throwing the axe as hard as he could at Samyaza's head.

Samyaza ducked to one side, and the axe blade nicked his shoulder, leaving a gouge on his armor but not slowing him down as he turned to swing his mighty blade to meet Jared's chest.

Or where Jared's chest would have been, but Jared had pushed right with his last step, and the tip of Samyaza's sword missed his neck by inches.

Jared's blade thrust upward toward Samyaza's chest—and was knocked away by the return swing of Samyaza's sword.

And then Jared was behind Samyaza, and they both turned to face each other again. Their swords clashed, striking blue and gold sparks as their blades slid against each other.

Jared heard a cry and saw motion out of the corner of his eye—distracted, he looked. It was his father, being held with a knife at his throat by a grinning orc. His father's eyes pleaded with him...

In the milliseconds he was distracted, Samyaza swung his sword again, this time connecting with Jared's armored chest. The blow didn't penetrate far, but the shock wave from the impact staggered Jared and he fell back as Samyaza pressed his advantage.

Jared saw an opening. He kneeled as Samyaza's sword whistled over his head, then thrust upwards with his sword. The point hit Samyaza's bare cheek and penetrated, blood spurting. The white of bone showed where flesh had been torn away as the sword carved back along the cheekbone until stopped by Samyaza's helmet, then dug deeper into his temple.

Sara cried out—and there she was, her naked human form crawling on the ground toward him. Jared knew this was another attempt to distract him.

Samyaza growled and tore away the gibbet of flesh hanging below his eye. He didn't slow as he attacked again.

And this time Jared was ready. He used the false Sara's body as a launch pad and soared into the air, somersaulting above Samyaza, swinging his sword down and across Samyaza's exposed neck. The sword parted skin and cut windpipe and arteries before crunching into vertebrae. It stopped before completely severing the neck, but the damage was enough to stagger Samyaza, who fell backward and slammed into the ground.

Jared stood over him and paused. He heard the gurgling of Samyaza's last breaths through blood and fluids, but he held the sword high and thrust it again through the gaping mouth and back through the brainstem. The body shook, then was still.

Around him the muttering of the troops rose in volume. Jared put his boot on Samyaza's head and his voice thundered across the battlefield: "The forces of Light have won this day! Tremble and flee when we invoke the Holy and terrible Name of Jesus!"

And the field dissolved into wisps of smoke as a new scene appeared.

He saw a room, figures watching as a doctor tended a woman giving birth—Sara, her legs parted, screaming as a baby forced its way into the world. He recognized his own sleeping body next to her on the table. But the image of Sara was doubled: he could see a shadow inside her which leaned forward to hold the baby in its ghostly hands, while dark tendrils streamed from below into the baby's head.

Jared cried out and he saw his body stir. Then looking down at his hands, he saw he still had the Sword of Righteousness. He flew toward Sara and swung it at the shadowy figure leaning out of her.

Blue sparks flew as the sword passed through the spirit of Lailah, and she screamed and dissipated into mist. He struck again at the black tendrils, and they were cut through and dissolved like smoke in the blue fire.

And then the baby came through, and the doctor picked him up as he began crying and gasping for air. Jared saw its spirit, bright and clean, and was proud.

46: Randy: Intervention

"Nothing seems to be happening," Randy observed. "Is your machine working?"

Kovac looked up from the display. "It is. We're getting readings that show decreasing activity, so some of the demons are leaving the area."

Jared's father fired again to keep the guards back, then looked over at Randy. "Doesn't affect the humans any, though."

They waited. The guards stayed inside, Randy firing occasionally to remind them why venturing out would be dangerous.

"We can't stay here too long," Roger said. "My people are tied down at the entrance. The bad guys won't give themselves up. If we don't get more state backup, we're sitting ducks when those guys inside the room decide to rush us."

And so they waited as the chanting inside rose to a crescendo.

Then something changed. They heard a wailing, and they could feel it in the air—the oppressive fear had lifted. Looking inside the throne room, they could see the crowd gathered between the thrones breaking up. They heard crying. Figures were slumped unconscious all around the table at the center.

"Boys, this might be our chance," Roger said, then strode forward. When he reached the doorway, he looked inside to either side, then motioned to them to follow. "These guys are out." The two guards at the door were unconscious on the floor.

Whatever had felled the observers in the room began to wear off, and they saw stirring as they walked to the front. Some had confused looks on their faces.

When Randy, Roger, and Kovac reached the raised platform, Jared was sitting up next to Sara, who was sleeping. Jared was holding a baby, still wet, and looking in wonder at its tiny face.

A man in surgical clothes and a mask stood up. He immediately focused on Sara and the baby. "Now we need to deal with the umbilical cord and afterbirth." He looked at Jared and the new arrivals. "Who are you guys?" He began the process of cutting the umbilical cord, dropping each instrument he used in a stainless steel pan on the cart nearby.

Kovac was looking at his field generator. "Spirits indetectable. But my field generator shouldn't have driven them off, just weakened them a bit. I didn't get a chance to use the projector close up. What just happened?"

Randy saw Jared's expression, and said, "I think Jared knows. When he's ready, I'm sure he'll tell us."

Sara heard confusing sounds around her. She had been watching the baby's birth through Lailah's eyes when the figure of a knight in armor appeared and slashed at Lailah with a blue-edged sword. Something snapped, and Sara's world had gone black for a while. She felt the absence of Lailah and tested her arms and legs, finding her body was hers again and they moved as she wished them to.

She raised her head and opened her eyes. To her right, Jared cradled something in his arms—their son. To the left, the doctor looked down at her, selecting implements from a tray and turning to snip at something.

She was exhausted but somehow happy. She could tell from Jared's expression that their son was fine. Whatever the demons had planned for him, they had somehow been foiled. Their son was still theirs.

She tried to sit up further but the effort hurt too much.

Then on the right, the faces of Mr. Wright and Jared's father appeared, looking down at her, concerned.

"Sara?" Randy asked. "Are you okay?"

"I'm—" The first word was hard, but after that they tumbled out, "—okay. Just tired. Water?"

"We'll get you some," Randy said.

Jared reached over and took her hand. "Hey."

"Hey," Sara said, trying to smile.

"We won this one," Jared said. Turning to look at his father, he said, "Thanks, Dad."

Roger Spendlove had been on the radio. "Looks like we're

getting some attention from the Feds and the state police. The logjam got broken. They're on the way."

The doctor propped Sara's head up with a pillow. "A fine, healthy baby boy, uncomplicated birth. And I still can't remember how I got here. Can one of you people tell me what's going on?"

48: Jared: Woke

Jared looked down into the baby's gray eyes. The little soul within looked back at him. It would be some time before the special nature of that soul would show itself. But Jared could tell that it was untouched by the foulness of Samyaza.

He reached over and squeezed Sara's hand again. Sara's former minions were waking up and starting to ask each other what had happened. Some would have hazy memories of their time spent in her service, some would remember nothing.

Sara smiled at him, more strongly this time. "That was you with the sword, right? You saved us just in time."

"I did. I think so, anyway." He looked distant for a moment —he heard Raphael's voice in the distance. "Ah, I see. I'm told that the demons fled to lick their wounds, but they aren't dead, just weakened."

"I'm in your debt, good Sir." She closed her eyes.

"How ever will you repay me?" Jared teased.

Sara's eyelids fluttered and she smiled. "I'll think of something. After I wake up." And she slept.

Jared's father was organizing the men to carry them back out of the mine, and they came to get Sara onto a stretcher for the trip out. The doctor fussed over her, but she didn't wake up.

Randy helped Jared hop off the table and held him up until his dizziness passed. Jared's father took the baby from his arms and cradled him, cooing quietly. "This bugger's going to be hungry soon. And we need a new wrap for him."

49: Randy: Debriefing

It took half an hour to get back to the mine entrance. When they came out into the twilight, the moon was full above them, and the sirens of multiple emergency vehicles were still getting closer. Already police and EMTs were waiting for them in the parking area. Jared and Sara were loaded into an ambulance van, which rumbled down the hill.

Kovac's men headed back to their chopper, and Kovac turned to shake hands with Roger and Randy. "Been a pleasure fighting evil with you, boys. One skirmish in the long battle, but we did well this time. Your boy is someone special," he said, gripping Roger's hand harder.

"Well, of course he is. We've always known—"

"Not 'special' as in smart and solid. 'Special' as in destined to defend us against the forces of chaos." Kovac gestured to his instrument case. "I may have been able to weaken the demons by disrupting their fields a little. But his sheer force of will is what sent them fleeing. He's a sheepdog—he instinctively defends his people."

Roger smiled. "I know where he gets that. And now that he has his own to defend—"

"—He's come into his heritage." Kovac looked over to where the helicopter's blades had started revving up. The noise level was increasing.

Two black cars drove into the parking area. Men in FBI jackets jumped out, two moving to block the exit and four more walking toward Kovac.

"Mr. Kovac? Tomo Kovac?" the leader said.

"Yes, gentlemen, I have had dealings with your superiors. What can I do for you?"

"I want your report on this incident by five PM tomorrow. There's been a significant breach of protocols. You were supposed to keep us informed of any … outbreaks."

"Ah, Washington," Kovac sighed. "Like I had time to ask permission. Am I free to go?"

"You are, yes. Just get that report in by five tomorrow. Everyone else here, we'll have to debrief. This could take some time."

Kovac nodded to the others and left, climbing into the Noumenal Institute chopper, which lifted straight up, then flew north.

Randy had to wait, then gave his statement, and the young man in black who recorded it pronounced it satisfactory. He signed nondisclosure papers requiring him to clear any interviews and keep all matters related to the incident secret—the stick if he should blab seemed to be prison time, but punishment was left specified by an ominous "18 U.S. Code § 798" reference. By the time the paperwork was done, most of the others had left. Randy worked his way through the shrinking crowd to the FBI leader, who he now suspected was nothing of the kind.

"Just a question for you," Randy said. "This place is dangerous—the leakage from below is strongest here. Why has it been left unprotected? There's no security."

The man—military in bearing, with steel-gray eyes and buzzcut hair—eyed him warily. "We didn't know there was an active problem until now. If we posted guards, we'd need a whole facility here, which would draw attention. Kovac is supposed to alert us to any threats. That didn't work this time. And there was a group inside the security agencies actively trying to keep us in the dark."

"Gotcha. But what now? There's a city down there—"

"There is? Just a legend, citizen. You never saw it." The grin spread. "Maybe there'll be some scientists here to make sure there's nothing. In fact, I guarantee it."

The next day Randy was drinking his first cup of coffee and thinking about visiting Sara in the hospital when his house shook. A few seconds later he heard a distant rumble. He went out his front door and looked toward the mountain, where a cloud of dust was rising from the mine buildings.

50: Sara: Recovery

Sara awoke. Her memory of nightmares and sirens in the night faded as her eyes opened to a shaft of sunlight from the window next to her bed. She could hear noises in the hall outside, and a nurse hovered in the doorway.

"Good morning," the nurse said. She took the chart clipboard off the hook at the foot of the bed and wrote down something. "How are you feeling?"

"Beat," Sara replied. "Like I was run over by a truck." A memory floated up. "Where's my baby?" She tried to sit up and failed.

"He's fine. Just rest. There are people waiting to visit, so if you don't feel up to it, let us know." The nurse put the chart back and headed for the door. "And breakfast will be along shortly."

Food sounded good. Suddenly she was famished. She dozed off again.

She woke to a knock on the doorframe.

"Are you feeling up to a visit?" Jared leaned in, smiling. "I just wanted to talk to you alone before the rest of the world gets here."

She smiled back at him and nodded. She felt a rush of well-being. She was not alone any longer.

Jared came closer and fiddled with the control on the bed, and the bed motor hummed as it moved slowly to the upright position.

"I'm told you can be released later today," Jared said, sitting on the edge of the bed. "They let me go last night. Our son—I'm still having trouble getting used to that!—is still being checked out, so they'll bring him by when they're done with tests." He took her hand and squeezed. "He's a normal baby. It was a close call."

"And thank God." She was remembering more. "You know none of that was me, right? It felt like I was sleepwalking through my own life. I did things—"

"I can guess, but you don't need to talk about it. You were under the influence, a lot of people were. But it's over." He leaned down to kiss her cheek. "You'll be back to your old self soon."

"Not my old self," she said, looking back on how fearful she used to be. "I might have been under Lailah's—or some demon's —control. But I was doing a lot of new things, taking a lot of chances. It wasn't all magic, I could do a lot on my own. I don't need to hide from the world. I can do big things."

"You always could. You just needed to know you could." Jared squeezed her hand. "I heard some stories. You had friends in high places. Or had—I hear some powerful people have fled the country. We're being asked to help in the investigation."

Sara realized it wasn't really over until the repercussions had played out. "I don't like the sound of that. I just want to move someplace where no one knows me and get on with my life."

"*Our* life," Jared said, "we're stuck with each other. We have a kid. Not that I'm complaining, and it might have been better if we'd had a more normal courtship, but…" He waited until she was hanging on the next word, "…will you marry me?"

Sara flashed back to when they had met, and the feeling she had had that anything was possible, before everything had gone sideways. "But—I'm damaged goods. You know."

"We're all damaged goods. I'm no saint," he said, remembering. "Your mom says they've done your bloodwork, and you're clean—good luck or divine intervention, I don't care. Nothing is going to keep us apart if the Lord of the Underworld couldn't."

The clouds in Sara's mind parted, and the sky above was clear and blue.

"Okay, then, yes. Yes, I will marry you."

Jared hugged her, and her tears were of joy, not sorrow.

A low-profile group from an unnamed federal agency had taken over a floor of the Comfort Suites by the highway for a week before leaving for Las Vegas and more weeks of interviews. The principal and staff at the high school were sworn to silence, and the only leak was a story in the *National Enquirer* that linked the Zion Mine events to Area 51 and alien visitations. Jared guessed the story had been planted to discredit any more credible stories that might have been written. The wire stories reported a standoff with a shadowy militia and an explosion at the mine when the authorities had detonated their weapons cache. Unfortunately the historic mine tunnels had been damaged and flooded, and the entire site was under Federal ATF jurisdiction while the investigators pored over it.

His own debriefing sessions lasted two days. His questioner was a diminutive black woman who told him to call her Nikki, strongly implying that was not her real name. She seemed to accept his testimony without question, only stepping in to ask for further elaboration on details—"Why did you think you could trust the Raphael persona? Did he ever indicate why his faction did not directly come to your assistance during the battle with Samyaza?" The questions made him think further about what it all meant. Were the Nephilim demons, or tools God used to challenge humanity?

'Nikki' asked him one question that revealed something he hadn't known. "Sara has told us she doesn't remember most of the names of the men she suborned to her cause. Do you believe she is telling the truth?"

"I do," he replied. "She was only along for the ride while something foreign directed her actions."

"We do have other means of confirming who she was working with. Many of the security camera tapes from the Luxor were mysteriously erased, but we have enough between those tapes we could recover and the statements of personnel to make our case. The biggest fish have left the country, though."

Jared had seen the notices of various politicians and CEOs resigning, and a few had been found dead—presumably by their own hand. It was lost in the usual noise of scandal and politics, with only the tabloids and conspiracy theorists taking note. Whoever was in charge of disinformation strategies for the national security agencies seemed to have prevented the real story from coming out.

When the debriefing was over, he had to sign more nondisclosure forms before he was allowed to leave. He wondered what would have happened if he refused to sign.

Real life started to return. Sara had tried an apology tour, trying to talk to the kids she had tangled with at school, with mixed results. Town gossip had cooled and the influence of the small number of people who knew what had really happened damped down the formerly prevailing view that she was a slutty Easterner who had brought evil to town with her. Sara's mother took a higher-paying job at a hospital in Salt Lake City and had started the process of enrolling Sara in a high school there. Everyone agreed she could not return to the same school to finish up, since so many parents wanted her gone.

Jared's family helped with the wedding plans. Since Sara was not LDS, a Temple sealing ceremony was out of the question. The bishop accepted Jared's decision to put off his mission until their child was older, but suggested Jared had already been a missionary in spirit, which made a kind of sense. Jared's mission might be more unusual than he had ever dreamed, and despite Jared's doubts the bishop encouraged him to think of his future role in the church, when he might be called upon to lead. Stranger things had happened.

The wedding was small, in the Spendloves' living room. Randy Wright served as best man, while Brandy Hansen was the maid of honor. Sara's father at first claimed he couldn't make it, but changed his plans and showed up just in time. Bishop Snow officiated. Sara's mother tended to the baby in the front row, but still cried. It was all very … normal.

Jared's sister Kristi hadn't been told exactly what had happened, but she treated him with new respect. Jared's father had signed the Federal nondisclosure form, but quietly supported him against the town gossips. "You took on the Devil himself and beat him. I'm proud of you and proud of Sara. Apple don't fall far from the tree…."

But Jared got a call in mid-June from Prof. Atwater at BYU. She had been consulting with Kovac and building support with other faculty to make Jared an offer: married student housing for him and Sara and their baby. Sara would enroll in BYU's Independent Study online high school as well as selected freshman courses at BYU. Stipends for research, scholarships for tuition. All irregular, but Kovac had leaned on his LDS contacts and made sure Jared and Sara would be nearby so he could get them involved in his research. And his other programs….

Kovac himself called the next day. "We know you'll be busy with college courses and raising a young child for at least a few years. But we have more work for you. Think of it as the Army

Reserve. We train to counter threats from supernatural entities. From above and below."

"I appreciate what you're doing for us, really," Jared said. "But we did our bit. We just want to be left alone for awhile."

Kovac laughed. "You may not be interested in tangling with them, but they are interested in you. You and Sara are marked—you still register as foci of interest on my instruments. So they'll be back, and the next time you need to be ready. We can help."

"Just how much commitment would you want from us?"

"Go through our training session in August. Not Sara, she can come later and has a child to take care of. But you should know who we are and what we can do."

Jared had hoped he had seen the last of the supernatural. But he wanted to help, and it would give them a way to live together independent of their families, but not so far away they'd lose touch with them. And if he needed allies to defend his family, he'd have them.

"Okay. Sign me up."

More by Jeb Kinnison

If you enjoyed this book, please check out other books by Jeb Kinnison:

https://jebkinnison.com/nephilim-also-by-jeb-kinnison/

Further Reading

Please visit the author's website for the current list of readings, including both books cited in the text and other interesting books on Mormon and US history:

https://jebkinnison.com/nephilim-for-further-reading/

About the Author

Jeb Kinnison grew up in Kansas City, Missouri, not far from Liberty Jail, where Joseph Smith and other Mormons were jailed in 1839-40 before fleeing to Illinois. He discovered science fiction in second grade, starting with Tom Swift books and quickly moving to Heinlein juveniles and adult science fiction.

He studied computer and cognitive science at MIT, and wrote programs modeling the behavior of simulated stock traders and the population dynamics of economic agents. Later he did supercomputer work at a think tank that developed parts of the early Internet (where the engineer who decided on '@' as the separator for email addresses worked down the hall.) Since then, he has had several careers—real estate development, financial advising, and counselling.

He retired from financial advising a few years ago and has done some work in energy conservation and relationship issues. He is known for his popular books on attachment types and began writing science fiction with the Substrate Wars series.

Visit his web site at JebKinnison.com for more: rail guns, Nazi scientists, the wreck of the Edmund Fitzgerald, the 1980s AI bubble, and current research in relationships, attachment types, diet, and health.

Visit the Substrate Wars website at SubstrateWars.com for more on upcoming books, physics, and the politics of the future.

Acknowledgements

I'd like to thank my intrepid crew of beta readers for their suggestions and corrections: Paul Perrotta, David Ochroch, Ken Walters, Joel Chesky Salomon, Bruce Sommer, Michael Zalter, Michael Cunningham, and Bridget Litchford Correia, as well as the members of the Manaña Literary Society who read parts: Sarah Hoyt, Julie Pascal, Jared Michael Anjewierden, Stephen Simmons, Blake Smith, Laura Montgomery, Melissa M. Green, Tiffanie Gray, David Burkhead, Joseph Capdepon II, Charlie Martin, Pam Uphoff, Jonathan LaForce, Jim Bellmore, and Kortnee Bryant.

Author's Note

January 23rd, 2018

This book came out of discussions with friends who grew up Mormon, and their stories of difficulties being raised surrounded by supportive family but without much experience with the kind of temptations they later met on the Internet or away from home.

I was raised as a Southern Baptist, but when I was five years old, my father started to hear voices and began preaching the gospel at Pentacostal services. I clearly remember when I was about four years old, running down the aisle at a tent revival in Independence, Missouri, toward where he was "healing" people by the laying on of hands. As his illness progressed, even his co-religionists realized he was becoming a danger to himself and others, and my mother had him committed. He spent the rest of his life in and out of mental hospitals, and I lost touch with him. When he was in his seventies, his half-brother found him and pulled strings to get him moved to a VA nursing home near Salt Lake City. I saw him for the last time there, where he explained he was waiting by the front door because Bill Clinton had told him he was sending a limo to pick him up. He died soon after and is buried in the veteran's cemetery south of Salt Lake City.

Are insane people who hear voices and experience hallucinations "possessed?" That was the explanation for thousands of years before medical science discovered some hints of the causes and found medications that could help. Was anyone in the past truly "devil-ridden?" And can we really be sure no one is possessed today? The Catholic Church now downplays popular interest in topics like possession and exorcism. But that doesn't prove it doesn't happen.

When we notice that folkways and religions around the world share many common features, the modern scientific view is that those features are artifacts of evolution and prehistory, narratives constructed to explain the world when gods, ghosts, and demons were thought to be real. The human mind has an evolved ability to see patterns in data, to construct explanations and stories to explain what has happened and predict what will happen. What we now diagnose as paranoia happens when this ability jumps the tracks of reason and sees patterns that aren't really there, constructing stories out of noisy data that aren't useful for guiding action and can even threaten survival. Paranoid schizophrenics are just mistuned, finding significance and danger where there is none.

Sara and Jared are the good kids of today, a bit lost in a world drenched in media and the Internet, looking for a future with someone they can trust who will help them grow into the adults they want to be, to start a family that will carry on the work of surviving and thriving into the next generation. It's harder than it used to be, perhaps, because of the faster pace of change in the world.

And it's even harder when they really are out to get you!

The history and doctrine of the Mormons is fascinating but not well known outside Mormon and Utah communities. Like Randy, I'm married to a sort of Mormon—R(eorganized) LDS, the much smaller group that decided to split from the group led west by Brigham Young after Joseph Smith's death. RLDS members settled in more scattered communities of the Midwest, and so never developed the intense local culture seen in Deseret, but their basic documents and teachings are broadly similar, diverging somewhat with time.

Jews, Christians, and Mormons all have common heritage in the earliest stories of the Torah and Old Testament Bible, with the tale of fallen angels and their children, seen as either heroic giants or evil that God had to flood the Earth to cleanse. The common story has one tenth of their number bound into the Earth as punishment. The story only confabulates a bit to imagine they still watch over us and try to persuade the weak to fall into sin. If you are a nonbeliever, they are a metaphor for the temptations that lead us away from being better people.

The Zion Mine in the story is based on the Dream Mine near Salem, Utah; a web search will bring up a lot more of its history. There were other "dream mines" (where prospectors said they had been led to look for ore by dreams or revelations) that did prove to be rich mines, but the Dream Mine never produced any worthwhile ore.

Sadly, there is no Noumenal Foundation, and no scientific evidence of magnetic forms of life dwelling in the Earth. But there's no scientific proof there isn't, either, and it is of such unknowns we spin our tale.

Notes

[1] Joseph Smith, Jr. *Teachings of the Prophet Joseph Smith.* Deseret Book, 1993.

[2] From George Washington's "Letter to the Hebrew Congregations of Newport, Rhode Island," 18 August 1790, Washington Papers, 6:284-85. Discussion at the Touro Synagogue web site: http://www.tourosynagogue.org/history-learning/gw-letter

[3] Letter from Thomas Jefferson to John Trumbull, Paris, Feb. 17, 1789. https://founders.archives.gov/documents/Jefferson/01-14-02-0321

[4] John Locke, Second Treatise of Civil Government, 1690, 4-22. http://www.bartleby.com/169/204.html

[5] "Joseph Smith—History," 33-35, from *Pearl of Great Price,* LDS Publications, https://www.lds.org/scriptures/pgp/js-h/1?lang=eng

[6] "Joseph Smith—History," 58-65, from *Pearl of Great Price,* LDS Publications, https://www.lds.org/scriptures/pgp/js-h/1?lang=eng

[7] Second Continental Congress, "Declaration of the Causes and Necessity of Taking Up Arms," 1775. https://en.wikisource.org/wiki/Declaration_of_the_Causes_and_Necessity_of_Taking_Up_Arms

[8] John Locke, Second Treatise of Civil Government, 1690, 4-24. http://www.bartleby.com/169/204.html

[9] "The Life of Porter Rockwell." https://sites.google.com/site/lifeandlegacyofporterrockwell/home/thelifeoforrinporterrock-

well

[10] "Insatiable Curiosity About Mormons Lured Explorer To Salt Lake," by Hal Schindler, Salt Lake Tribune, 11/20/1994. http://historytogo.utah.gov/salt_lake_tribune/in_another_time/112094.html

[11] Doctrine and Covenants, Section 89, 2013 Edition, Church History Library. https://www.lds.org/scriptures/dc-testament/dc/89?lang=eng

[12] *Gospel Doctrine*, Salt Lake City: Deseret Book, 1939, p. 208; emphasis added.

Made in the USA
Columbia, SC
02 October 2022

68556889R00181